T0131489

# THE LEGEND

*of the*

# LADY IN THE LAKE

A LITTLEROOT MYSTERY

J.M. SEWALL

author HOUSE®

*AuthorHouse™*
*1663 Liberty Drive*
*Bloomington, IN 47403*
*www.authorhouse.com*
*Phone: 1 (800) 839-8640*

*Published by AuthorHouse   04/03/2020*

*ISBN: 978-1-7283-5841-3 (sc)*
*ISBN: 978-1-7283-5842-0 (e)*

*Print information available on the last page.*

*This book is printed on acid-free paper.*

# CHAPTER ONE

Terry Welling lies in bed on a lazy Saturday afternoon. The sun is shining in his room, and his room is a bit of a mess. His clothes are all over the floor, food wrappers are piling up in his trash bucket, and his pillow is wet with drool.

He has just come off a double shift at Games 2 Go, and he hasn't had time to tidy up his room. But right now, all he wants to do is sleep in and doesn't want to be disturbed. He starts tossing and turning, trying desperately to sleep, until he moves his arm slightly, causing him to wake up and make a face. He grabs his arm in pain, wishing it would just stop already.

It's been three months since he and his friends encountered Dr. Kaminko, who had disguised himself as Mayor Angus Hamilton and was embezzling the town's money for his experiments. Three months since the house was destroyed, and three months since he broke his arm.

Though it has mostly healed, he still gets the occasional twinge of pain and he was given medicine for it. The doctor, however, told him that his arm may never be one hundred percent again; there will still be pain and it might take some physical therapy to get it back to at least seventy-five percent strength. He gets out of bed, wearing only a pair of dark red boxer shorts, opens his desk drawer, and takes out the bottle of medicine the doctor prescribed him. He goes out to the hall and enters the bathroom.

He opens the medicine bottle and puts a pill in his hand. Normally he'd just drink out of a water bottle, but right now he just wants to sleep, so he turns on the faucet, lets the water run for a few seconds, almost forgetting why he came into the bathroom in the first place, then he puts the pill in his mouth, sticks his lips to the running water, takes a huge drink from it, then swallows so the medicine can go down.

He turns the water off and looks at himself in the mirror. He notices the deep red burn mark from where Dr. Kaminko phased his hand through his chest and remembers how much it hurt.

Even though it doesn't hurt anymore, it still reminds him of the night he and his friends discovered Kaminko's plan. He tries so hard not to think about it, but every time he looks at the burn, it only makes him remember that scars don't heal, no matter how much you want them to. He and his friends were lucky that night. If it weren't for Dr. Kaminko's son Anton, they probably would be floating endlessly in the ghost dimension right now.

Because of the mark, he won't even go to the lake or the pool without wearing a shirt because he doesn't want people taking pity on him or his friends for what Kaminko did to them that night. He knows that he'll have to put up with it, eventually, because he is looking forward to the family trip to Pushaw Lake sometime in the summer. Ever since that night, his parents have been trying to spend more time with him.

They've been eating more dinners together, swapping stories, telling jokes, playing games like Cribbage, and just being with each other. He's been enjoying each minute he can spend with them and is very excited for the trip to Pushaw Lake. Perhaps it's the one place where nobody will take pity on him and ask questions non-stop. Part of him wishes he had never stepped foot in that damn house in the first place.

Perhaps if he had listened to Billy, they never would have even approached the house and it would still be standing. Then again, who knows how much more money Kaminko would have embezzled from the town? He probably would have bankrupted the entire town if it meant nobody could ruin his experiments.

He keeps looking in the mirror for a few more moments and notices his jet-black hair has grown a little past his neck and that he's looking a little bit scruffy with a bit of a goatee growing on his face. He thinks about shaving it off, but he decides against it for now and heads back to his room so he can try and get back to sleep.

After at least three more hours of vacationing in Dream Land, his cell phone rings and shocks him awake. He grabs the phone, turns the ringer off, wishing people would just leave him alone when he's trying to relax. He sees that his mom Julie is calling him, so he presses a button and says "Hello?"

"Hi, honey. How's your day going?" Julie asks on the other end of the line. "Groggy." Terry replies. "I came home from work a few hours ago but I can't seem to get any sleep."

"Oh, I'm sorry to hear that, sweetie." Julie says empathically. "Your father and I are still in town, and we're going to grab some Chinese food for dinner tonight. Why don't you ask Billy to come over? He likes Chinese, doesn't he?"

"He does, but I think he mentioned something about a new video game he just bought."

"Did he stop at the store to buy it?"

"No. He bought it online. He hasn't been in the store for quite a while. My boss is starting to wonder if he's still alive. Plus, I'm sure he'll be up for days trying to complete it one hundred percent. In other words, I probably won't hear from him until Monday when he'll talk to me about the game non-stop during class and how I should play it."

"I thought you like to play video games. Isn't that one of the reasons you work at the store?"

"I do, and it is, but right now it's the last thing on my mind. I don't really have the energy to play games. For the moment, I just want to get some sleep."

"Okay, hon. I'll call you later. Love you."

"Love you too, Mom." He hangs up the phone, puts it on the floor, and goes right back to sleep.

Another hour or two passes before Terry wakes up, feeling fully refreshed. He stretches for a quick second, then he decides to take a shower and heads to the bathroom. He turns on the water, waits for it to warm up, turns on a radio that sits outside the bathroom, then he undresses and steps inside the shower.

He lets out a sigh of relief as he feels the grime of the day wash off his body while the music plays on the radio. He closes his eyes and starts to imagine himself as the lead singer on stage playing the song with the rest of the band, singing while thirty thousand fans cheer their lungs out.

*"Wow. That would be so cool."* he thinks while the water runs down his face. *"Having so many fans who enjoy our music AND seeing us on stage. That must be how the members of Dime Front feel every day. But if Billy were a part of the band, we wouldn't have any fans at all. He'd need a bucket just so he could carry a tune."*

He lets out a small chuckle just as he starts rinsing the shampoo out of his hair. When he's done, he turns off the water and steps out of the shower, steam filling the room, like a fog just rolled in. He stumbles through the steam to open the door to the towel closet. He grabs a couple of towels and starts drying himself until he says to himself "Good enough," then heads back to his room.

He gets dressed, his attire consisting of a black t-shirt, dark blue jeans, and a new pair of black boots he just bought. He considers drying his hair, but decides against it, thinking it's best to just let it air-dry. He heads downstairs to the living room and notices his parents aren't home yet. He plops on the couch, grabs the remote to the television, and turns it on. He begins flipping through channels, hoping to find something worth watching, but as he's channel surfing, he finds himself saying the same thing repeatedly. "Seen it. Seen it. Seen it. Seen it. Seen it. Seen it. Seen it. Seen it. Seen it."

Just then there's a knock at the door, interrupting his "fun time" of finding nothing to watch. He gets up, walks into the kitchen, and approaches the door. His parents always emphasize to check who's at the door before opening it when they're not home. He looks through the peephole, and the other side of the door he sees what appears to be a female news reporter with long blonde hair, a blue jacket with a press badge on it, and beside her is a cameraman. "Who is it?" he asks.

"Is Terry Welling home?" the reporter asks.

"Speaking. May I ask who you are?"

"Brenna Kinsley for Channel 8 News. I'm doing a follow-up story on how you and your friends exposed the corruption of the late former mayor Angus Hamilton."

"Uh…I don't know about this…did you already talk to the others?"

"We tried. First, we started with Billy Martin, but he wasn't available. He said something about defeating the, uh…what did he say again, Jeff?"

"I believe he said the Evil Zombie Potato King." the cameraman says.

*"Sounds about right."* Terry thinks to himself, then asks "What about Allison Libby or Casey Martin?"

"Ms. Libby is apparently camera shy," Brenna replies, "and, well, I'd rather not say anything about Ms. Martin. She has…quite the vocabulary." Terry lets out a snicker in spite of himself. *"That is definitely Casey."* He keeps looking out the peephole and asks, "Is this really necessary?"

"Please, Mr. Welling, this is very important." Brenna replies. "You and your friends are the only ones who know what really happened that night three months ago. Will you do it?" Terry thinks about it for a few moments, wishing they would just leave, but he also knows if he doesn't do the interview now then she'll just keep bugging him about it until he finally gives in, so he starts to unlock the door.

"Get ready with the camera!" Brenna says to Jeff, and the second Terry opens the door, Jeff points the camera right in his face. "Hey! What the--?" Terry exclaims, trying to shield his eyes from the camera's incredibly bright light. Jeff moves the camera over to Brenna, who is readying her microphone. He makes a counting down motion with his free hand, points to Brenna, and quietly says "Action!"

"This is Brenna Kinsley reporting for Channel 8 News." she says with a tone that projects professionalism and confidence. "I am here at the house of Terry Welling, one of the four students from Littleroot High School who, three months ago, exposed and put an end to the corruption of the town's former mayor, Angus Hamilton. Despite failed attempts to speak with the other three students, we are lucky enough to get a follow-up interview with the brave leader of the group." She sticks the microphone in Terry's face and begins the interview.

"Mr. Welling," she begins, "you and your friends were hailed as town heroes after revealing the truth about Angus Hamilton. Could you please tell us what was going through your mind during the whole ordeal?"

"Uh, well…" Terry replied nervously. "Fear. Anxiety. Curiosity. Mostly curiosity. In the beginning, I was just trying to do a report for History class. But, once we learned Hamilton may have been hiding something, we were determined to discover the truth. And the deeper we went, the more we uncovered."

"And then Mayor Hamilton attempted to hold you and your friends hostage in the basement. Correct?"

"Um...yes. We discovered he had lied about who he really was, and he was determined to keep his identity a secret. So, he said we weren't allowed to leave."

Brenna starts flipping through some notes she jotted down on a pad of paper and replies "Right. He claimed to be the town's legendary mad scientist Dr. Ivan Kaminko. Then the four of you managed to escape the house before it was destroyed in a mysterious explosion. Care to elaborate on it?" Terry, realizing this was beginning to turn into an interrogation, starts to slowly back away from the microphone. "I think I've answered enough questions," he says quietly. "To be honest, I'd really rather not talk about this anymore."

"We would really like some answers, Terry. How is it possible the four of you escaped the house before the explosion?" She shoves the microphone even further in Terry's face. "Is it true you caused the explosion because you had a deep hatred for Mayor Hamilton?"

"What?! No! Why would you say--"

"Mayor Hamilton claimed you and your friend Billy Martin tried to break into his mansion a couple of nights before you went into Dr. Kaminko's house. You were labeled as punk delinquents and the entire town hated you. Is that why you blew up the house?"

"I didn't blow up the house. I have no reason to do such a thing."

"Then why won't you answer the question? You and your friends are the only ones who know what really happened that night. And what was the deal with claiming you saw the ghost of Dr. Kaminko's son Anton?"

"Please. Stop. I don't want to--"

"So, do you admit to destroying the house of Littleroot's most infamous urban legend? What led you to such an action?" Then, before she knew it, Terry walks back into his house and starts to shut the door in her face. "I've more than answered enough of your questions, Ms. Kinsley." he replies. "Please leave now."

"But, Mr. Welling--" Brenna begins, but before she could finish her sentence, the door closes completely shut, and she hears the faint sounds of the door's locks clicking. She starts to knock on the door in frustration in hopes Terry will come back outside, but there's no answer. She then motions to Jeff, who proceeds to turn off the camera.

"One way or another, Mr. Welling," she shouts, "we WILL get to the truth! You can't hide forever!" She and Jeff head back to their news van, while Terry watches them through the peephole. He sees them leave, relieved, then heads back into the living room and lays down on the couch. He puts his arm over his eyes and lets out a loud sigh, wishing the people of the town would start talking about something else other than Dr. Kaminko's house for a change.

# CHAPTER TWO

Monday rolls around, and that can only mean one thing. A new week at Littleroot High School has begun, but Billy Martin wishes it was still Sunday. Or at least Saturday. He was so close to completing his new game, *Zombie Potato Warfare,* but now he must endure the same old classes and the same old people he sees every single day.

He wishes something exciting would happen, but it's been kind of boring since the night at Dr. Kaminko's house. He wishes to forget that night ever happened, but it's proven to be very hard to do. The second someone walks into the main lobby of the school, the first thing they see is a huge trophy case with every award the school has ever won, ranging from sports tournaments to special accommodations past students have received over the years.

The latest addition is a framed copy of the newspaper of the town's new mayor, Barbara Daniels, awarding them for their hard work in exposing the corruption of her predecessor, Angus Hamilton.

At first, he liked all the attention he was getting; people opening doors for him, doing his homework, even giving him food at lunch time. However, even though the attention was much positive than what he normally gets as the school's Prankster Prince, he began to feel a little crowded as time went by.

His fellow students started following him and his friends everywhere. They couldn't even use the restroom without accompanying them in some way. They could be in the stall when a classmate would start asking them questions such as "Was it scary to be in that house?" and "Did you really see the ghost of Dr. Kaminko's son?"

Eventually the praise began to feel like harassment, and Billy finally reached his boiling point. Normally he'd never hurt a fly but, one day at lunch, all he wanted was to eat in peace. He never got the chance when a group of students gathered around him and Terry to watch them eat, as if there was something remarkable about their eating habits and got to the point where he started to feel claustrophobic. He had trouble breathing and was getting incredibly uncomfortable.

What exactly was it that made him snap? A student who took pictures for the school's newspaper, the Littleroot High Weekly, shoved their camera in Billy's face. Terry tried calming Billy down, but to no avail. He put his fork down, slid his tray to the side, stood up, and punched the student right in the face, breaking the camera in the process.

The principal, Mrs. Doyle, suspended him for three days, but she could understand why he hit the student. He, like the others, just wanted to be left alone and forget about Dr. Kaminko's house. They couldn't get any privacy anymore, not even at their own homes.

Luckily, Billy's father, Gene Martin, is the town sheriff. He said he would arrest anyone, mostly the press, who came to their house, or those of his son's friends, asking questions about Dr. Kaminko. Mrs. Doyle announced that, during school hours, Dr. Kaminko was not to be mentioned or discussed in class. She even said she would give detention to anyone who hounded Billy and his friends about that night. She was also beginning to get tired of hearing about Dr. Kaminko. She felt like it was watching a rerun on TV; when it first happens, it's great, but when it was on non-stop, it would drive you crazy and make you wish there was something else to talk about.

Billy walked past the trophy case and approached the hall just in time to see Terry struggling to open his locker when he grabbed his arm and dropped his book. Billy quickly walked up to him and picked up the book.

"Hey, buddy. Lose something?" he said with a sly grin across his face. Terry grabs the book, putting it back in his locker, and replies "Thanks, Billy." As he shuts the locker door, Billy asks "Is that a new book?" Terry shakes his head. "Nope. It's a classic," he replied. "*The Adventures of Tom Sawyer* by Mark Twain."

"What are you doing with a book like that?"

"I bought it to read during summer vacation. I guess I forgot I had it in my backpack."

"Summer vacation sounds good right now."

"We still have a month left before school's out, Billy."

"Don't remind me. So, I heard some reporter was bugging you the other day."

"Yeah. Brenna Kinsley from Channel 8 News. She wanted to do an interview about Dr. Kaminko." Billy rolls his eyes. "When will people stop talking about that stupid house? My ribs hurt just thinking about it."

"I can imagine. How are they, anyway?"

Billy pats his stomach. "Just dip them in barbecue sauce and dinner will be served."

"Very funny."

"I thought it was. How's the arm?"

"I won't be playing professional basketball anytime soon."

"You suck at basketball. I've seen your free throws, Shaq."

"Shut up. You're not exactly Michael Jordan on the court, either. Besides, didn't that reporter try to interview you first?"

"Actually, she tried Casey first. But she used some words I promised my parents I would never use. Plus, I was busy playing my new game."

"That reminds me. How are you doing on it?"

Billy holds up a hand. "Just five levels to go and I can finally face the Zombie Potato King."

"May I ask why you didn't pick it up at the store? I would've given you a discount so you don't have to pay full price." Billy looks away. "I don't know, Terry. I just...didn't feel like going anywhere. I wasn't really in the mood to leave the house."

"Fair enough."

"When the reporter was bugging you, why didn't you call my dad? He would've made sure she'd leave you alone. That's his job, after all."

Terry lets out a soft sigh and replies "Your dad's job is to keep the town safe. He's got more important things to do than arrest nosey reporters."

"Like what? Figure out who stole the last sprinkled donut?"

"I'm serious. But she did say something about getting to the truth, whatever that means. So, if she comes to my house again, I'll be sure to give your dad a call."

Billy then turns around and points to his backpack. "Hey, Terry. Can you reach in there and grab something for me?" Terry replies "Sure thing, buddy." He puts his hand inside and starts fumbling around, not sure what he's looking for, until he grabs something and pulls it out. In his hand is a black beret. Confused, Terry asks "Billy? Is this what you wanted me to grab?"

"Yup. I'm going to wear it to impress the French teacher." Still confused, Terry asks "Umm…WHY? You hate French class!" Billy puts on the beret and remarks "I don't hate it…anymore. I just have a new-found appreciation for the language. With this baret, she's sure to notice me now!"

"Billy, wearing a hat doesn't mean she's going to…" Terry stops for a moment, blinks twice, and says "What did you just say?" Billy adjusts his beret. "What? I was just talking about my awesome baret and how the teacher will notice me."

"Billy, it's not called a baret. It's called a BERET."

"Tomato, po-tato."

"And for the last time, that is NOT how you say it!" Before Terry can finish his sentence, the two of them hear a familiar voice say to them "You're wasting your time, Terry. No matter how much you try, you'll never get it through his incredibly thick skull."

They turn around to see Casey and Allison standing behind them. Casey eyes Billy for a second and says, "What the hell are you wearing on your head, cousin?" Billy points to the top of his head and replies "Oh. This? It's a--" Terry clasps his hand over Billy's mouth and says "It's a beret. He's trying to impress the French teacher."

"Again?" Casey asks. "Didn't he learn from last time?" Terry shakes his head. "Sadly, no." Terry clears his throat and says "So, Casey, the, uh… year-end school carnival is next month, and I was wondering if you'd like to go. With, uh, me, that is."

Allison looks over at Casey, who is completely stunned at what she just heard Terry say. "Well, Terry, I…" she begins, but suddenly stops. She's not sure what to say now, which is surprising considering she always has something to say. She simply stares at Terry for a few moments, then finally says "I don't know about this, Terry. I must go. Come on, Allison." She and Allison turn and head out the hall, with Allison saying "We'll, uh, see you guys later."

Terry watches them leave, dumbfounded, wondering why Casey turned him down like that. Billy looks at him, then looks in the direction in which the girls were leaving and says "Wow. That was harsh." Terry replies "I can't really blame her, Billy. Things between us have been…"

"Awkward? Strange? Creepy? Disgusting?"

"Let's just stick with 'awkward' for now."

Ever since she kissed him at the award ceremony Mayor Daniels held in their honor, she's tried so hard to avoid him, worried the kiss might mean something. It does, of course, but she won't admit it in fear things between them will change. She has a reputation to maintain, after all. Allison pretends not to notice, but she finds it quite difficult. She tried getting her to talk about her feelings, but she kept refusing, telling Allison to drop it time and time again.

Billy just wishes he never had to see his cousin kiss his best friend at all. He keeps saying it would "gag a maggot" (whatever that means), and it was enough to make him toss his cookies; in fact, after the ceremony, he ate a bag of cookies, just so he could toss them.

"So, on a scale of one to ten, how awkward is this right now?" Billy asks. Terry answers "Seven. Definitely a seven." Surprised, Billy remarks "Really? Sounds like the equivalent of coming to school without pants."

Terry gives him a look. "You would know what that's like, Billy."

"I was half asleep and running late! Don't judge me!"

"It was in the middle of winter, Billy. How could you forget your pants?"

"Very easily. Now, can we talk about the elephant in the room?"

"Hallway."

"Right. Hallway. How much longer must Allison and I endure the strangeness between you and Casey? It's been three months!"

"She'll talk when she's ready. Now let's hurry up. I don't want to be late for class." The two friends proceed to walk to French class. When they approach the door, Billy whispers "Do you think she'll like my hat?"

"She didn't really notice the crude picture of that French poodle you drew for her last week. I doubt the beret will get her attention." They open the door and a young woman, late twenties, dark brown hair, and green eyes is sitting at the teacher's desk. Her name is Abigail Granger, Littleroot High's new French teacher.

You see, Billy's pranks finally pushed Madame Michaud to her breaking point. She assigned the entire class a family tree project. Sounds easy enough, but there was a catch; they had to do the entire project in French. Billy refused, saying he will never use French in his lifetime and he'll hire an interpreter if he ever decides to visit France when he's older.

So, Madame Michaud made him stay after school every day until he got it done. However, instead of using his time in detention wisely, he was planning to make his comeback as the Prankster Prince, and he chose Madame Michaud as his target. But he started to wonder how he could pull a prank that would one to remember without getting arrested or expelled. He had to think out every detail carefully. So, he snuck out of detention after school one day and went into her classroom while she was out.

He brought with him a box Styrofoam packing peanuts, a small container of powdered paste, and a bucket of water. He set up everything perfectly, so when she returned, he would finally have his revenge.

The second she opened the door, the bucket of water fell on her and soaked her from head to toe. While she was trying to process what had just happened, Billy quietly walked inside the classroom, turned on the ceiling fan, and quietly walked back out. The powdered paste was set on top of the fan blades, so when he turned it on the paste flew all over the classroom and landed on her entire body, making her look like a walking talking marshmallow.

She tried to remove the paste, but she lost her balance and fell back into her seat, which was where Billy had hoped she would go. The second she landed in her chair, she unknowingly activated the final phase of Billy's prank. By pushing the chair back when she landed into it, she pulled on the rope it was tied to, which released the Styrofoam peanuts right above her head. She screamed in anger while Billy sat right outside her classroom covering his mouth, trying so hard not to laugh.

She then ran outside the room, her face covered with packing peanuts, not knowing Billy was right there. She immediately knew he was responsible, but she couldn't prove it. She went to the restroom and cleaned the paste and packing peanuts off her face, then ran straight to the detention room. She was surprised to see Billy sitting there acting all innocent.

He even had the nerve to say "Why, Madame Michaud, what on Earth happened? Did someone pull a nasty practical joke on you? Who would do such a terrible thing?"

Mrs. Doyle soon arrived, saw Madame Michaud covered in packing peanuts, and asked what happened. She told her, but there was no evidence of Billy doing it, because every time Mrs. Doyle walked by the detention room, Billy was still there.

This was enough to drive Madame Michaud over the edge, and she immediately handed in her resignation. She walked out to her car, screaming countless obscenities, and as she drove off, she shouted, "I HATE YOU, BILLY MARTIN!" Of course, he already knew that.

After Madame Michaud quit, Mrs. Doyle had trouble finding a replacement. Everyone who normally took French class now had to go to the library for study hall. The reception to Billy's prank was mixed; half of the student body thought it was a hilarious return for the school's most notorious prankster, while the rest thought it was immature and hated Billy for making such a popular teacher quit. No matter what people thought about it, Billy was just glad she was gone and hoped Mrs. Doyle would never find a replacement teacher.

After about two weeks of no French class, everyone started thinking they would never take it again. That is, until Mrs. Doyle held a school assembly. She announced she had finally found a new French teacher to replace Madame Michaud, which made Billy scream at the top of his lungs "DAMN IT!"

He already started planning his next prank, until he saw Madame Granger for the very first time. The second he saw how beautiful the new French teacher was, he (along with nearly every boy in the room) immediately shut his mouth. Even Terry was taken aback by Madame Granger's beauty, but then he noticed Billy just staring at her, his mouth gaping open. "Hey. Billy. You okay?" he asked. It was that moment he realized what was happening with his friend. *"Uh oh."* He thought. *"It's the seventh grade all over again."*

It wasn't the first time Billy acted like this. In seventh grade, they had a substitute teacher for their math class. She had blonde hair, blue eyes, and was quite lovely. Billy was instantly awestruck with her, and he tried to impress her by answering every single math problem. But math wasn't, and still isn't, his best subject, so he got every one of them wrong. Every attempt to get her attention resulted in either humiliation or detention.

He didn't it let bother him, until he found out she was engaged, then he feigned illness for an entire week and refused to get out of bed. Terry thought he would learn his lesson after that, but he was wrong.

Madame Granger sees them walk inside and says with a smile on her face "Mr. Welling. Mr. Martin. You were almost late." Terry replies "Sorry, Madame Granger."

She says "It's okay, Terry. Just take your seats." Billy approaches her, takes her hand, and says in the cheesiest French accent you had ever heard, "Oh, how I have missed you Mademoiselle. Let us run away together and go somewhere exotic. Like Pittsburgh." Terry pulls him away, apologizes to Madame Granger, and drags him over to his desk.

"Billy", he whispers, "the only French words YOU know are 'French Fries', 'French Toast', and 'French Vanilla Ice Cream'!" Billy sits down at his desk, stares intently at Madame Granger, and replies "Say whatever you want, Terry, but I know she wants me."

# CHAPTER THREE

Being the sheriff of a small town such as Littleroot, Maine can certainly have its disadvantages, and for Gene Martin, it can sometimes be an absolute bore. He always dreamed of being a police officer; it runs in the family. His father, Joseph Martin, was a police officer, as was his grandfather John.

He started his career at the Bangor Police Department, and it was during his time there that he met a young woman named Amy Miller. They dated for a few years before getting married, and sometime after that she was pregnant with Billy. He couldn't wait to have his son possibly continue the Martin legacy in the Bangor PD one day.

But then something happened that made him transfer to the police department in Littleroot when Billy was six years old. The reason for the transfer is something he prefers to keep a secret from his son. Many times, has Billy asked him about it, but Gene, being a stubborn man, simply said to him was "Trust me, son. It was for the best. That's all you need to know." To this day Billy still doesn't know the truth behind the transfer, and it is one of the reasons he wants to be a detective someday.

Gene hopes Billy will become a detective at some point in his life, but first, according to him, he needs to stop being a coward all the time and grow up. And by growing up, he means stop pulling pranks and believing in things that don't exist such as ghosts and Bigfoot.

He's frankly getting a little tired of his son being afraid of everything around him and constantly being a wiseass to his teachers. At least once a month he gets a call from the school saying his son made some inappropriate joke or was being disrespectful in some form. A week ago, he got called in to speak with Mr. Elliot, Billy's history teacher.

Apparently, Mr. Elliot was trying to teach the class about art from ancient history, to which Billy said aloud "Ancient history? You mean back when Mrs. Doyle was a kid?" While the entire class roared with laughter, Mr. Elliot did not find it at all amusing and told him to stay after class.

When Gene asked Billy why he would say something like that, Billy replied "I guess he meant thousands of years, not hundreds." Gene told him they would discuss it more at home, and when he got back to his car, he let out a loud chuckle in spite of himself. He knows his son shouldn't have said that about the principal, but he still thought it was funny and did all he could not to laugh while in Mr. Elliot's classroom.

Gene sits at his desk looking through some paperwork, pretty bored out of his mind. Not since the night his son and niece went to Dr. Kaminko's house has anything exciting really happened. But he didn't become a police officer for thrill seeking adventures; he did it to keep his family safe.

Jeremiah Martin, Gene's older brother and Casey's father, owns the Littleroot Federal Credit Union and offered a him a job because "nothing ever happens in this quiet little town." Gene, however, refused the job, stating even though his brother might be right, he couldn't imagine doing anything else even if nothing at all happens. But today is not one of those days. He soon gets a call about someone finding a body near Littleroot Lake and steps out of his office to investigate.

Littleroot Lake is one of the town's most popular hangout spots for the student body in the summertime. It's surrounded by many trees for miles and miles all around. Unless you've been a resident of Littleroot for most of your life, it can be easy to get lost on your way there.

The lake is approximately five miles wide and during the summer, when the sun sets, the light shines off the water and creates a dazzling view for everyone to see. This has become known to the residents as the "Littleroot Lights". It is one of the reasons the lake is so popular during the summer, especially when tourists visit.

But there is one more popular attraction at the lake. In the middle of it is a rock on a small island, shaped like a woman gazing up at the sky.

Historians local and from all over have tried to figure out what it means for years, but right now it's just one of Littleroot's many myths and legends.

Sheriff Martin arrives at the lake and he sees it's already been taped off as a crime scene. He steps out of his car, crosses over the crime scene tape and approaches one of his deputies, Franklin Judd. "What have we got, Judd?" he asks.

"A woman and her dog found the victim this morning." said Judd. "The medical examiner's on her way to look at the body."

"Any idea who it is?"

"Not yet, sir. We have dogs canvassing the area. Hopefully they find something that will give us a clue as to who we found."

"I'm sure they will." They approach the body, completely covered with a sheet. Gene lifts the sheet to get a look at the victim's face. "Male. Caucasian. Early to late nineties." says the officer standing next to the body. Gene examines the body a little closely, and sees he's wearing a blue jacket with white arms and the Littleroot High logo on the shoulder.

"Strange…" he says to himself.

"What's strange, sir?" Judd asks.

"The victim's wearing a letterman's jacket from Littleroot High School." Gene replies.

"Maybe he's a former student."

"I'd consider it as a possibility, except the jacket is recent. The booster club had the jackets updated a few years ago. The old jackets had the logo on the chest, not the shoulder."

"So how did this guy get it? Maybe he has a grandson on one of the varsity teams."

"We won't know until we can properly ID him."

"What for?" said the officer. "The poor S.O.B. went for a walk and dropped dead from a bad ticker. Simple enough."

"Have some respect for the deceased, officer." Judd chimes in. This man must have some family who's worried about him."

"Hey. No ID, not our problem."

"It's our job, officer." Gene snapped. "We don't decide what to investigate. The least we can do is locate his family so they can give him a proper burial."

Just then, he hears the medical examiner's van drive in. The door opens, and the M.E., Dr. Linda Taylor, steps out. She crosses over the tape, bag of supplies in hand and asks Gene "What do we have, Sheriff?"

"Male. Caucasian. Early to late nineties. We don't know who he is yet, but we're hoping to find something that will give us a clue as to he is." Dr. Taylor starts doing her preliminary examination. "Hmmm…no signs of assault, no defensive wounds…"

"Is it possible he drowned?" asked Judd.

"Not unless he decided to go for a swim in his clothes." the doctor replied. "It could have been a heart attack, but I won't know until I get him back to my lab and do a proper autopsy."

Then, an officer comes out of the woods and runs up to the sheriff. "Sheriff Martin!" he exclaims. "We found a wallet." Gene approaches the officer and takes the wallet from him. He opens it up and finds an ID with a picture of a young man with dark red hair and brown eyes. He reads the name out loud so Judd and Dr. Taylor hear him.

"Trent Alexander. Age seventeen." Suddenly, the entire area grows quiet for a few moments. Judd breaks the silence by saying "Isn't Trent Alexander the student from Littleroot High who's been missing for almost a week?"

Gene thinks for a minute or two, then replies "He is, and the last time anybody saw him he was…"

"He was what, Gene?" Dr. Taylor asked.

"He was wearing a black shirt, dark green pants, black boots, and a Littleroot High jacket." Again, the area grows silent, with nobody saying a word. Gene returns to Judd and Dr. Taylor, completely perplexed. "How is this possible?" Dr. Taylor asks.

Gene's train of thought is soon derailed, however, when he overhears a commotion happening on the other side of the tape. "I'll be right back." he says, and he rushes over to see what's going on. He isn't surprised to see Channel 8's very own Brenna Kinsley trying to cross while officers hold her back.

One of the officers yells "Stay on that side of the tape, lady!" She screams back, "The people have a right to know what has happened!" She then sees Gene approaching her. "Oh, Sheriff Martin! Help me out here, please?" Gene tells the officers to let her go. They comply and walk over to another part of the crime scene, but Gene steps in front of Brenna tries to cross again. "What are you doing here, Ms. Kinsley?" he asks.

"My job. What does it look like?"

"It looks to me like you're trying to interfere with an ongoing police investigation. And you can quote me on that."

"What's the big deal, Sheriff? Surely someone in your position would jump at the chance to tell people that something exciting has happened in this town since--"

"Ms. Kinsley, I've already told you a hundred times. The events that took place at Dr. Kaminko's house are done and over with."

"But do you believe what happened that night and what the police have just discovered are somehow connected? And what about the disappearance of Trent Alexander? Have there been any new leads?" The sheriff sees Brenna's cameraman Jeff standing behind her, looks back at Brenna, and replies "There is no link between our current investigation and Dr. Kaminko's house. We don't know who the victim is. Yet."

"Well surely your son and his friends might know. Perhaps you could ask him to help with--" Gene grabs her microphone and throws it in the woods.

"This interview is OVER, Ms. Kinsley. And if you even THINK of interviewing my son or his friends about this case, I will have you arrested for obstruction. Now get out of here." He motions for some officers to keep her from crossing while he returns to the body. Without making a fuss, she takes Jeff by the arm and they start walking back towards the news van.

"So?" asked Jeff. "Anything?" Brenna replies "No. He wouldn't even budge. But that won't stop me from getting to the truth. I'm sure that if I ask Terry Welling and his friends, they could give me some answers."

"We're not supposed to go near them, remember?"

"He's bluffing. His son Billy will talk to us, I'm sure of it."

When Gene sees the news van leave, he breathes a sigh of relief, hoping she won't bother him anymore. He looks back at Dr. Taylor, who's preparing to have the body taken to her lab and becomes really confused. He scratches his head while she finishes her preliminary examination, wondering if they have indeed found the missing student. *"If that is indeed Trent Alexander,"* he thinks to himself, *"then what the hell happened to him?"*

# CHAPTER FOUR

A bell rings throughout the halls of Littleroot High School, meaning the first class of the day has ended. As the students leave their respective rooms and prepare for their next class, Terry can't be any more relieved that French is over, because he doesn't have to watch Billy make a fool of himself anymore until tomorrow.

He heads to his locker to grab his History book while Billy follows behind not saying a word. As he fumbles with the combination lock, Billy just stands there with a silly smile on his face.

"I think I'm wearing Madame Granger down," he says. "It won't be long until she falls for me."

Terry rolls his eyes and replies "Billy, you have a better chance of getting Rihanna to fall in love you. Besides, you can't date a teacher."

"Why not?" Billy asks.

Terry responds "Because she's older than you and she could get arrested for it. Plus, she's a TEACHER."

"What's your point?"

"What part of her being a teacher did you not understand?"

"So? She could tutor me in French so I can actually speak the language."

"But didn't you always say you would never have a reason to use French in life?"

"But, Terry, French is the language of love."

Terry continues fumbling with his locker. "Billy, you can barely speak English. And you're failing that class, as well."

"Says who?"

"Uh, the English teacher, your report card, Mrs. Doyle, your parents, me, Casey, Casey's dad, Allison, Allison's parents, the school district…"

"Okay, I get it."

"And my parents."

"Shut up."

Terry chuckles and finally gets his locker open and searches for his History book. "Where the hell is that thing?" he says to himself. "I know I put it in here." He keeps his hand inside the locker and continues searching until he finally grabs a hold of the book he was looking for. "Finally."

He shuts his locker, looks at Billy, and asks "Aren't you going to grab your book out of your locker?" Billy walks up to his locker, pretends to fumble with the combination, and flatly says "Darn. I can't remember my combination. I guess I can't get my History book now."

Terry sighs and does the combination to Billy's locker. When he finishes, he opens it up, grabs the book, shuts the locker, and remarks "Problem solved. Now let's get going." As they start walking to their next class, Billy accidentally bumps into Jeremy Hodges, Littleroot High's resident bully. Junior, seventeen years old, and big-boned, Jeremy is someone you do not want to mess with.

Billy thinks he'll be the spokesperson for a weight-loss company, prison division someday. If you even look at him wrong, he'll beat you senseless. Of course, his favorite punching bag is none other than Billy Martin.

For no apparent reason, he'll just do whatever he wants to make Billy's life miserable; one time during Billy's freshman year, Jeremy stole his clothes while he was in the shower after Gym class then pushed him out of the locker room and shut the door so he couldn't get back in. Most of the time, though, Billy could be minding his own business when Jeremy decides to mess with him by either taking his lunch money or just by pushing him against the lockers in the halls.

The second Billy's arm bumps up against Jeremy's, the bully takes notice, turns around and says "Hey! Martin!" Billy stops right in his tracks and mutters "Crap." He then looks at Jeremy and says "Oh. Hi, Jeremy. How can I help you on such a great day?"

"You bumped into me."

"I did? Oh, I am so sorry, Jeremy. How can I make it up to you?"

"Did you bring your lunch money today?"

"Yes, I did. Why do you ask?" Jeremy starts cracking his knuckles. "I hope you don't plan on eating today. Give me your lunch money." Billy scratches his head for a few seconds, then replies "Um, yeah, how about I don't and say that I did?"

"What was that?"

"I don't think I'm going to do that today, Jeremy. By the looks of it you've taken enough of people's lunch money." Terry puts a hand on Billy's shoulder. "Okay, Billy, that's enough. Don't make him angry."

"Are you calling me fat, Martin?"

"No! I would never call you fat, you BIG FAT FATTY OF A FAT MAN." At that moment, Jeremy clenches his fists walks straight up to Billy, then grabs him by the collar of his shirt and slams him against a locker. The impact is enough to get the attention of every other student in the hallway, including Casey and Allison.

Jeremy gets right in Billy's face and screams "NOBODY CALLS ME FAT, YOU LITTLE PRICK!" Billy sarcastically responds "I didn't call you fat. If I did, though, I would have made some 'You're So Fat' jokes."

Terry, trying to loosen Jeremy's grip on Billy, shouts "Billy, stop! You're only going to make him angrier!"

Billy remarks "Ah, what the heck, I'll make some jokes."

He reaches into one of the pockets on his jeans and pulls out some not cards. He clears his throat and says, "You're so fat, that when you cut yourself shaving, marshmallow fluff comes out." The other students start giggling, and Billy continues. "No? Okay, how about this one? You're so fat that your yearbook photo was taken from a helicopter."

Jeremy screams some more. "DO YOU WANT TO GET YOUR ASS KICKED, LOSER?!" Billy reads another note card. "You're so fat, that when you step on a bathroom scale it reads 'One at a time'!"

Jeremy makes a fist and prepares to punch the wiseass he has in his grip. Terry grabs his hand and says "Jeremy, don't. I won't let you." Jeremy looks at him, looks back at Billy, then returns his gaze to Terry. He surprises everybody in the hall by releasing Billy and says to Terry, "You won't LET me? Who do you think you are?"

He then grabs Terry by the arm and starts twisting, making him scream in agonizing pain. "You think you're so tough, don't you, Welling?"

he shouts while twisting Terry's arm. "You and your loser friends go into a stupid house, meet the so-called Dr. Kaminko, then blow up the house, and suddenly you think you're somebody? You're still nothing!"

Terry starts to feel tears rolling down his face; the pain is too much for him to bear. He knows people can see him crying, but he doesn't care. For the past two years he's watched Jeremy bully the hell out of his best friend while everyone else just sat back and did nothing to stop him.

Just when Jeremy is going to twist his arm to the point he might rip it out of his socket, however, he hears a familiar say "That's enough! Out of the way!"

Terry looks up and sees his history teacher Mr. Elliot making his way through the crowd of students, trying as hard as he can to stop the situation. He gets through the crowd and confronts Jeremy, saying "Let the student go, Mr. Hodges. Now!" Jeremy, with a sly grin on his face, releases Terry's arm and stares Mr. Elliot down, trying to show he's not afraid of him.

Mr. Elliot continues to look the bully in the face, refusing to even blink an eye. Billy helps Terry up, whispering "You okay, Terry?" "Yeah. Thanks." he replies while rubbing his arm. They watch as Jeremy and Mr. Elliot continue their little stare down for at least five more minutes, until Jeremy finally looks away and says "Whatever. Just keep those losers away from me."

As Jeremy walks down the hall away from everyone else, Mr. Elliot walks up to Terry and Billy while everyone else continues walking to their classes. "Are you two alright?" he asks them. Terry responds "Yeah. We'll be fine, Mr. Elliot. Thanks."

Mr. Elliot eyes Billy and says, "What did Mr. Martin do to anger Mr. Hodges this time?" Billy exclaims "What? Why do you always think it's my fault he went all bull-crazy?"

"Because it usually is. I've never known Mr. Hodges to get that angry at anyone else besides you. Are you wearing a target on the back of your shirt, Mr. Martin?"

Billy shakes his head. "Nope."

Mr. Elliot points to his classroom. "You two had better hurry up," he says, "or you'll be late." Billy walks on ahead with Terry following but is stopped when Mr. Elliot puts a hand on his shoulder. "Mr. Welling", he begins, "are you sure you're okay?"

"Yeah." Terry replies. "Why do you ask?"

"I know it's been a rough few months since you and your friends went to Dr. Kaminko's house. I'm concerned."

"Concerned? What about?"

"You. You are one of the best students I've had the pleasure of teaching all year, but lately you've been quiet. You rarely answer my questions anymore and your grades are starting to slip a little. You are one of the brightest students in your class. I'd hate to have to fail you. You have a bright future ahead of you."

"I appreciate the concern, Mr. Elliot, but I'll be fine."

"I hope so, Terry. Just remember, if you ever need someone to talk to, my door is always open."

"Thanks, Mr. Elliot." Terry smiles a little and walks into the classroom with his favorite teacher not far behind him.

The rest of the day goes on without a hitch, and the entire student body couldn't be any happier when the final bell rings. As they rush out the doors, Casey and Allison stay in the lobby so they don't get run over by the stampeding students. While the remainder of them head out the door, Casey is looking in the trophy case, adjusting her hair. Allison looks at her and says, "Can I ask you a question, Casey?"

"Sure, Alli. Go ahead."

"Well, it's about Terry."

Casey jumps and remarks "What about Terry? Is he okay?"

"He's fine. I was just wondering why you turned him down when he invited you to the school carnival."

Casey rolls her eyes. "It's nothing, Allison. I'm just not a fan of carnivals."

"Now that's a lie. You went to the carnival last year and you had fun."

"I went with you. There were no boys involved. Why are you making a big deal out of this?"

"Billy and I noticed that things between you and Terry have been...

let's say…uncomfortable. Is this because of the kiss?" Casey blushes. "No! Of course not! How did you know about that?"

"Casey, the entire school saw you kiss him on the cheek. We all know how you two feel about each other."

"Just drop it, okay? I don't want to talk about this anymore. Let's talk about you and Billy."

"What about me and Billy?"

"Aren't you upset he's flirting with the French teacher? Doesn't it bother you at all?"

Allison starts to feel her face turn hot. "Well," she replies, "maybe a little. He's wasting his time with an older woman. But it's none of my business. He'll stop eventually."

Just then Casey and Allison hear voices coming the hallway, and they see Terry and Billy. Casey quickly runs to the other side of the trophy case while Allison remains where she stands. She whispers to Casey "Relax. It's only Terry and Billy."

"I know!" Casey whispers back. "I'd prefer to avoid them. I don't want Terry to see me."

"They don't even notice we're here. I just saw them go into the boys' room."

"That's a relief."

In the boys' bathroom, Terry is in a stall while Billy sits by the window. "So, want to come to my house for dinner tonight?" he asks. "My mom's making her famous chicken and rice casserole."

Inside the stall, Terry replies "I'd like to, Billy, but I have to work tonight. There's a new shipment of games and my boss needs my help putting them on the shelves."

"You're so lucky. I wish I could work at a place that sells comic books and video games."

"You could have if you didn't try to leave with those cutouts of the plumber and the blue hedgehog."

"How was I supposed to know they weren't free giveaways?"

"The manager said not to touch them, Billy."

"I thought he was testing me."

Then, Terry steps out of the stall wearing his work uniform consisting of a black t-shirt with his name and the Games 2 Go logo on it, dark blue jeans, and black shoes. "If he was testing you," he says, "you would have failed miserably."

The two friends leave the bathroom and continue walking in the hall until they reach the lobby, where they see Allison standing next to the trophy case. "Hey, Allison." Billy says.

Allison waves. "Hey, guys."

Terry looks around. "Where's Casey?"

"I don't know. I haven't seen her around."

Billy rolls his eyes and remarks "She's hiding from you, Terry." Terry shoots him a look.

"No, she's not, Billy. It's not a big deal. I need to get to work. See you guys later." The second Terry steps out the doors, Casey comes out from around the trophy case.

"That was close." she says with a sigh of relief. "Thanks, Allison."

Billy eyes her and says "This is getting annoying, Casey. You should stop hiding from him. You can't avoid him forever."

"Shut up, Billy. This is none of your business. Don't you have a ghost or a running leaf to hide from?" Allison chimes in and says "Billy's right, Casey. Eventually you'll have to talk to Terry. I can't keep lying for you."

Terry walks down the steps and heads to the sidewalk, not realizing someone is watching him. The second he gets to the end of the sidewalk, the Channel 8 News van pulls over right in front of him. "What the hell?!" he shouts.

Brenna Kinsley and cameraman Jeff open their doors and get right in Terry's face. "Terry Welling, Brenna Kinsley for Channel 8 News. Mind if we ask you a few questions regarding the body the police found earlier this morning?"

"What are you talking about? What body?"

"The one found at Littleroot Lake, of course. What do you know about it?"

"I don't know anything about a body. I'm going to be late for work. Please leave me alone." Jeff sticks his camera even further into Terry's face and exclaims "Just answer her question, kid. She thinks you know something."

"Why the hell would I know anything about a body the police found?"

Brenna sticks her microphone in his face. "Did you know the body is believed to be that of missing Littleroot High student Trent Alexander?"

"Trent's dead? How do you know that?"

"Reporter's instincts, Terry. Now…" While Brenna continues pestering Terry, Billy, Casey and Allison step outside, unaware of what's going on.

"Remember, Billy," Casey says, "I'm having dinner with you and your parents tomorrow night, so don't do anything stupid to ruin it."

"Why do you assume I'll ruin it?"

"The last time I had dinner at your house, you flung mashed potatoes and it landed on my skirt. I couldn't get the gravy stains out."

"I was doing a science experiment measuring the velocity and distance of lumpy foods. I'd call that a success."

Before Casey can deliver a retort, Allison looks over to the sidewalk and says "Isn't that Terry over there? Who's he talking to?" Casey clenches her hands into fists. "It's that stupid reporter Brenna Kinsley. She's bugging him. Come on, guys."

Brenna keeps pestering Terry, making him uncomfortable. "Please stop," he begs. "I don't know anything about a body."

"You know more than you think, Terry. There's a connection between the body and Dr. Kaminko's house. What did you see there?"

"I told everybody what I saw. Leave me alone!" Before Brenna can continue asking Terry questions, she sees Billy, Casey, and Allison running up to her.

"Ah, perfect timing!" she exclaims. "Hi, my name is--" Casey interrupts her. "We know who you are, Kinsley. What are you doing with Terry?"

"I'm doing my job. A body was found at Littleroot Lake this morning, and it's believed to be Trent Alexander."

"The student who went missing last week?" Billy asked. "Why would you ask Terry about it?"

"I believe there's a connection between the body and Dr. Kaminko but I can't prove it. I thought maybe Mr. Welling and the rest of you might know something."

At that point Casey walks up to Brenna, gets right in her face, and says "Listen here, princess. We're done talking about Dr. Kaminko's house. We've told everybody what we know, and we're getting sick of you hounding us, especially about a body that has no connection like you claim. Why can't you leave us the hell alone like everyone else? Go report on traffic or something. Better yet, go to hell and stay there."

Brenna tries to keep her composure and replies "Ms. Martin, please. The legend of Dr. Kaminko was only the beginning. Let me do this follow-up on you guys. This could make you famous! Picture it: talk shows, book deals, maybe even a movie! What do you say?"

"I already told you. Go. To. Hell. Let's go, Terry." Casey grabs him by the arm and pulls him away from Brenna and Jeff while Billy and Allison follow behind her. Brenna and Jeff get back into their van, and she shouts "This isn't over! You'll see!"

As they drive away, Terry releases himself from Casey's grip and says "Thanks, guys. One more second and I doubt I could've kept my cool for much longer."

"No problem, Terry." Billy says. "But I must say it would be cool if somebody made a movie about us. I know who I want to play me."

"Who?"

"Denzel Washington."

Rolling her eyes, Casey ignores Billy and turns back to Terry. "If that B-word bothers you again, give my uncle a call. He'll take care of it."

"Thanks. I will." He looks at her for a few moments, and she looks back at him. She then feels her face turn red and says "Well, I got to get going. See you later. Come on, Allison." She turns and walks back toward the school with Allison right beside her.

Billy looks at Terry and says, "Well at least she's talking to you now."

Terry chuckles. "Yeah. I guess. I'll talk to you later." He heads down the sidewalk and crosses the street, hoping he isn't late for work.

Terry walks through the doors of Games 2 Go with only two minutes to spare. The manager, Eddie, looks at his watch and says to Terry without even looking at him "You're pushing it a little close today, dude."

"I know, I'm sorry, Eddie." Terry replies. "So, what's the new game we're putting on the shelves?"

Eddie points to a pile of boxes. "It's called *Soldier of Valor*, one of the most anticipated games of the season. Open up the first two or three boxes and put the copies on the shelves, then take the cutout in the back room and put it on display outside." Terry nods, grabs a box cutter Eddie left on the counter, heads over to the boxes and cuts the tape off the top of one of them.

He grabs a few copies of the game, as many as he can carry, and starts putting them on the empty shelves. While he's doing that, Eddie asks "So is your friend Billy coming to buy a copy of the game? I haven't seen him come in for some time."

"I doubt it, boss. He might just buy it online again, just like the other games he bought. I'm worried about him."

"I'm sure he's fine. But it's a shame he hasn't been here in a while. He's one of my favorite customers. I hope he comes back soon."

"You and me both."

Terry spends the next forty-seven minutes opening boxes and putting copies of the game on shelves while Eddie deals with customers at the register. "So," a customer holding a damaged game system asks, "how much will a replacement cost?"

"Used," Eddie starts, "will cost about a hundred and fifty. New, two hundred. But if you buy it used, you will get a ten percent discount on your next game purchase."

Terry chimes in "You'll also get store credit you can use on another game system should you choose to buy it brand new." The customer gleefully says "Sounds like a good deal. I'll take it."

Eddie directs him to the register, rings him up, hands him a receipt, and says "Thank you for shopping at Games 2 Go. Come again." As the customer walks out, Eddie looks at Terry and says "Thank goodness you're here, Terry. I totally forgot about the store credit deal."

Terry opens another box and replies "No problem, boss."

"Haven't I asked you to stop calling me that?"

"Yes, but it's fun." He goes into the back room and grabs the cutout of the soldier character from the game. He asks Eddie "Which side do you want this on? Left, or right?"

Eddie responds "Uh, put it on the right side so people on the street can see it." Terry opens the door and sets the cutout down, but then gets the feeling he's being watched. He turns around and isn't at all surprised to see Brenna Kinsley and Jeff walking up to him. But before she can even get a word out, Terry shouts "Are you crazy?! You can't follow me to work! I have a job to do! Just leave me the hell alone!"

Eddie hears the commotion and says, "Something wrong, Terry?" Terry turns to him and says "Eddie, can you please call Sheriff Martin?" Eddie nods and heads back inside to call the sheriff. Brenna asks, "Is that really necessary, Mr. Welling?"

"YES! I am getting sick and tired of you and your lap dog cameraman following me around. No matter where I go, you're there. You bugged me at my house, then at school, and now where I work. This is going to STOP."

In no time at all, Sheriff Martin's car pulls into the store parking lot. He gets out and asks, "What's going on, Terry?" Terry points to Brenna and Jeff, who are acting innocent. Sheriff Martin sighs, says "I see. Thanks for telling me. I'll take care of this." He walks up to Brenna with a pair of handcuffs and says, "Please turn around, Ms. Kinsley."

"Why?"

"You're under arrest for harassment. I warned you about this, but you didn't listen. You were told to leave my son and his friends alone, and yet you ignored what I said."

"I was doing my job!"

"Doing your job doesn't mean following people around hoping they'll talk to you, nor does it mean giving out information on an ONGOING POLICE INVESTIGATION. You had your chance."

As Sheriff Martin puts Brenna in the back of his car after reading her rights, Terry walks up to him. "Uh, Mr. Martin?" he asks.

"Yes, Terry? What is it?"

"Is it true you found a body at the lake?"

Sheriff Martin lets out a sigh through his nostrils, nods, and replies "Yes. We did. This morning."

"Is it Trent Alexander?"

"I honestly don't know yet, Terry. You know I can't talk about it. The medical examiner hasn't started the autopsy yet. We're hoping to get some answers soon."

Terry looks at Brenna. "What about her?" he asks.

"She'll probably make bail as soon as I get her to the station, but I'm sure she'll think twice before hounding you again."

"How did you know she asked me about the body?"

"Billy called and told me. She was giving you a hard time at school, right?"

"...Yeah."

"Don't worry. She won't be going anywhere near the school again. If she does, she'll be arrested for trespassing."

"Thanks, Mr. Martin."

Gene chuckles. "No problem, Terry. Have a nice day." He gets back into his car, starts the engine, and drives off while Terry walks back inside the store, happy Brenna Kinsley is out of his hair. At least for now.

# CHAPTER FIVE

The Littleroot Public Library is the most likely place where Allison Libby can be found after school, doing her homework without anyone distracting her. She sits by a window in a corner by herself, doing her homework without any distractions. She prefers it this way; she feels she can get more done when nobody's around to bother her.

Unless, of course, Billy just happens to walk in, then she's more than happy to let him sit with her and keep her company. However, the chances of Billy Martin walking into a place that doesn't have video games or comic books are small. But at least it's the one place her mother won't send a search party to look for her if she doesn't come home on time.

After Dr. Kaminko's house was destroyed and Allison broke her wrist, her mother, Kimberly, became overprotective of her. She started watching her like a hawk, making sure she doesn't get hurt; if she even gets a paper cut, she'll flip out. She even quit her job as a cashier at the local store to keep an eye on her only daughter.

Though Allison won't say anything to her, she's beginning to feel a little smothered, almost claustrophobic. With her mother watching her every move nearly twenty-four hours a day, she's surprised she hasn't hired a bodyguard for her yet. But she will finally reach her breaking point if she does that, and she's hoping she doesn't.

Her father, on the other hand, is a different story. David Libby works at Thorne Construction, operating the crane. He enjoys it, but he wishes the crane was a dinosaur so he could slide down its tail and shout "Yabba-Dabba-Doo!" like his favorite cartoon character. He wishes television now was more like the shows of days gone by; he doesn't understand why every other show is about singing or people famous by being famous.

One year for Christmas, Allison gave him a box set of DVDs that had some of his favorite shows growing up. They watched it together and had a great time, but Kimberly couldn't understand why a grown man could enjoy cartoons involving a screwy rabbit or a cat and mouse constantly hitting each other. His reason was simple. He told her "Because they're funny."

He loves his wife, but it just perplexes him when she spends too much time keeping a close eye on their daughter. Of course, he was worried when she broke her wrist, but he also chose not to obsess over it like Kimberly has done. He feels as though she's spending too much time trying to keep their daughter safe from the entire world and kind of neglecting their nine-year-old son Jake. This has caused some tension in the Libby family household. He's sleeping in the spare bedroom these days.

Allison finishes up the last of her homework, although a small part of her doesn't want to. She knows as soon as she steps through those library doors, her mother will call and text constantly until she answers. So, she takes her time finishing her assignments, puts her books in her backpack, gets up from the table, and walks as slowly as possible to the doors. When she finally steps through the doors and finds herself back into the real world, just as she expected, her cell phone rings.

She tries resisting the urge to just let it go to voicemail, because she knows it's her mother calling. If she ignores it, her mother will jump in her car and embarrass her somehow, maybe by dragging her down the steps by her arm and throwing her into the car while everyone watches.

Not wanting to be humiliated, she finally answers. "Hello?" she says with a slight hint of anger in her voice. "Allison, where are you?" Kimberly asks on the other line. "Do you have any idea what time it is, young lady?"

Allison, trying so hard not to scream, replies "Yes, Mom. I know what time it is. I was at the library doing my homework. That's where I always go after school, remember?"

"Don't give me any lip, Allison. I want you home right now."

"I'm on my way." She hangs up, puts her phone in her jeans pocket, and proceeds to walk the long way home.

It takes at least twenty-five minutes for Allison to get from the library to her house, but that's only if she goes the normal way. These days she prefers to go the long way, which adds about another twenty minutes to her walk home. The longer she takes to get to her house, she figures, the more time she has to herself before her mom gives her a lecture for not being home on time.

She walks through the woods, where she sees the beauty of Littleroot Lake and can stop for a few moments to admire it. But today seems different, somehow. While she's walking, she notices a few police cruisers parked by the lake.

*"Strange,"* she thinks to herself. *"Why are the police at the lake? Did the seniors drive Mrs. Doyle's car into it again?"* She decides her mom can wait a few more minutes for her to come home and walks up to an officer standing by the edge of the lake.

"Excuse me," she says. "But what's going on here?" The officer turns and replies "I'm sorry, miss, but the lake is closed until tomorrow. I'm afraid I'm going to have to ask you to leave."

Allison doesn't question him and heads back into the woods, but she's still confused. What happened to make the police keep people from coming to the lake? It can't be anything big; nothing ever happens in this little town, at least not since the night at Dr. Kaminko's house. Of course, that was three months ago. Well, whatever it is, it's probably nothing to be concerned about. Besides, she needs to get home before her mom calls in the National Guard to find her.

When Allison finally walks into the driveway of her house, she sees her brother Jake sitting on the deck playing a video game. He looks up from it and sees his big sister coming up the steps. "Hi, Alli!" he exclaims, giving her a hug.

"Hi, Jakey!" she responds, giving him a hug of her own. "How was school today?"

With a big smile on his face, Jake says "Oh, it was awesome! During lunch Henry Collins told a joke that was so funny, it made peas shoot out of Lance Getchell's nose!" Trying to keep a straight face while not looking disgusted, Allison says "Oh, really?"

"Yeah, but I couldn't tell if they had snot on them."

"But they probably didn't beat your distance record from when milk came out of your nose."

Jake shakes his head. "Not even close!" Just then, Kimberly steps outside and says "Allison. You're late. You know the rules." Allison walks inside the house and replies "Sorry, Mom. I stopped by the lake on my way home. I noticed some police officers there and I was curious."

Kimberly follows her inside with Jake behind her. "Why were the police at the lake?" she asks.

"I don't know, Mom. They told me to leave."

"Well, it's probably for the best. I don't want you at the lake. You could get hurt." Allison walks into the kitchen, goes to the fridge, grabs a small bottle of juice, and replies "How can I possibly get hurt walking by a lake, Mom? It's not like I'm going to break my arm just from staring at it. What's the big deal?"

"The big deal," Kimberly begins, "is you almost got yourself killed when you and your friends ventured into that accursed house. You shouldn't have gone there. It was too dangerous, not to mention foolish and stupid."

Allison takes a sip from the bottle, doing her best to stay calm. "How many times do I have to apologize?" she asks. "I said I was sorry already. I wasn't expecting the night to be so…eventful. I thought it was going to be a simple night of looking for answers that probably didn't exist."

Kimberly rolls her eyes. "It doesn't matter, Allison. The point is I don't think you should be hanging out with your friends anymore. They're a bad influence on you." Allison starts choking on her juice, and when she finally stops coughing, she exclaims "What the heck is THAT supposed to mean, Mom? How are my friends a bad influence on me?"

Kimberly grabs a towel and wipes up some of the juice Allison spit up, looking her in the eyes and says, "If it weren't for them, you never would have gone into that stupid house and you never would have broken your wrist." Allison puts her juice bottle on the counter, but she doesn't say anything, knowing her mom will continue the most pointless argument she's ever heard in her life. But before she can even leave the kitchen to go upstairs, Kimberly stands in front of her.

"We're not done with this conversation yet," she says. "So, you are to stay here until we are." Allison just stares at her mother, not saying a word. Just then, the front door swings open, and David walks inside after a long day of work. He puts his lunch bucket down by the door and tries to walk into the kitchen, only to see his wife and daughter engaged in an old-fashioned stare down for some unknown reason.

"Uh, hello, family of mine," he said hoping to get their attention. "May I ask what's going on here?"

"Dad, Mom's being completely unfair." Allison replies. "She's telling me I shouldn't hang out with my friends anymore. She thinks they're a bad influence." David sighs, rolls his eyes, and calmly says "Kimberly…"

His wife turns to face him and exclaims "David, don't start with me. Our daughter's "friends" are nothing but trouble, especially that Casey Martin. She puts her down constantly and doesn't value her opinion at all. She's nothing but a selfish, narcissistic little…"

Suddenly, without warning, Allison screams "STOP!" at the top of her lungs, shocking both of her parents and her brother. Kimberly looks at her with a look of surprise on her face while David has a grin on his.

"Allison Libby, what has gotten into you?" Kimberly asks.

Allison takes a deep breath and replies "Do not talk about Casey like that. She's my best friend, and I'm tired of you always saying bad things about her."

"Sweetie, you know it's true. She never respects you. Why are you defending her?"

David remarks "Because you finally pushed her buttons. We're all getting fed up with how you talk badly about her friends, whether it's Casey, Terry, or Billy."

"It's their fault my baby got hurt at that stupid house! Terry's a self-righteous punk who thinks he's got something to prove, Billy's afraid of a running leaf as well as his own shadow, and Casey only thinks of her own well-being instead of those around her."

Allison responds "Mom, stop. Casey may have her faults, but she's been my best friend for nine years. Yes, she can be a little selfish, but she cares about me. And she DOES value my opinion. I let her know what I think about things, and she does her best to respect that. And Terry is not a punk. He's smart, determined, and cares about the town a great deal. He wanted to expose the truth about Hamilton because nobody else dared to go inside the house and put an end to the legend of Dr. Kaminko. If he didn't go inside, Hamilton probably would've bankrupted the entire town. And Billy may be gullible and quite cowardly, but he's more than that."

"Oh? What else is he?"

"He's…sweet, funny, honest, and he doesn't let anything bother him. He also cares about me. So does Terry. That's why they're my friends, and I won't listen to you talk badly about them anymore."

David puts a hand on Allison's shoulder and whispers "Good job, kiddo."

Kimberly shouts "Don't encourage her, David! Children aren't supposed to talk to their parents that way! Where does she get the nerve to talk to me like that?"

David shouts back "I'm glad she did! Ever since she went into that house, all you've done is try to shelter her from the rest of the world! You won't let her volunteer at the animal shelter anymore, she's not allowed to go anywhere unless you're with her, and you won't stop bad mouthing her friends! You've suffocated her with your overprotectiveness, and she's had enough! She's sixteen years old, for crying out loud! You need to stop trying to keep her safe from the world! Let her live her life!"

The shouting between David and Kimberly continues, while Allison and Jake try their best to ignore it. Eventually the arguing gets to the point where Jake wants to be anywhere but the house. Allison sees her brother becoming uncomfortable, so she takes him by the hand and they walk over to the front door. Kimberly notices and says, "Where do you two think you're going?"

"Anywhere that's NOT here," Allison replies. "Come on, Jake, grab your coat."

"Where are we going, Alli?" Jake asks, to which Allison says, "The one place Mom can't yell at us." And with those words, the sister and brother duo open the door and head outside.

Casey Martin spends most of her time after school going online, checking the latest news in social media and fashion. She's always looking for inspiration in hopes of being able to create her own signature look. After all, if she's going to be a big name in the industry, she needs to create a style all her own instead of just copying someone else's work and trying to pass it off as her own.

These days, though, she hasn't really felt inspired. She just can't bring herself to look at the latest fashions. All she can think about is kissing Terry the day of the awards ceremony. Why did she do it? Should she have done it to begin with? Would Terry have done it first if she didn't make the first move? Why is this bothering her so much? She likes him, a lot, but what if they became more than friends? If it didn't work out, would their friendship even survive it? How would it affect Terry's relationship with Billy?

Sure, Billy can be a real pain in the neck, but he's still her family, and his opinion, whether she'll admit it or not, matters to her; after all, she knows how uncomfortable it makes him whenever she flirts with his best friend. Should she tell him she wants to be more than friends with Terry? Should she keep it to herself? Should she call Terry right now and tell him she'd like to go to the school carnival with him? But what if he says no and decides he wants to go with somebody else? Does he still plan on going? Maybe he still wants to go with her.

She thinks to herself *"I'm going to do it. I'm going to call Terry and tell him I would like to go to the carnival with him. It's a month away, and that will give me plenty of time to decide on an outfit. He'll love it."*

Just as she's about to dial Terry's number on her phone, her mom Angela calls her from downstairs, saying "Casey! Allison and her brother are here!" Startled, Casey puts her phone on her desk and heads downstairs. Sure enough, Allison and Jake are standing in the doorway, taking off their coats.

Angela takes Jake into the kitchen for a snack while Casey and Allison head back upstairs. "What's the matter, Alli?" Casey asks her.

"Let's just say I finally reached my breaking point with my mom." Allison replies. "She pushed me too far, and my dad came to my defense. Jake and I were getting tired of listening to the fighting, so we decided to come here. I hope that's okay."

Casey opens the door to her room. "Of course, it's okay. You and Jake are always welcome here, especially if you need to get out of the house for a little while."

The two friends enter the room, which hasn't changed much in the past three months. Normally Casey makes some slight changes to the room every few months, such as a new poster or she'll move some of her favorite outfits around in her closet. But, because of the incident at Dr. Kaminko's house, her injury made it difficult to make any changes, so she left it the way it was and never got around to doing anything with it.

Allison notices Casey's phone on her bed, sees Terry's number was the last one she dialed, then says "So what did Terry have to say?" Blushing, Casey replies "Nothing. I started calling, but then my mom said you and Jake were here, so I quickly hung up. Luckily, he won't know I called. It didn't ring long enough for his phone to let him know it was me."

"Plus, he's working right now. He wouldn't have been able to pick up." Allison adds. Casey sits on her bed, and tries to change the subject by saying "So, how silly did Billy look with that hat he had on today?"

Allison remarks "I know he's trying to impress Madame Granger, but eventually he'll realize it's a waste of time and give up. So, what were you going to say to Terry?"

"I was just going to say I'd go with him to the school carnival. That is, if he's not going with anyone else."

"Casey, I don't think he'd want to go with anybody besides you. Trust me." Just then, Allison says "By the way, do you know why the police have closed off the lake?"

Casey shakes her head. "I didn't even know they did. I'd ask my uncle Gene, but he probably can't tell me because it's an ongoing investigation or something like that. I'm sure it's not a big deal."

Allison turns on Casey's computer to check her e-mail. "You're probably right. Nothing exciting about the lake, anyway."

"Of course, I'm right. When was the last time the police of this quaint little town ever needed to close off the lake?"

Later that night, the Littleroot Police have left the lake for now. It was decided the body they found was merely a coincidence and that there was no reason to alarm the townspeople. After all, Littleroot Lake is a big tourist attraction in the summer, and it wouldn't be right to keep them away. The lake tends to be a popular spot at night, when teenagers come to party when everyone else is asleep.

There have been noise complaints in the past, but nothing serious.

Tonight, though, only two young people dare to venture to the lake at this time of night.

A young man stands beside the edge of the lake, simply enthralled by its beauty. "Come on! The water's fine!" he says.

From the shadows, a woman says "I don't know if I should. Isn't this lake supposed to be haunted?" The boy rolls his eyes. "Really? Don't tell me you believe in that old legend, too! There's nothing to fear! Besides, aren't YOU the one who wanted to come out here?"

The woman says, "I am, but I didn't assume it would be so creepy at night."

"It's just an old superstition, like the legend of Dr. Kaminko, except Dr. Kaminko was real! The story of Littleroot Lake is just that! A legend! Now come on!" The woman approaches cautiously, stands next to the boy, and says "I guess you're right. I feel safe with you already."

The boy replies "You should. The lake is harmless. I'll make sure nothing happens to you." The boy looks up at the night sky and doesn't notice the woman's eyes turn black. She then says with a sly grin on her face "Oh, I know you will. In fact, I'm sure you can do so much more…"

# CHAPTER SIX

It didn't take long for the body of the young man to be discovered at the lake the next morning. It was all over the news, but Terry was somewhat oblivious to it as he groggily stumbled into the kitchen and sat at the table. "Morning, sweetie." Julie said as she cracked open a couple of eggs. "You want some scrambled eggs?"

She doesn't get an answer. "Terry? Do you want scrambled eggs?" She turns around, only to see Terry asleep, face on the table. Marcus enters the kitchen and sees his son sleeping at the table.

"What's with him?" he asks.

Julie replies "He was up late doing his homework last night. He came home from work, made a sandwich, went into his room and didn't come downstairs."

Marcus sits at the table, lifts Terry's head up, and notices a line of drool coming from his mouth while he snores. "He seems to be sleeping a lot lately." Marcus says. "When was the last time he actually stayed awake?"

Julie turns on the stove, puts the egg yolks in a pan, and responds "I honestly don't know. I think his pain medication is doing it. Maybe he should stop taking it."

The smell of eggs being cooked brings Terry out of dream land. He yawns, stretches for a few moments, then says "Scrambled eggs…" Julie puts the eggs on a plate when they're finished and hands it to him. "Morning, sleeping beauty." Marcus says with a slight chuckle while Terry grabs a bottle of milk from the fridge.

"Morning, Dad. Morning, Mom." When he pours some milk into a glass, he sits back down, ready to enjoy his breakfast.

"Late night?" Marcus asks. Terry grabs his fork and stabs part of the scrambled eggs with it. "Yeah, you could say that. Work was exhausting." Terry replies.

Julie sits down next to Terry, and calmly says "Honey, listen. We think it's best if you stop taking the medication the doctor prescribed."

Confused, Terry asks "Why?"

"We think it's keeping you awake. You sleep in until noon and you can barely get through a shift at work without needing to rest every ten minutes. Your boss called and said he's concerned."

"The medicine isn't making me tired, Mom. I'm just having trouble sleeping, that's all."

"Is it affecting your school work?"

"No, Mom. I can stay awake through class, but when I have to work, I just want to come home and relax."

"Why don't you tell your boss?"

Terry rolls his eyes. "I doubt that would go well with him. He expects me to do my job and not complain about it."

Marcus chimes in and replies "If he's going to work you until you can't stay awake, then maybe you should take some time off until you're feeling one-hundred percent."

"I can't do that, Dad. I don't want him to think I can't handle it anymore and fire me as a result."

"Do you work today?"

"No. Why?"

"After school, I want you to come straight home and sleep. Don't worry about your homework until you're awake. Okay?"

Terry thinks about it for a moment, then says "Okay, Dad." He continues eating his breakfast until he looks at the television. "Hey, Mom, can you turn up the volume please?" he asks.

Julie turns up the volume enough for Terry to hear what the newscaster on the screen was saying. *"This is the second body found at Littleroot Lake as in many days,"* the reporter says. *"Police are not releasing the identity of the victim, along with the first victim they found. The police have closed off the lake until the investigation is complete. No entry will be allowed until further notice. This has Gary Duschene reporting for Channel 8 News.*"

Julie turns the television off. "Wow," she exclaims. "Two bodies found at Littleroot Lake. That's rare."

Marcus sips from his coffee cup. "Who could they be?" he asks.

"I think one of them is Trent Alexander." Terry chimes in.

"What makes you think that?" Marcus asks as Terry gets up from the table.

"I talked to Billy's father at work yesterday. He was there to deal with Brenna Kinsley, and she said it was Trent Alexander."

"Hasn't he been missing for a few days?"

"Yes. Sheriff Martin doesn't know if it is him, but he probably wouldn't rule it out as a possibility."

"Well, whatever's going on, please stay out of it, Terry. It's a matter for the police." Terry grabs his backpack and heads for the door.

"I don't plan on getting involved. It's none of my business. I'll see you guys later. Love you!" He opens the door and heads off to school, with the thought of the lake in the back in his mind.

He quickly forgets about the lake the second he arrives at school. While a lot of the students stand outside the doors waiting for the bell to ring, he heads inside so he can get to his locker. He notices Billy isn't around, which kind of surprises him; he knows Billy doesn't care for school, but he at least tries to show up early so they'd have some time to talk before their first class starts.

He opens his locker, puts his backpack inside, then hears a voice from behind say in a cheesy French accent "Bonjour, Monsieur Terry!"

He knows it's Billy and turns around. "Hey, Billy, what's…" His jaw drops the moment he sees Billy standing there in a beret, a black-and-white striped long sleeve, a pencil mustache, tight black pants, black shoes, and a bubble pipe in his mouth. He stands in shock, not moving a muscle; almost like a statue.

He finally closes his mouth, and says "What the HELL are you wearing, Billy?"

Billy replies in his French voice "I am not Billy Martin. I am Pierre Cousteau, French class extraordinaree. I have traveled all over France, learning all its customs. I have even been to that city in Canada, the one that starts with the letter 'Q'."

"You mean Quebec."

"Zee *Jeopardy* guy?"

"No."

"Who is zee *Jeopardy* guy?"

"It's not zee… it's not him! It's the name of the city! And what's with the bubble pipe?"

Billy laughs and replies in his French voice "Silly Terry. I am only sixteen. I am not old enough to buy tobacco."

Terry rolls his eyes. "Is this another attempt to impress Madame Granger?" he asks.

Billy blows into his pipe, making small bubbles come out of it. "This is not any attempt," Billy says. "This time she won't be able to resist me. She will see that I am a master of the language of love."

"Even though you don't know how to speak it?"

"…To each his own."

They head down the hall, but when they approach the door to Madame Granger's room, they notice a sign that says *French class has been cancelled for today. Please go to study hall in the cafeteria. Merci Boqué, Madame Granger."*

The bubble pipe falls out of Billy's mouth as he stands in shock. He throws his hands in the air and screams "OH, COME ON!! NO FAIR!! WHY IS THIS HAPPENING TO ME?!" He soon attracts the attention of a few other students in the hall, causing them to stare at him and Terry, who grabs him by the shoulders and shakes him.

"Billy, snap out of it! Calm down!"

"But it's not fair!"

"It's not a big deal! She's probably sick! She's only human, after all!"

"No, she's not! She's a goddess! Perfectly flawless! She can't be sick!" Then, Terry realized he would need to resort to desperate measures and gave Billy a quick slap across the face. Everyone in the hall was shocked at what he did; it was so loud it echoed all the way down the end of the hallway. Billy, however, didn't seem to be at all surprised.

Instead, he calmly says to Terry "I don't think I needed that." After his little moment of weirdness ends, he and Terry head to the cafeteria for study hall.

Upon entering the cafeteria, they almost every table in the room is taken, except for the one Casey and Allison are sitting at in the corner by a few windows. They weave through the crowded cafeteria, trying not to bump into anyone along the way. But, as Terry expected, Billy accidentally steps on the foot of his favorite person Jeremy Hodges, who happened to be sleeping, not caring why he was in the cafeteria if it got him out of class.

Then, he felt someone step on his foot. The moment he felt someone's shoe on top of his, he woke up and found none other than Billy Martin, dressed up in the most ridiculous outfit he had ever seen. He immediately got out of his seat and grabbed Billy by the shoulder. "Hey, Martin!" he shouts. "What's the big idea?"

Confused, Billy replies "What the hell are you talking about, Hodges?" Jeremy points to his foot.

"You just stepped on my shoe. Why don't you watch where you're going? And what the hell are you wearing, anyway?"

In his lame French accent, Billy says "I am Pierre Cousteau, French class extraordinaree. I have traveled all over France, learning all its…"

Terry grabs Billy and says "No. I'm not listening to that again. Let's get going." He drags Billy away before Jeremy can say anything else, and they make it over to Casey and Allison's table. "Hey, guys," he says. What's going on?" Shrugging her shoulders, Casey replies "We have no idea, Terry. What about you?"

"Madame Granger's out today, and there was a sign that said all of her students were to come to the cafeteria for study hall." Terry looks around and observes every student in the cafeteria. "But there's no way every student in the school can be in her class. Something strange is going on."

"Speaking of strange, what's with the getup, cousin?" Casey asks Billy, who seems confused at the question, but when he tries to speak in his French accent again, Terry quickly puts a hand on his mouth and says "What did I just get done saying to you? You're NOT Pierre Cousteau. You're Billy Martin. So, talk normal already!"

He removes his hand from Billy's mouth, ready to put it back on in case he decides to speak in that awful accent again. Instead, Billy says in his normal voice, "Party pooper."

Then, Allison chimes in and exclaims "I think I know what's going on." "What?" Terry asks. "Well," she replies, "when I was walking home yesterday, I passed by the lake and saw the police there. I asked what was going on, but the officer didn't answer and asked me to leave."

"It might have to do with the body they found yesterday."

"What body?" Allison asks.

"My dad said they found a body at the lake," said Billy. "Rumor says it's Trent Alexander."

"There's no way to prove it's him, Billy." Terry says. "Trent's been missing for a week, but it doesn't mean he's dead. I'm sure the police will find him soon."

"I hope so. The last thing this town needs is a ghost running amok."

"Billy," Casey begins, "there are no such things as ghosts!"

"Oh, really? Then explain what we saw three months ago! Magic trick gone wrong? Very realistic special effects? I don't think so."

Just then, Mrs. Doyle walks in, and as she heads up to the stage, she notices Billy's outfit and asks, "Do I want to know what's going on, Mr. Martin?"

"Probably not, Mrs. Doyle." Billy replies. She shakes her head and raises her hands above her head to get everyone's attention.

"Quiet, please! People, quiet!" The entire room goes silent, giving Mrs. Doyle a chance to speak. "I'm sure a lot of you are confused as to why you're all doing in the cafeteria instead of going to class right now. There is a reason, and here to explain it is Sheriff Gene Martin."

Gene walks in, and just like Mrs. Doyle, he notices what his son is wearing, but instead decides not to say anything and walks onto the stage.

"Thank you, Mrs. Doyle." Gene says. "Now, I know you have been hearing rumors about what happened at the lake yesterday. Normally I don't do this, but the sad truth is, two bodies were found at the lake yesterday and this morning. The first one has been identified as that of your fellow classmate Trent Alexander."

A chill in the air fills the room immediately after the announcement. Nobody could believe what they had just heard; one of their classmates, dead? It just couldn't be true. How could someone they know be gone just like that? They had hoped he would be found unharmed, but to hear they will never see him again was too much to bear for some.

Terry and the others were just as devastated as everyone else. He didn't know Trent very well, but he knew he was very popular. He was on the wrestling team, an MVP, and a decent guy.

"I just can't believe it." Allison mutters. "He volunteered at the animal shelter just like me. He liked playing with one of the dogs, a Lab-Akita mix named Maverick. He planned on adopting him one day. Now he'll never get the chance…"

Billy takes off his beret in silence. He thought Trent was a cool guy; he tried to teach him how to play basketball once, but he kept missing the basket. He didn't get mad at Billy even once. Instead, they sat on the bench and swapped stories about family, friends, and favorite hobbies. Trent was the only person in the school, besides Terry, who treated him with respect.

Then, Mrs. Doyle speaks up and says "Thank you, Sheriff Martin. Now, I know this must be tragic news for most of you, so grief counseling will be available for anyone who feels they need it. And for those who don't have study hall, please head to your scheduled classes. That is all."

The students leave the cafeteria to head to their classes, but some feel as though there's no point in going. Trent was their friend, their teammate. To have his young life cut short is enough to make some of them sick to their stomachs. Terry and Billy remain at their table, since they have study hall, but Casey and Allison don't move a muscle.

"Uh," Billy says, "don't the two of you have Algebra or something?"

"How can we go to class after what we just learned?" Allison replies. "It just can't be true. This is just a bad dream, right?"

"I wish it were, Allison." Terry remarks. "That nosey reporter said they found his body, but I didn't believe her; I just wanted her to leave me alone. She was telling the truth."

"That doesn't give her the right to be such a pain in the ass, though." Casey exclaims. "What happened to her, anyway?"

Billy clears his throat and replies "My dad arrested her outside Games 2 Go yesterday. She'll probably make bail soon, but my dad said he'll make sure she doesn't bother us anymore."

Terry says nothing and instead stares out a window, hoping he and his friends will never have to deal with Brenna Kinsley again. And yet he has a feeling he'll be seeing her again at some point.

The school day ends on a somber note, with most of Trent Alexander's friends being sent home early due to being so distraught they ended up becoming sick, and as if to fit the mood the entire student body was feeling, grey clouds covered the sky and a downpour began. It didn't take long for students to feel themselves being soaked by the heavy rain as it fell from the sky and onto their bodies.

While most of them ran to their cars as fast as they could, some chose to stay behind and wait for someone to pick them up by the main doors. Quite a few of them didn't have backpacks, so all their books and homework would be ruined by the rain; they weren't going to take that chance, especially if they have an assignment that is worth a third of their final grade. They decided to wait for their friends who had vehicles to drive up to the steps and gift them a lift home; others called their parents to pick them up.

Billy was one of the others. He takes out his cell phone and presses his mother's speed dial, asking her to stop by the school and give him a lift home.

Twenty minutes later, Amy Martin pulls up to the steps in her purple 1998 Mercury Grand Marquis. Billy runs to the passenger side door as fast as he can to minimize getting soaked.

He throws his backpack in the back of the car, and once he finishes buckling up, Amy asks "Billy, honey, don't you think it's past time you consider taking Driver's Ed? I can't keep picking you up every time it rains cats and dogs. Sooner or later you'll have to bring yourself home from school."

As the car leaves the school yard, Billy sighs, "Yeah…no. I have absolutely no interest in driving. You've seen me drive in video games."

"Billy, those are games. This is reality. You must learn to drive at some point. Your father and I aren't your personal chauffeurs, you know."

"You're not? And I already bought those funny looking hats, you know."

"Speaking of funny hats, how'd the outfit go? Did it impress the girl you like?"

"No. she wasn't in today."

"Oh, I'm sorry, sweetie. Maybe she'll be there tomorrow. By the way, don't forget Casey and her parents are having dinner with us tonight, so don't do anything to ruin it."

"Why do you always assume I'll ruin something?"

"Remember what happened last time they had dinner with us?"

"I already told you it was a science experiment."

"Well make sure your inner Einstein doesn't make an appearance tonight."

"No promises."

The minute the car pulls into the driveway, Billy runs inside the house while Amy heads to the kitchen to start dinner. He quickly goes into his room, shuts the door, turns on his television, and starts playing a video game. He figures he has time to kill some zombies before dinner, but before he knows it, two hours pass, and he hears Amy yell from downstairs, "Billy, Casey and her parents are here! Come down and say hi!"

Billy shuts off the game, and reluctantly leaves his room. But the minute he gets to the bottom step, before he has a chance to say hello, Casey says "Just look at him! He's not even ready for dinner! He's still wearing the clothes he wore at school today! That stupid outfit!"

Billy, looking at Casey's black dress, replies "So what? Why should you care how I dress? And why are you dressed so fancy? We're not going anywhere that requires you to look like a total snob. It's my house, so I can dress however I want!"

Casey's father, Jeremiah chimes in and says "Now, now, guys. There's no need to start ripping off each other's heads. We're here to have a nice dinner tonight. So, what are we having tonight, Amy?"

"We are having oven-roasted chicken," Amy replies, "with mashed potatoes, gravy, biscuits, and stuffing." She then looks at Billy and whispers "Billy, please change into something more appropriate." Billy whispers back "But, Mom…"

"No buts, Billy. Go change. Now."

Billy lets out a small growl and stomps back upstairs, not knowing Casey is right behind him. She follows him into his room and is immediately shocked at what she is seeing.

Billy's room is a total mess; bed not made, clothes on the floor, video game wires all tangled up, trash bin overflowing with food wrappers and soda bottles, and there is a terrible odor she can't identify.

She sees Billy walk over some box to get to his closet. Just as he picks out a shirt and jeans, Casey says "Uh, Billy…"

He turns to see Casey standing in his room, and replies "What do you want, Casey?"

"Uh, nothing. I just couldn't help but notice that your room is a little…untidy. Have you considered cleaning it up a little?" Billy pretends to think about it, for only a second, then just as quickly, replies "Nope. Not interested."

"But, Billy, no smart human being can possibly live in such…horrid conditions. How can you even sleep in this mess?"

Billy removes his striped shirt and proceeds to put on the other one, albeit grumpily, then Casey turns around while he puts his jeans. "The answer is very simple, Casey". Billy said. "Because I'm comfortable in it. I see no point in cleaning it up since I spend most of my time in here. If I had a fridge and a bathroom, I could live up here."

Casey rolls her eyes and remarks "You practically do! But you can still clean up this mess. I mean, old food wrappers, soda bottles, messed up bed, comic books completely unorganized, DVDs and CDs all over the floor, and…what is in all of those boxes?"

Billy shrugs his shoulders, pretending to ignore his cousin's complaints. "I have no idea," he says. "I just like to have them in here on the off-chance I might need them."

"Then use them to pick up the comics, CDs, and DVDs! This room is a pigsty! You seriously need to clean up some of this crap!"

"You call it crap, I call it necessities." Casey picks up an old pizza box, intensely disgusted by it. She can normally ignore a room if it's messy, but when her cousin lets his own room get as bad as it has become, she can't keep her mouth shut.

"THIS is NOT a necessity, Billy! This is just disgusting and lazy!" she yells. "Clean this up, will ya?" Billy throws his French outfit into the hallway and attempts to walk out but finds himself blocked by Casey's person.

"Excuse me," he calmly says. "Can you move aside, please?" Unmoving,

Casey replies with a motherly tone "Not until you clean up this battlefield you call a room."

Normally Billy would just pretend she wasn't there and move her to the side so he could go downstairs and eat, but for some reason he feels a little irked at the thought of her trying to give him orders, especially when it comes to how he keeps his room; yes, it's disgusting, but it's his room and he prefers to clean it, if he decides to clean it, on his own time, not when someone tells him to.

"Casey, I am not going to clean my room just because you stand in my doorway and tell me to. You're not the boss of me, so get out of my way."

Casey shakes her head, refusing to move an inch. Instead, she yells "Aunt Amy! Could you come up here, please?" Within thirty seconds Billy's mom comes to the door to his room, and Casey moves out of the way to show her the land of the lost that is his room. At first, she says nothing, as if she was only imagining things and her son's room isn't as bad as it really is.

Then, without warning, Amy screams "WILLIAM EDWARD MARTIN! WHAT IS ALL THIS?! YOUR ROOM IS DISGUSTING! I WANT IT CLEANED UP RIGHT THIS MINUTE!"

Shocked by his mom's sudden outburst, Billy says "But what about dinner?" Amy replies "You're not eating until all of this garbage and useless junk is gone and this room is spotless! It may not have been perfect in the past, but at least I could see your floor! This is the last straw! You, mister, are grounded! No TV, no comic books, and no video games until I say so!"

Billy shouts back "But that's not fair!" Amy rubs her temples, trying to calm herself down, looks at her only child, and remarks "Life isn't fair, Billy. Now not another word from you. I'll be back with some trash bags so you can get started on cleaning this mess."

She looks at Casey and says "Thank you, Casey, for telling me of this monstrosity. Keep an eye on him while I get the trash bags." She turns and goes downstairs while Casey eyes Billy with a look of arrogance and confidence, but he doesn't even look at her. He suddenly feels like crying, his eyes becoming a little misty.

He could handle being grounded for his messy room, but he hates being treated like a child by anyone. He stands in his room in shock, still trying to process what just happened. One minute he was being told to change for dinner, the next he's grounded because his cousin couldn't keep her mouth shut.

When Amy returns, she's carrying two large trash bags in her hand. She passes them to him, then goes over to a corner of the room that has a small bookcase. It's where Billy keeps his collection of Sherlock Holmes books, and he hates it when anyone touches them. She pulls them out of the bookcase and hands them to Casey, causing Billy to shout "What the hell are you doing? Those are mine! You can't do that!"

"Your father and I paid for them, so actually we can." Amy replies with a hint of sadness in her voice. "You'll get them back when we decide to give them back."

She goes back downstairs, but Casey decides to stay and watch Billy clean until his father comes home. He starts throwing the wrappers in one bag and soda bottles in the other.

Casey walks over to him and whispers "You'll thank me for this one day, cousin." He simply gives her an ice-cold stare and doesn't blink.

She couldn't believe what she was seeing. Her cousin, the biggest coward in all of Littleroot, was mad. He was mad at HER. She didn't understand why; she was only trying to help him not be a slob but he just couldn't see it yet.

Instead he keeps his angry gaze upon her and says "Leave me alone and get the hell out of my room. I will never forgive you for this."

Trying to explain why she did it, Casey replies "Billy, I was only…" but he interrupts her and screams "I SAID GET OUT! GET AWAY FROM ME!!"

At that moment, Casey finds herself shocked at Billy's sudden outburst. He has never talked to anyone like that, not even her. He always kept to himself instead of getting involved in anything. But today was different, and she couldn't for the life of her figure out why.

Instead of trying to ask him what the matter was, however, she decided he just needed time to calm down and proceeded to walk downstairs and let him clean up his room.

After she left, Billy stopped cleaning and sat on a section of his floor that was clean. He released his grip on the trash bags, trying to collect his thoughts without losing his temper again.

He felt hurt. He felt betrayed, like he had just been stabbed in the back with a very sharp knife and someone kept twisting it while also taking away one of the few things that meant a lot to him. At this point, he was starting to feel low and began to wish he never had a cousin.

He suddenly felt the tears fill up in his eyes and decided to finally let them roll down his face, unable to hold them back any longer. He stands back up and proceeds to go to his bed, plopping and lying face down, crying himself to sleep.

# CHAPTER SEVEN

The Littleroot town jail isn't very big, but it's enough to keep troublemakers out of peoples' hair until they're released. Many police officers often joke about holding an adoption fair to see if any of the punks would be taken to good homes. However, Sheriff Martin tends to ignore them, saying the prisoners are not there for their entertainment. Of course, the latest troublemaker in the cell might be an exception.

Brenna Kinsley sits in a corner at the far end of the cell, wondering when her boss would arrive to pay her bail. She couldn't understand why she was even in jail in the first place; she was just trying to do her job. After all, the people have a right to know about the deaths at the lake and if they're connected to Dr. Kaminko somehow. Dr. Kaminko's house was all people were talking about after it was destroyed thanks to Terry Welling and his friends. She knows they're hiding something but won't talk about it. They'd rather get on with their mediocre lives than be famous. But, no, they had to whine to the sheriff and have her butt thrown in jail like she was a common criminal.

Why can't they respect the Fourth Estate? Freedom of the press, people! How is she supposed to move up in the world of journalism if she can't even get a simple interview with the town's new celebrities? The sooner she finishes her story, she'll be one step closer to getting a better chance at being a famous name in the media and finally leaving the quaint (and very annoying) town of Littleroot, Maine. She may have grown up here, but she wants to get out as soon as possible. She got sick and tired of the quiet, peaceful atmosphere Littleroot provides. She wanted to see some action, so as soon as she got the chance, she interned at the Channel 8 studio before they told her to study journalism at the Maine School of Communications. When she graduated, Channel 8 offered her a job and she gladly accepted, hoping it would lead to a big career.

Five years later, however, she found herself in a dead-end job reporting on parades and town events. Then, three months ago, she was sitting at home when her boss called her. He said there had been an explosion at Alden Hill and Dr. Kaminko's house was destroyed. She rushed to the scene just as the fire department were trying to put out the flames erupting from the remains of the town's most infamous urban legend. She looked over at some ambulances being loaded up with some people who were obviously injured by the explosion somehow. She walked past a fire engine and approached the closest ambulance. She asked the EMT what had happened, and they only replied that they don't know, but four teenagers were found unconscious at the bottom of the hill. She looked over their shoulder to see a sixteen-year-old boy with black hair lying on a stretcher wearing an oxygen mask. She attempted to ask him questions, but the EMT told her to get back and let them do their job so they can get the boy and his friends to the hospital.

She immediately became intrigued at the possibility of a big scoop that has finally come to Littleroot, but when she asked the four teens if she could get an interview, their parents were quick to tell her to leave them alone and let them rest. That only made her more determined to get the whole story, so she tried buttering up Sheriff Martin, but she was welcomed with a slammed door in her face after she learned one of the teenagers was the sheriff's son. Using her various resources, she managed to dig up information on the young Martin. It made her more curious about the foursome and again requested the sheriff to interview Billy, and again he slammed the door in her face.

Her attempts at speaking with Littleroot's new celebrities were met with reluctance; they finally agreed, hoping she would finally leave them alone. The story brought the station its highest ratings in years. Every other news station came to Littleroot, wanting a piece of the action that surrounded the story. Then, the excitement and hype began to die down, and almost nobody was talking about Dr. Kaminko anymore, which brings us to now. Brenna pitched the idea of a follow-up interview to her boss, and he approved, not knowing the kind of trouble she would eventually find herself into.

Brenna's cameraman Jeff approaches the cell, and she couldn't be any happier to see him, although she's also a little annoyed at the same time. She was glad he arrived, but mad that he took so long. She runs up to the bars and says "What the hell took you so long, Jeff? I've been in this stupid cell for nearly twenty-four hours!"

Jeff replies with a neutral tone in his voice "The boss wasn't too happy about you being arrested and was trying to decide if he should pay your bail or let you sit in there and think about what you did."

"And what did he decide?" Brenna asked. Just then, Mr. Rowan, the head of Channel 8 News, comes through the door, but he doesn't look very happy to be in the police station where one of his best reporters is being held. He walks up to the officer behind the desk and says, "I'm here to post bail for Brenna Kinsley." The officer hands him a clipboard and replies "Fill out the paperwork and she will be released shortly." Brenna lets out a sigh of relief, knowing she can finally leave and get back to work on her story. But while Mr. Rowan is filling out the paperwork, he walks over to the cell and tells Brenna "Don't think you're off the hook for what you did, Ms. Kinsley. You are on thin ice as of now."

Confused, Brenna asks "What do you mean, boss?"

"Do you have any idea how much trouble you've caused the studio? Not to mention the legal fees we must pay because of you? The families of those kids are filing for restraining orders against the entire Channel 8 news team thanks to your overzealousness."

"I was only doing my job, boss. Everyone else in this town may have forgotten about what happened at Dr. Kaminko's house, but I haven't. The town hasn't felt the same since that night. Something happened in that house that changed the town. I just know it! I only need some proof, and I know those kids have the answers! Let me interview them again! Please let me speak to them!" Brenna pleaded, but Mr. Rowan didn't seem moved by her request. "Are you crazy, Brenna?" he said with a sincere tone of anger in his voice. "You are not to go near those kids! If you even set one step near their homes or the school, their families will sue you for everything you have. They already threatened to sue the studio because of what you did yesterday. But luckily, I convinced them not to press charges. On one condition." Jeff slowly backs away, afraid of what Brenna will do when she learns of what her boss had done.

"And what is the condition, boss?" she asks, confused at Jeff's movement. Mr. Rowan returns the clipboard to the officer and hands him the bail money, then he looks at Brenna. He gathered up the courage to speak, knowing he didn't want to say it, but he swallowed his fear and said "When you return to the studio, hand in your press pass and never return. I'm afraid I must let you go. I'm sorry, Brenna."

Before Brenna can even say a word, Mr. Rowan and Jeff leave the holding area, leaving her in complete and total shock. What had just happened? Was this a bad dream? How could Mr. Rowan just fire her like that? It didn't make much sense. She worked her butt off at that studio for five years, and this is the thanks she gets for all her hard work? The second the officer opens the cell, she storms out of the police station, her blood boiling to a level of anger she never felt before. She walks about for two or three blocks before stopping into the local coffee shop. She orders a plain coffee, black, and sits at a table by a window to gather her thoughts.

Then, just before she can call her boss and tell him what he can do with her press pass, Allison Libby walks in. What a twist of fate this was. Perhaps she could get her job back if she managed to get at least one follow-up interview with one of the four teenagers from that night at Dr. Kaminko's house.

Allison doesn't seem to notice her at all, just keeping to herself. She orders a mocha latte and sits at the far end of the building. She hears her cell phone ring and pulls it out of her jeans pocket. She sees it's Casey and quickly answers. "Hello?" she says. "How's the dinner going?" After a few seconds, she exclaims "What? Billy was grounded? What did he do to make that happen?" Just then, she notices Brenna eyeing her.

*"Not very subtle in her spying."* she thinks to herself. "Uh, Casey, I got to go. I'll talk to you later." She hangs up and turns her phone off, then she walks over to Brenna's table. "Um, what do you want, Ms. Kinsley?" she asks as politely as she can, considering who she's talking to.

Brenna takes a sip of her coffee, then replies "Hello to you too, Ms. Libby. Could I possibly have a few minutes of your time?" Allison knows she should just turn around and go back to her table; this reporter's been a real pain in her neck, and the necks of her friends. But something doesn't seem right. Brenna didn't seem like herself, as if she didn't have a friend in the world. So, against her better judgment, she sits down in the chair across from Brenna's. "What exactly is it you want, Ms. Kinsley? My parents told me I'm not supposed to be talking to you. So where is your cameraman? Hiding in the bathroom?"

Brenna shakes her head. "No cameraman, Allison. He's not here. He's probably back at the studio working with someone who still has a job."

"What do you mean?" Allison asks, and Brenna takes out her press pass. After a moment, she quickly tosses it into a nearby trash bin. "I don't work for Channel 8 anymore. My boss fired me so your parents and the parents of your friends wouldn't sue the studio."

Allison isn't sure what to say about Brenna's situation. She may have been annoying and got on her nerves, but even she didn't deserve to lose her job to prevent a lawsuit from occurring. Perhaps there was a way to help her. She adjusts her glasses, then quietly asks "Is there anything I can do to help you?"

Brenna shakes her head. "I thought about approaching you and politely asking for a quick interview, but I decided against it, because that's what got me canned in the first place. I just wanted someone to talk to, that's all." Allison starts to feel sorry for her, then says "So, what did you want to ask me?"

Brenna picks her head up in slight disbelief. Could Allison Libby really want to be interviewed? She takes a tape recorder out of her coat pocket and asks, "Is it okay if I record this?" Allison nods, and Brenna presses the record button. "So, Allison, have you noticed any changes in the town since the night you and your friends went to Dr. Kaminko's house three months ago?"

"Uh, um…not really." Allison says. "It's been quiet, I guess. Things went back to normal for us. Why? Is there something weird going on?"

"You don't think it's weird the bodies of Trent Alexander and some other victim were found at Littleroot Lake, exactly three months after the night at Dr. Kaminko's house?" Allison shakes her head. "No, but I knew Trent. He volunteered at the animal shelter and wanted to adopt one of the dogs there. His name's Maverick."

"I have reason to believe there is a connection between Dr. Kaminko's house and the victims." Brenna says. "Both victims were found aged differently. Trent Alexander was seventeen, but when they found his body, he appeared to be his late eighties or early nineties. Same with the other victim."

Flabbergasted, Allison asks "What? Aged differently? Are you sure of this? How is that even possible?" Then, Brenna leans in a bit closer and says, "Let me ask you, Allison, and this is a very serious question."

"Uh, okay, Ms. Kinsley." Allison replies. Brenna then says, "Have you ever heard of...the Lady in the Lake?"

# CHAPTER EIGHT

CHAPTER EIGHT

Another day at Littleroot High School begins, but quite a few students have decided to stay home. A candlelight vigil for Trent Alexander is planned for later that night, and they want to use the time to prepare. They'd like to do everything they can to honor the memory of a fellow student whose life ended so abruptly and mysteriously. They just couldn't figure out how he died; the police weren't going to release that information until the autopsy was finished, and that could take another few days.

Some were confused, some were upset, but most were angry. They wanted to know if Trent died accidentally or if it was foul play, and if that's what it was, then they'd be ready to find the one responsible and make sure their friend was avenged. But luckily Sheriff Martin was also ready for such a possibility and would arrest anyone who even tried to take the law into their own hands. As much as he'd like to know how Trent died, he had to make sure nobody turned their grief into revenge, especially if Trent's death was just an accident. He'll just have to wait until the medical examiner can give him the results of the autopsy, and so will everyone else.

Billy stands at his locker, waiting for Terry to arrive, but he isn't his normal self. He spent the night before cleaning his room after Casey told his mom about the mess it had become and ended up being grounded for it. He had hoped his dad would convince her to ease up on him a little, but it turns out he was just as steamed as she was after seeing his room. He is now grounded for two weeks. No games, no comic books, no TV, no internet, and he can't even read his Sherlock Holmes books. Amy put them away, and he can't think of where they'd be. He hates not being able to read his favorite of the series, *The Hound of the Baskervilles*. Don't ask him why it's his favorite; it just is.

But until he can get them back, all he can focus on is his room. Every inch is to be cleaned until it is spotless. No trash on the floor, the bed must be made to his parents' standards, and dirty clothes are to be thrown into a hamper right outside his door. He doesn't want to do it, but he knows it's the only way he can get his stuff returned to him. But his thoughts of his things get interrupted when Casey approaches him.

"Hey, Billy. How are you this morning?" It's obvious she's trying to apologize for what she did, but he will hear none of it. He just looks at her with the same expression he gave her last night. Billy's never been one to hold a grudge, but this is different. It is to him, at least.

"Oh, come on, Billy, are you still mad about last night?" she asked. "I had my reasons for telling your mom. That room needed to be cleaned. Have you finished it yet?" Billy says not a word; instead he lets out a low growl, then he turns and goes to the cafeteria to get something for breakfast. He didn't have time to eat at home. He was so tired from cleaning he almost overslept and had to rush out the door so he wouldn't be late for school. As he storms away, Casey decides not to follow him, and Terry finally arrives just in time to see him leave.

"Hey, Casey," he says as he starts to do his locker combination. "What's wrong with Billy? I thought he was waiting for me here." Casey rolls her eyes. "He's kind of mad at me." Terry opens his locker. "Really? Why? What happened?"

Nonchalantly, Casey replies "Because I told his mom his room was a mess and she kind of…grounded him." Terry says nothing for a few moments, trying to process what Casey just said, then remarks "Wow. But that's no reason to be mad at you."

"Yeah, well, good luck telling him. He won't even talk to me. He keeps giving me an icy-cold stare, as if he wishes to melt me with laser vision or something." Terry grabs a few books, then closes his locker. "I'll try talking to him, see if I can calm him down. I know him. He's not normally one to be angry at anything." He proceeds to walk down the hall after Billy when Casey stops him. "Uh, Terry?"

"Yes, Casey?" Before she can even say anything, she starts to feel her face turn red. "Um, there's something I wanted to talk to you about, but I guess it can wait for a while longer. Go. Talk to your friend." Terry heads down to the hall and yells "Hey, Billy! Wait up!"

Casey kicks a locker. Not hard, but enough to let out some of her frustration. *"Stupid, stupid, stupid!"* she thinks to herself. *"Why didn't I ask him when I had the chance? At this rate, I'll never get to ask him to go to the school carnival with me! I wouldn't be asking him at all if I didn't kiss him during that stupid ceremony! What was I thinking?"*

Terry catches up to Billy, but he doesn't seem to notice. He appears to be lost in his little angry world. "Billy, I've been calling your name. Didn't you hear me?" Terry asked.

"Oh, sorry, Terry. My mind was somewhere else."

"Is it because you're mad at Casey?" Billy keeps walking toward the cafeteria, with Terry right behind him. "She had no right to do that! It just pisses me off!" Billy exclaims. "Thanks to her, I am grounded until further notice! She treated me like a child, and I want nothing to do with her!"

The two friends enter the cafeteria, where Billy grabs a chocolate milk and puts scrambled eggs on his tray. "Billy," Terry begins, "I know Casey can be a little…irritating at times, but you know she did it because she doesn't want you to live like a slob."

"Slob? You think I'm a slob?" Billy asks as he and Terry sit at a table. "Why would you say I'm a slob?"

Terry replies "I didn't say you're a slob, Billy. It's just there have been times where I wished your room could have been a little neater. Aren't you afraid of attracting mice with all of the old food you leave in there?" Thinking for a moment before shoving some scrambled eggs into his mouth, Billy says "No, not really."

"I haven't been in your room in quite a while, Billy, so I'm just going to ask. How bad has it become since the last time I was there?"

"Uh, not that bad." Billy says while taking a sip of chocolate milk. "Why do you ask?"

Terry sighs. "If it weren't bad, you wouldn't be grounded and angry with Casey right now. So, how bad is it?"

"Uh, trash overflowing, food wrappers on the floor, bed wasn't made, clothes everywhere, and maybe a few boxes that I couldn't find much use for."

Terry lets out a loud chuckle. "Well, it's no wonder you're grounded, Billy. You're living in a pigsty." Billy finishes his milk and aims for the nearest thrash bin. He misses by a long shot. "It's not a pigsty, Terry," he says, "it's comfortable living."

"I'm a little concerned, Billy. You live in a messy room, you never come by the store anymore, and you buy most of your games online. What's the matter?" Terry asked him.

"Nothing's wrong with me. I just haven't felt like going out lately, that's all."

"It's been three months, Billy. Did that night at Dr. Kaminko's house affect you that much?" Billy says nothing. He instead looks out the window, really hoping Terry will change the subject. But Terry presses on. "Come on, Billy, you can tell me. I'm your best friend, remember? If you can't talk to me, who can you talk to?" Billy remains silent. "Billy…"

"I'm not sure I want to talk about it right now, Terry." He gets up from the table, grabbing his backpack and heading out of the cafeteria while Terry follows him, refusing to drop the subject.

"Billy, you can't ignore this. Leaving it bottled up inside isn't healthy at all. You need to let it out."

"No, I don't. You know why? Because I'm not bottling anything inside. I am fine, and you don't need to stand up for Casey. As far as I'm concerned, she can go jump in the lake for all I care. What she did was unforgiveable. So, can we just drop it, already?"

The bell rings, and the two of them head to the door of their French class. They open the door, and Madame Granger is sitting at her desk. "Bonjour, Monsieur Martin. Bonjour, Monsieur Welling. You're right on time. I'm glad." Madame Granger said as they walked into the classroom.

Billy looks up and immediately smiles. *"She's back! Yes! I have another chance at winning her over!"* he thinks while going to his desk. *"Now I wish I brought my Pierre Cousteau outfit today."*

"Uh, Madame Granger," Terry speaks up.

"Yes, Terry?" Madame Granger responds.

"What happened to you yesterday? We saw the note on your door and we thought maybe you were ill."

"Oh, thank you for your concern, but I merely had a twenty-four-hour bug. Nothing to be worried about." Terry then notices one of the hairs on her head doesn't seem to be the right color, but he could just be imagining things due to a lack of sleep. "Alright, class, please open your books to page forty-seven and we shall begin our lesson."

Terry leans over to Billy and whispers "Hey. Does something seem a little off with Madame Granger today?"

"I don't know. Why do you ask?" Billy whispers back. Terry points to the teacher's hair. "A few strands seem to be a little discolored. She's a brunette, but those hairs look white. Or maybe even grey." Billy squints a little, looks at Madame Granger's hair for a moment, then replies "I don't think so, Terry. Maybe you're just seeing things. When was the last time you had a decent sleep?"

Madame Granger catches them whispering and clears her throat. "Excuse me, gentlemen," she said. "But can you please continue your conversation after class? I won't ask again."

"We are sorry, my dear," Billy says. "I can promise it won't happen again." He picks up his French book and turns his attention to Madame Granger.

"Kiss-up." Terry whispers.

"Paranoid." Billy whispers back. Terry starts flipping through his book, wondering if Billy was right. Was he only imagining things because he wasn't getting enough sleep? It's not common for a woman of Madame Granger's age to have grey hairs, but he was still confused.

What are the odds that she would be out sick the same day the police confirm they found Trent's body at the lake? Could it just be a coincidence? He had a funny feeling in the pit of his stomach, and it probably wouldn't be going away anytime soon.

As luck would have it, Allison was having a similar feeling in the pit of her stomach during Algebra class. Not many of her classmates were in today. They were at home, preparing for the vigil, but that wasn't what had Allison so distracted. Her conversation with Brenna Kinsley was firmly in the back of her mind.

Is it possible a "Lady in the Lake" was responsible for the death of Trent and the currently unidentified victim? She didn't think so, because such a thing couldn't possibly exist; sure, the legend of Dr. Kaminko was proven to be true, but that was different. There is just no way someone could live in a lake and just randomly kill people.

She was somewhat familiar with the legend of the Lady, but never paid much attention to it. It's just another one of Littleroot's urban myths and legends. So, for the time being, she decided to keep her little chat with Brenna a secret. She doubts anyone would even listen to her, anyway.

Casey notices Allison's lack of attention to what the Algebra teacher is saying. It wasn't like her to not be distracted in class. She would always listen to her teachers so she wouldn't miss a single detail on any subject. Casey rips out a piece of paper from her notebook, writes a small message on it, then crumbles it up and throws it as far as she can to Allison's desk. Instead, it hits her in the head. Not hard, but enough to derail her train of thought. She opens the note, which reads

*"Are you okay? You seem a little sidetracked. Don't let the teacher catch you daydreaming."*

Allison looks over at Casey, who's quietly waiting for a response from her. She waits until the teacher has their back turned, then she jots down a note of her own and quickly throws it at Casey's desk.

Casey picks the note up from the floor and reads what it says.

*"Everything's fine. I am not distracted. I was just thinking about something. Nothing important."*

She starts to write another note when someone approaches her desk. She looks up to see the Algebra teacher, Mr. Vaughn, standing by her desk, eyeing her. "I assume what you're writing on that piece of paper is more important than what I'm teaching you, Ms. Martin." Mr. Vaughn said with a slight tone of sarcasm in his voice.

"Uh, nope. Not at all, Mr. Vaughn. Just gibberish, that's all." Casey replies with a chuckle as she tears up her note and shoves it in her desk. "Good. Let's try to keep it that way, shall we?" Mr. Vaughn says as he turns and continues his lesson. But Casey just couldn't pay attention to what he was saying. Something was bugging Allison, and she wanted to know what it could possibly be.

The first half of the school day was finally over, which meant it was time for lunch. Terry and Billy find themselves near the end of the lunch line, which seemed to be moving slower than normal. It felt as if time had slowed down at that moment, and Billy let his frustrations be heard.

"Oh, come on!" he shouts. "I've seen snails move faster than this stupid line! Can you people hurry it up?!" Terry ignores him, focusing on a book he had been wanting to read but never found the time. As he turns a page, Billy taps his shoulder. "Hey, Terry." Billy says.

"Yes, Billy?" Terry replied.

"Do me a small favor and make this line move faster, will you?" Terry rolls his eyes. "And what makes you think I can do that even if I wanted to?"

"Just tell them you cracked a rat. Maybe that will do the trick." Terry again ignores him, focusing on his book the best he can. "Come on, Terry, do it. Announce to everyone that you cracked a rat!"

"Billy, I don't even know what the hell that means!" Billy gets a blank look on his face, then says "Really? You don't know what it means to crack a rat?"

Terry shakes his head. "No, I don't, and I'm pretty sure I don't want to know what it means. It sounds wrong."

"Trust me, Terry, it's not wrong. It just means you had to fart. Really bad." Terry closes his book, trying to process what Billy just said. "Let me get this straight, Billy," he says. "You want me to just announce to everyone in line, and in the cafeteria, that I farted really bad?"

Billy nods. "Exactly." Terry gives him a quick smack on the side of his head. "Forget it. I'm not saying that. Where did you even come up with the phrase 'crack a rat', anyway?"

"Oh, I was watching a funny show on TV last week. It's a hidden camera show about four lifelong friends who compete to embarrass each other. It was called 'Impractical' something."

"Billy, what did we say about you taking things from TV and using them in real life?"

Billy shrugs his shoulders. "I don't know. Did we say we liked it?"

"Never mind." The line starts moving a little faster, much to Billy's delight. Then, just as quickly, his delight turns to anger when he hears Casey's voice behind him say "What's for lunch?" Terry turns his head to see her and Allison, then says "We don't know, Casey. The line is moving slower than Billy when Mr. Vaughn asks him to complete a problem on the board."

"Hey! I resemble that remark!" Billy exclaims.

"Billy," Allison says, "it's 'resent', not 'resemble'. 'Resent' means you hate it, and 'resemble' means you look like it."

"Terry, did she just say I look like a math problem?" Billy asked. Terry shakes his head. "No, Billy, she didn't. She was explaining that you were trying to say you hate what I said."

"Oh. I knew that."

"Uh-huh. Sure, you did." The line moves some more, and the four friends are finally able to get their lunch. Their choices are a chicken burger, French bread pizza, or ravioli. Terry grabs the pizza and some apple juice, Billy chooses a chicken burger and some chocolate milk, Casey picks a pizza and flavored water while Allison grabs a bowl of the ravioli and skim milk.

They find a table near a window and sit down, but then Billy speaks up and says, "I don't remember asking HER to sit with us", pointing a finger right in Casey's face.

"Do you want to lose that finger, Billy?" Casey asks. "I suggest you get it out of my face before you force me to break it." Billy keeps pointing. "What did I say about telling me what to do? I DON'T have to listen to you!" he yells, attracting the attention of everyone in the cafeteria. "Billy, keep your voice down", Terry whispers. "You're making everybody stare at us."

"I don't care right now, Terry." Billy replies. "She keeps bossing me around and I'm sick of it!" Allison puts a hand on Billy's shoulder. "Billy, please calm down," she says in a calm and soothing tone. "Just eat your lunch." Billy lowers his finger and takes a huge bit out of his chicken burger, followed by a huge sip of chocolate milk.

"Billy, you can't be mad at me forever. Eventually you will need to forgive me," Casey tells him. "Right, Terry?"

"I'd rather not be in the middle of this right now, Casey." Terry says before taking a bite out of his pizza. "It's none of my business, and it's none of Allison's. You two need to work this out by yourselves."

The rest of the lunch period soon becomes quiet for them. Terry and Allison talk to each other about various topics, such as their Algebra homework, upcoming school events, and anything else they can think of so they won't have to deal with Casey and Billy giving each other the cold shoulder.

The tension between them was so thick, Terry and Allison felt they were caught in a fog. Instead, they just stare at each other without saying a word. Finally, Casey says "Billy, lunch is nearly over. Can't we just forget about this whole silly thing and pretend it never happened?"

"I wish I could, Casey," Billy remarks with an angry tone in his voice, "but I can't. You got me grounded and I had to miss dinner because of it. I just wish you would mind your own damn business and keep your big mouth shut!"

Casey yells "Excuse me?! Maybe if you weren't such a slob, I wouldn't have had to say anything at all! How ANYONE could live in such a mess is way beyond me! Why can't you learn to pick up after yourself?!"

Billy gets out of his chair, slamming both of his hands onto the table, loud enough for everyone in the cafeteria to hear. "I don't see how that's any of your business, Casey," he loudly replies. "You think that just because you have a certain standard of how to live and how to dress, you expect everyone to do what you want. Well, guess what? I don't have to!"

Casey gets out of her seat. "And what is that supposed to mean, Billy? What standard do I have, exactly?" She looks at Terry and Allison, but they keep quiet. "Well? What does he mean, guys?"

"Don't ask them, Casey. You want to know what I mean? Fine!" Billy shouts. "You're snobby, obnoxious, selfish, rude, and you think everyone else is below you just because their daddy doesn't own a damn bank!"

Casey slams her hands on the table. "Don't you dare bring my dad into this! Don't forget that he's your uncle, too!"

"Yeah, I know! You remind me every single chance you get! But part of me wonders. How can you possibly be his daughter? Because if I were your father, I'd be ashamed to have you for a daughter! The way you talk about my dad behind his back pisses me off! We may not be rich like your family is, but that doesn't matter! My dad helps keep the town safe, while yours just sits on his ass and counts money like he's the most important man in the world or something!"

Casey says nothing. Instead, she just stares at Billy, while Terry, Allison, and everyone else in the cafeteria watch her, waiting for her to say or do something. Then, without any kind of warning, she raises her right hand and slaps Billy across the face. The slap was heard throughout the cafeteria and through the halls of the school. Students were absolutely shocked at what she had done. Murmurs soon filled the room, while Terry and Allison get up from their chairs and back up against a wall.

"Should we do something, Terry?" Allison whispers. Terry shakes his head. "At this point, I'm not sure there is anything we can do," he whispers back.

Billy rubs his face, shaking off Casey's slap. Sure, it hurts, but to him, it didn't hurt as much as what she did to him last night. He then takes a glob of chocolate pudding from his lunch tray, holds it for a few seconds, then throws it right in Casey's face.

Loud gasps can be heard throughout the room, but they don't seem to notice or even care. The pudding starts to run down her face, and soon spills all over her pink shirt. Mr. Elliot runs over to the table and says, "What's going on over here, you guys?"

Casey doesn't speak a word to him; instead, she leans over the table, gets in Billy's face, and says with a low snarl "I wish I never had you for a cousin."

Billy snarls back "Well, at least that's something we can actually agree on." He grabs his backpack, takes care of his tray, and storms out of the cafeteria without saying a word to Terry, Allison, or anyone else while Casey heads to the bathroom to wash the pudding off her face.

Mr. Elliot looks at Terry and asks him "Care to explain this, Mr. Welling?" Terry looks at the floor and shakes his head, replying "Honestly, Mr. Elliot, I'm not sure that I can."

# CHAPTER NINE

It is never a good thing when people get into an argument and refuse to speak to each other afterwards. What's worse, however, is when their friends are caught right in the middle and are forced to choose a side.

Terry and Allison never imagined it would happen between Billy and Casey, but it did, and now they must decide if they should side with one or the other, because there was no way in a million years they could get the two of them to even acknowledge each other's existence at the moment.

The best thing would be to ignore the entire situation and hope it dies down so they can talk to each other again. But if there is one thing that Billy and Casey share, it is their stubbornness and refusal to let things go.

The rest of the day went on with a bit of an uneasy feel and everyone could sense the tension between Billy and Casey. She spent the rest of lunch in the bathroom washing the pudding off her face, but then she noticed some of it had stained her pink blouse and it wouldn't come out. She was forced to call her mom and ask her to bring a clean shirt. She never told her the truth about how her blouse got stained with chocolate pudding; instead she said she accidentally spilled it at lunch, although she wasn't sure how much of that story her mom believed, but she stuck to it anyway. All she knew for sure was she would never speak to Billy again.

Billy, on the other hand, was enjoying his newfound freedom from his least favorite (and only) cousin. Sure, he was still grounded, but he didn't care. He no longer had Casey breathing down his neck over every single detail of his life; how he dressed, how he ate, how he spent his free time, and how to basically live. He spent the rest of the day quietly humming a happy tune to himself without a care in the world. His attitude made Terry a little suspicious. He may look happy on the outside, but he's got to be hurting on the inside. After all, Casey is his family, and the only cousin he has. How anyone could feel so happy after an argument like that is obviously hiding what they're truly feeling. Terry attempts to get him to talk, but he simply states that he never felt any better than he did at that exact moment. A few of their teachers started wondering if he was taking some sort of drug that was making him act so weird. Terry assured them that Billy was fine, he was just in high spirits right now and hopefully he would be back to normal soon.

When the day finally ends, Terry sees Billy standing at a vending machine underneath a set of stairs getting ready to buy a soda. He walks over to him and says "Hey, Billy. Can we talk?"

"Terry!" Billy said with an upbeat tone in his voice. "What up, my man? Soda?"

Terry declines. "Billy, are you sure you're okay? What happened at lunch today was…"

"Awesome, right? I know! Never have I felt so free! Now I don't have to worry about some snobby witch breathing down my neck about everything I do. It's like releasing an animal back into the wild!"

"Did you just call Casey a wild animal?" asked Terry.

"Of course, not," replied Billy. "She can't be considered a wild animal. She can't even be considered human."

"Then what would you consider her to be?" Billy thinks for a few moments, then says "Uh, would it be mean if I considered her to be a Gorgon?"

"Yes. It would."

Billy puts his money in the slot. "Then that's what she is." Terry shakes his head. "Billy…"

"Don't try to defend her, Terry. She's evil and you know it." The soda falls to the bottom slot of the machine and Billy grabs it, waiting a few seconds before opening it so it doesn't spray all over him. "But she doesn't turn people to stone, Billy." Terry remarks.

"How do you know?" Billy asked.

"Because she can't." Terry replied. "It's not even remotely possible! The two of you need to sit down and work this out, because Allison and I refuse to be caught in the middle of this." Billy just stands there, confused. "And why would I want to do that?"

"Because she's your family." Billy takes a sip from his soda, then laughs. "That's a good one! 'She's your family'? As far as I'm concerned, she's nothing but a distant memory in the back of my mind." Terry puts some money in the vending machine. "But it's only been a couple of hours."

"What's your point?"

"The point is, you can't let something like this get between you two. Just bury the hatchet and forget this whole thing started." Billy thinks for another moment, then just as quickly replies with a stern "Nope!"

"Come on, Billy, you need to talk to her so the two of you can work this out. Won't you at least think about it?" Terry asks as his soda falls to the bottom slot of the vending machine. "Forget it, Terry," replied Billy. "As far as I'm concerned, she is dead to me. Cascy Martin doesn't exist anymore." Terry rolls his eyes and shakes his head in frustration. "Surely, you can't be serious." he says.

"I am very serious." Billy said. He puts his bottle of soda in his backpack, then puts the backpack straps over his shoulders and proceeds to walk to the main doors in the lobby. Then, before walking outside, he turns to Terry and says with a goofy grin "And don't call me Shirley." As Billy heads outside, Terry smacks himself in the head, thinking to himself *I knew he was going to say that! I knew it! Why didn't I keep my mouth shut? I walked right into that trap! His parents never should have let him watch that stupid movie!*

Meanwhile, in another part of the school, Casey sits in the hallway near the doors to the library and tries to finish up her Algebra homework but can't seem to concentrate. She couldn't get what she said to Billy out of her head. She didn't mean it at all, but Billy sounded so serious when he said he agreed. Did he really wish she wasn't his cousin? Is there a way they could sit down and talk about what happened? She heard him whistling in the hall earlier in the day after lunch, so maybe he didn't want to hear whatever she had to say. Perhaps he was glad to be rid of her, or maybe he was acting that way to hide his true feelings. She would probably never know since he decided he would never talk to her again.

Allison walks in and sees her struggling with her homework. She walks over to her table and says, "You look like you could use some help."

"Is it that obvious?" Casey asks. Allison sits down and replies "Yes, it does, but I don't think it's the homework that's giving you trouble. I think something else is bugging you." Casey crumples up her homework and throws it over her shoulder. "Today started out so easy," she starts. "I was all ready to ask Terry to go to the school carnival with me, but Billy ruined the moment just because he won't speak to me. And then we had that stupid argument."

"Well, Casey, I'm sure he didn't think it was stupid." Allison remarks. "Maybe he was trying to make a point. Perhaps he wasn't entirely wrong."

Casey raises one of her eyebrows. "What is THAT supposed to mean?" she asked. Allison adjust her glasses. "Well, Billy might have been truthful when he said you can be a little bossy."

"Truthful? How?" asked Casey. Allison takes a deep breath, prepared to deal with Casey's response, and says "I feel that there are times where you don't respect me, that you treat me more like a secretary instead of your best friend like you claim to be. I feel like you're taking advantage of me."

"How so?"

"Well, when we were doing our report for Mr. Elliot's class, I really wanted our topic to be Senator Susan King, but you wouldn't even budge on the subject and told me we would do it on Christina Meir, even though I didn't even know who that was, but you insisted on it. I was afraid to tell you no, so I agreed to do it."

"Allison, I…" Casey starts, but Allison puts up a hand and continues. "And that night Terry and Billy went to Mayor Hamilton's house, you decided to try on clothes while I worked on the report by myself. You ignored my request for help and focused completely on your outfits."

"Allison, do you seriously think I'm taking advantage of you?" Casey asks. "I would never do that to you!" Some other students in the library shush her, then Allison whispers "Well, you did, and I was getting a little tired of it, but never said anything until Billy finally stood up to you. I mean, you told his mom that his room was messy and you got him grounded. You are always bossing people around because you want them, us included, to behave and dress a certain way. Are you truly surprised that he wished you weren't his cousin? I can't believe it took him this long to finally say something."

Casey doesn't say a word; instead, she just sits in silence, thinking about Allison just said. She never thought herself to be such a bossy person or imagined she tried to ever tell anyone how to dress or how to live their lives, but perhaps what Allison said was a little bit true. Maybe she really IS somewhat of a bossy person who takes advantage of her friends and tries to mold them into her image, but she just never realized it until now.

She then pushes her chair out, gathers her things, then walks out of the library in a hurry with Allison following her. "Casey, where are you going?" she asks, but Casey doesn't respond. She keeps walking down the hall and down a flight of stairs as fast as she can while Allison tries to keep up with her. "Casey! Slow down!" she calls out. "What's wrong?"

Casey finally stops, turns around, and shouts "Why would you say that, Allison? How could you possibly think I'm that kind of person?"

"Casey, I didn't mean to upset you," Allison says. "But I felt that you needed to know the truth. You needed a bit of a wake-up call. All Billy did was set the alarm." Casey clenches her fists but bites her tongue. "You call that a wake-up call?" was all she could say.

"You're right. I should've hit the snooze button before I opened my mouth."

Casey unclenches her fists, then takes a few deep breaths before asking Allison "Do you really think I'm that bad of a friend?" Allison shakes her head. "No, of course not, Casey. But sometimes I feel as though you treat me more like a sidekick than anything else. And Billy…"

"I was only trying to help him." Casey replied. "Living in a room like that isn't good for anyone's well-being. I didn't want him to get sick. He may be annoying and quite immature, but he's still my cousin."

"But you act like a mother to him, and he already has one. I'm sure she would have asked him to clean up his room without you saying anything. If that happened, he wouldn't be angry at you. But I'm sure there's a reason for his room being a mess." Allison remarks.

"What possible reasoning could there be for his room being a pigsty?" Casey asks.

"Well, when was the last time any of us had seen him go do anything since that night at Dr. Kaminko's house?" Casey shakes her head. "I am not sure, but I do know he hasn't stopped by Games 2 Go in a while. He prefers to buy all his stupid games and comic books online now. I just assumed he was being lazy and acting as though he's allergic to fresh air or something."

"I don't think he's being lazy on purpose, Case. I think he's scared."

Casey scoffs. "Obviously, he's scared. He's afraid of his own shadow. Why do you think we had six more weeks of winter earlier this year?"

Allison adjusts her glasses. "That's not what I mean." Casey thinks for a few moments, then it hits her; going to Dr. Kaminko's house, meeting Anton, coming face-to-face with Dr. Kaminko himself, almost getting thrown into the ghost dimension, then the house being destroyed and Billy breaking his ribs. She looks at Allison and says, "Do you think Billy was really affected by what happened at Dr. Kaminko's house?"

Allison shrugs her shoulders. "The only way to know for sure is to ask him yourself." Casey shakes her head. "I can't. He won't even speak to me. Terry tried talking to him, but he wouldn't budge. He's either not scared or in denial."

"Casey, what you need to do is wait. Don't push him into talking. When the opportunity presents itself, I am sure he will open up to you." Casey collects her thoughts, then as she and Allison start walking down the remaining stairs, she says "I hope you're right, Alli. I really do…"

✦✦✦✦✦

One job that quite a few people would never want is being the medical examiner. They can't imagine cutting open the bodies of the deceased and looking for a cause of death, but for Dr. Linda Taylor, it can be quite the adventure. Most of the time she only must examine traffic accidents and patients who died during surgery, but never has she had to figure out a seventeen-year-old boy aged so rapidly into an eighty or ninety-year-old man. She was both disturbed and intrigued about the cause of Trent's death. She knew his family wanted answers so they could finally let him rest in peace, but she also had to examine the other body that was recently found at the lake.

She was convinced it was a mere coincidence both bodies were found at the lake, but the recent body was also young, yet when they found him, he too appeared to be in his eighties or nineties. After restless hours of examinations, she may have found a cause. She takes out her cell phone and calls Sheriff Martin and tells him and Officer Judd to her lab.

About twenty minutes later, Gene and Franklin arrive, hoping Linda had some news about the victims. "Okay, Linda, we're here." Gene announces. "Do you have an answer as to how these two died?" Frank takes ten dollars out of his pocket. "Ten bucks says they both drowned," he says proudly, "because they were both found at the lake."

Linda shakes her head. "Seriously, Frank, you're betting on the deceased now?"

Frank grins. "There's no racetrack around here." Gene ignores him. "And I thought my son was a smartass. Now, what do you have, doctor?"

"Well," Linda begins, "it's nothing definite, but I have reason to believe the victims died of progeria."

Frank, confused, asks "Isn't that the opening of a book?" he asks.

"No, Frank, that's a prologue." Gene replies. "Progeria is a disease that makes someone look older than they really are." He then looks at the bodies and remarks "But I thought progeria made you age ten years, not ten seconds. How can you be sure that it was the cause?"

"I'm not entirely sure, but it's a possibility." Linda replies. "It might be a new variant. I'll know more once I complete my examination. But there's another reason I called you guys here."

"And what would that be?" Frank asks.

"I don't think it was a coincidence both bodies were found at the lake. Is it possible whatever caused these deaths left them there for a reason? What are the odds both bodies would be found there only a couple of days apart?"

"We know where you're going with this, Linda", Gene replied, "but there is no reason for alarm just yet. Now, we are not sure what killed these boys, and until we know for sure, we just need to keep doing our jobs until we find a cause."

Just then, another officer runs into the lab, nearly out of breath, then shouts "Sheriff Martin! Deputy Judd! I am so glad I found you before you left!" said the officer between breaths.

"Calm down, officer." Frank replied. "What's going on?"

"We need to get to Littleroot Lake right away!" Confused, Gene asks "Why? What's happened?"

The officer replies "Someone just called it in five minutes ago. Two more bodies were just discovered at the lake."

# CHAPTER TEN

Wallace Paisley and Henry Reeves. Those were the names of the latest victims found at Littleroot Lake. Both were only seventeen, but appeared to be in their eighties or nineties. A young couple discovered them while walking through the woods, and even though the police had it sealed off, that didn't stop them from sneaking over and taking a closer look. Horrified, they quickly called the police and left the area before anyone showed up; they were afraid they would be arrested for entering a crime scene of an active investigation.

Sheriff Martin could not believe Linda was right. The fact that two more bodies were found at the lake, in the same way as the others, gave him great cause to worry about the safety of the town he was sworn to protect. So, to that end, he arranged a press conference for the very next day and made the announcement.

"Two more bodies were found at Littleroot Lake yesterday afternoon." Gene said in a stern and professional, yet somber, voice. "Their names are Wallace Paisley and Henry Reeves, age seventeen, both students from Belfast. We do not know the cause of their deaths, but we now treating them, as well as the deaths of Trent Alexander and the second victim, now identified as sixteen-year-old Jacob Whitely, as homicides. So, until we catch the one responsible for these heinous acts, Littleroot Lake will be closed until further notice. No one will be allowed to enter under any circumstances. There will be no exceptions. That is all. Thank you for your time."

The reception to his announcement was mixed throughout the halls of Littleroot High School. On one hand, the students were devastated at the loss of their classmates, but they were also mad that their favorite hangout spot was closed off to them until the killer could be caught. And they let their anger be known, particularly to the sheriff's son.

One student yelled to Billy as he walked by "Hey, Martin! Your dad sucks!" Another threw a can of cheese spray at him, making him smell like bacon and cheddar. He was hoping nobody would notice his cheesy aroma. As he approached his locker, Terry, who was already getting his books, took a sniff, looked at Billy and said, "Uh, Billy?" Billy, trying to ignore the smell, fumbles with his locker combination, then replies "Yes, Terry?"

"Are you aware that you smell like…?" Billy grabs his books, eyes Terry and says "Yes, Terry. I smell like cheese whiz. What of it?" Terry puts the last of his books in his backpack and says nothing for a few moments. Then, he remarks "Uh, nothing at all. I was just wondering…"

"What?"

"Did you maybe eat a lot of grilled cheese sandwiches?" Terry takes another sniff. "With maybe a side of bacon?"

"No, Terry, there was an accident in the middle of town involving a meat truck and a gigantic cow. I decided to get caught right in the crossfire hoping to get cheese and bacon related superpowers!"

"Wow. The sarcasm is on fire today. What happened?"

Billy opens his locker, looking for his books. "Nothing," he says. "I believe you heard the news about the lake?"

"That your dad closed it down because he's ruling all the deaths of Trent and the other victim as homicides?" Terry says. "Yeah, I heard. But that still doesn't explain why you smell like a sandwich."

"Well," Billy starts, "a few students let their frustrations be known. One of them threw a can of cheese spray at me and it kind of…sprayed on me. But there's something else. Two more bodies were found at the lake this morning. Students from Belfast."

Wide-eyed, Terry says "More victims? Seriously? What is going on here?" Then, before Billy can answer, Casey and Allison approach them. Billy turns away, still refusing to look Casey in the eye. Instead, he says "Hey, Alli."

"Hi, Billy." Allison replies. "How are you today?" Then, she takes a quick sniff. "And why do you smell like cheese?" Billy rolls his eyes and doesn't reply. Instead, he looks away, pretending to look for something in his locker. Terry says to Allison "It's a long story, Alli. So, did you two go to the vigil held for Trent last night?"

"We did." Casey replies. "It was really nice. We knew Trent was popular, but we had no idea exactly how popular he was until last night." Billy turns to look at his cousin with a confused look on his face, but still says nothing. Terry steps in for him, asking "What do you mean, Casey?"

"Well, his family was there, obviously, but a lot of townspeople were also there. There was a moment of silence, then a few people shared stories about Trent. Not just stories relating to sports, but about who he was as a person in general. They talked about his hobbies, his dreams, his time at the animal shelter. They had nothing but praise for him."

"That's not surprising, Casey." Terry said. "He just died. It would be rude to say anything negative about him in a time of mourning, but maybe there wasn't anything negative to say about him, anyway. At least his loved ones were there and got support from the town. They are going to need it right now."

The four friends go quiet, processing everything. It is never easy when someone loses a person they love, so they couldn't even begin to imagine what Trent's family was going through right now. The hurt, the heartbreak, the feeling of emptiness, the anger, the question of *"What if I had been there? Could I have saved him?"* But as much as everyone wants to hold on to a memory, or wonder if they could have changed fate, they can't stop time from moving on.

"So, uh," Billy speaks up, "perhaps we should get to class now. What do you say, guys?" Terry clears his throat, closes his locker, and replies "Uh, yeah. That's probably a good idea. So, Casey, Allison, we'll see you at lunch, okay?"

"Uh, yeah, sure." Casey says. "Lunch. Until then. Come on, Allison, let's go." She looks at Allison, who's in deep thought, but what she's thinking about is a mystery to her. Terry and Billy have already left for their class, so Casey is left wondering what is going on inside her friend's head. *"It's certainly better than trying to get inside Billy's head,"* she thinks to herself. *"Then again, Allison's head isn't full of cobwebs like Billy's is. It's just as bad as his room. Disgusting.*" She waves a hand in Allison's face, trying to get her attention.

"Allison? Hello? You there?" she asks, but Allison doesn't budge. She is as still as a statue. She is only like this when something is bothering her, but never says a word. Casey thinks it's a little creepy and wants her to stop, because she fears she will attack her like they're in one of those stupid movies Billy is too afraid to watch. Of course, she knows such a thing could never happen. Allison would never attack her. At least, she hopes she won't.

Casey finally decides to flick Allison's nose in hopes it will finally snap her out of her little trance. It does the trick, as Allison reactively grabs her nose and starts rubbing it. She looks at Casey and shouts "Ow! What was that for?" Casey shrugs her shoulders and replies "Sorry, but you weren't moving a muscle and it was creeping me out."

"So, that makes you decide to flick my nose? That really hurt, you know."

"It was either flick your nose or smack you in the head like Terry does to Billy, but I'm not a total savage. Now, come on, let's get to class before we're late."

As the two friends head for Algebra class, they pass by a group of students heading in the opposite direction. Allison can't help but overhear their discussion as they walk by. "So, do you think it's true?" one student asks.

"It has to be," says another. "It's the only explanation." The students keep talking. "How else would you explain what happened to those guys? It has got to be only one thing."

Allison stops in her tracks, wanting to listen in on the group's conversation, which Casey notices. "Allison, come on!" she says, but Allison walks towards the students. "Excuse me!" she shouts, getting their attention.

"Yes?" one student asks her as they turn around.

"Well, I was curious, and I wanted to know. What are you discussing?" One of the students gives her a look, and replies "What business is it of yours?"

"I am terribly sorry about this," Casey interrupts, "but my friend doesn't know when to stay out of other people's conversations, so we'll just get out of your hair and head off to class now." She grabs Allison by the arm and tries to drag her away from the group. "Let's go, Alli, before we get in trouble."

Then, another student speaks up. "Wait!" they exclaim. "We'll tell you. We're surprised you haven't heard. Everyone in school is talking about it."

Confused, Casey replies "Talking about what, exactly?"

"Why, how Trent and the other victims died, of course. Everybody knows how it really happened. It wasn't accidental drownings like the rumors people are spouting. It's something much worse."

"What else could it be if they didn't drown?"

"Think about it. Trent and the other victims were found at the lake with no plausible cause of death. Since they didn't drown, the only possible explanation is…"

"Don't stop now, guys. What is it?" Casey asks, but they go silent. Then, Allison speaks up and replies "The Lady in the Lake."

Lunch time arrives quite slower than normal for Casey and Allison, almost as if time just stood still. They decided to skip the lunch line and immediately sit at their usual table, waiting for Terry and Billy to arrive so they could discuss what they had heard earlier in the day. But the line seems to be standing still for some reason, and Casey starts to lose her patience waiting for Terry and Billy. "Where the hell are they?" she asks furiously. "We should have seen them in line by now!"

"Relax, Casey, they'll be here." Allison replies. "You know Billy wouldn't miss a chance to criticize lunch. We'll see them soon enough." Ten minutes pass, and just like Allison said, Terry and Billy make their way to the front of the line. They grab their lunches and head to the table where Casey and Allison are sitting. Billy sits next to Allison, just so he didn't have to look at Casey, while Terry sits between Casey and Allison.

"So," Terry begins, "what's on today's agenda today, ladies?"

"We heard a rumor before Algebra class this morning," said Casey. "Apparently, Trent and the others didn't drown. Everyone in school is saying it was something else."

Billy mutters under his breath "They probably saw you without makeup. That's what killed them."

Terry reaches over and smacks him in the arm, whispering "Not now,

Billy. Let her finish. So, exactly what caused Trent's death?" Casey takes a sip of her milk, takes a deep breath, and says "The Lady in the Lake." At that moment, Billy spits up his chocolate milk and starts to cough. Allison pats his back while Terry asks "The Lady in the Lake? That old legend? That's what killed Trent?"

Billy catches his breath then remarks "Okay, I was ready to accept that Dr. Kaminko was real, but there is no way in hell a woman living in a body of water killed Trent and the others. That's just stupid!"

Casey rolls her eyes at Billy's remark, saying "This coming from the kid who reads 'Fake Science Monthly' and who also believes in ghosts and the Loch Ness Monster, yet he can't believe in the Lady?"

"I don't read, I skim. And who said I was even talking to you?"

"Then who were you talking to, you little brat?"

"None of your business, spoiled princess!"

"Alright, that's enough!" Terry exclaims. "Casey, you have to admit that it does sound a little far-fetched. I mean, I am not entirely familiar with the story, but didn't she supposedly drown back in the twenties?"

"Yes, but what if it's true? If Dr. Kaminko was real, then why can't the Lady be real, too?"

"Casey, Littleroot has a lot of urban myths and legends. The story of the Lady in the Lake is just one of them. It's merely a story kids tell to scare each other around a campfire, just like the legend of Dr. Kaminko."

"Except Dr. Kaminko was REAL, Terry! We went into his house, we discovered the truth, and we proved he existed! We got hurt because of it!"

"I'm trying to keep an open mind, Case, but there has to be another explanation behind these mysterious deaths that doesn't involve the spirit of a woman who drowned in the lake over nine decades ago."

"Why not? Think about it. Four bodies were found at the lake within only a matter of days, and the spirit of the Lady is said to haunt the lake where, per legend, she will end the lives of anyone who dares to enter her territory. Supposedly it's her way of getting revenge on the town because they let her drown."

"Except two of the victims aren't even from Littleroot, they were from Belfast! So, that can only mean the Lady of the Lake doesn't even exist! Just let the police do their work, will you?" Casey looks at Allison, who's trying to ignore the heated discussion. "Well?" Casey asks her.

"What?" Allison says.

"Tell them what you told me earlier." Allison shakes her head. "I'd rather not. I'd prefer to forget it even happened." Billy looks at her and remarks with a chuckle "Did you go skinny-dipping again?"

"No! I thought we agreed to never bring that up again!"

"Sorry. Now, what were you going to say?" Allison takes a deep breath, then replies "I spoke with Brenna Kinsley the other day." Terry exclaims "What? Why?"

"Because she told me she believes there is a possible connection between what happened at Dr. Kaminko's house and what's happening at the lake. Of course, that's nonsense, but then she mentioned the Lady, asking if I was familiar with the legend."

"And?"

"Like everyone else, I only know what is told through legend. Woman drowned in the twenties; spirit declares vengeance on the entire town."

"Not exactly an open and shut case." Terry chimes in.

"I know, but there's no other explanation for the deaths yet. There's nothing wrong with being mildly curious. Maybe we should go to the lake later tonight and check it out for ourselves." Then, Terry gets up from the table. "I don't think so, Allison."

"I think that's a great idea, Alli." Casey exclaims. "That way we can search for answers. If the Lady is real, then we'll know for sure. If not, then we can let the police do their work, though I doubt they'll have much luck solving this little mystery."

"Didn't you hear what I just said, Casey?" Terry asked. "I don't think it's such a good idea. Let's just forget about it."

"Why? What's the big deal?"

"Well, for starters, the lake is now a crime scene, so nobody except the police are allowed in. And, secondly, how exactly did you plan to find evidence of the Lady's evidence? It's not like she leaves a calling card, if she even exists."

"I didn't say she exists, now did I? I'm just exploring the possibility that something strange is going on in this town. Don't you think so, Terry?"

"I will admit that the town hasn't been the same since we went to Dr. Kaminko's house, but that doesn't mean the alleged spirit of a supposedly haunted lake is killing people."

"Perhaps she's killing her victims by feeding them this poor excuse for food." Billy chimed in, examining his lunch, wondering if he should send it to the medical examiner and ask her to perform an autopsy. "Is this supposed to be a hamburger or something the science lab uses for dissection?"

Ignoring Billy's rants about the food, Terry continues. "Casey, it just doesn't make sense. Why would this 'Lady in the Lake' suddenly appear after all this time? If the legend was true, then the lake would've been closed a LONG time ago. Don't you agree?"

"Well, I guess you make a good point. But I would still like to check out the lake and try to find a clue or something. Perhaps Billy could talk to his dad…"

"No! Leave me out of this!" Billy screeched. "My dad will NOT let us go to the lake just because you want to investigate a haunted lake and search for the Lady!"

"I thought you didn't believe in the Lady, Billy." Allison said.

"I don't. But I'm not taking any chances. I'd rather stay grounded than go anywhere near that freaky lake, so count me out!"

The school day ends, and Billy is not happy about it. As he opens the main doors, Terry follows behind him. He doesn't seem too happy, either.

"So, are we really doing this?" he asks Billy.

"Yep." Billy replies.

"We are really going to walk down to the police station, and ask your dad if we can go to the lake tonight and look for signs of the Lady?"

"Uh-huh."

"How did Casey manage to convince us to do this again?"

"Don't ask me. We were tricked somehow; I don't know how that happened."

"Simple. It's Casey."

"Don't remind me…"

"Well, the sooner we ask, the sooner we can get it over with. What do you think he'll say?"

"I have a pretty good idea."

They remain silent for the remainder of the walk to the police station. They open the front doors, speak to the officer sitting behind a desk by the entrance, who calls ahead. A few moments later, the officer lets them walk into Sheriff Martin's office. They see him sitting at his desk going over some paperwork, and before Billy can even open his mouth, and without even looking up from his papers, Gene says "No."

"I haven't even said anything yet!" Billy exclaims.

"You don't need to." Gene replied. "I already know what you're going to say. You, Terry, Casey, and Allison want to go down to the lake and do your own little investigation. And my answer is 'no'".

"But it's for a good reason, Mr. Martin." Terry tells him. "If you let us help, we might find something you can use. Perhaps we can figure out what killed Trent and the other victims."

"Forget it, Terry. The lake is the scene of multiple homicides. I can't let any unauthorized personnel in there, not even my son and his friends. Besides, I'm pretty sure I already know how they died."

"Really? You figured it out already?" Billy asked.

"Dr. Taylor believes all of the victims died of an advanced case of progeria."

"You think they died from taking a blue pill?"

"Billy," Terry interrupts, "your dad said 'progeria', not…never mind. Progeria is an age-related disease that makes you look older than you really are."

"Huh?"

"For example, if you had progeria, you would still be sixteen, but you would appear to be twenty-six. Get it now?"

"Exactly." Gene said. "Dr. Taylor should be finished with her examinations soon, but it still doesn't explain how the victims all died of the same disease. It doesn't make any sense."

"Do you think the Lady of the Lake had anything to do with it?" Billy asks, while Terry slaps himself in the forehead. *"I can't believe he just asked that stupid question,"* he thinks to himself. *"We're in for it now."*

Gene finally looks up from his paperwork. "Seriously? The Lady in the Lake? That old legend? What kind of nonsense are you talking about, son?" he asked.

"That's what the kids at school are saying. They think the Lady is responsible."

"Billy, Dr. Kaminko is one thing, but a lake spirit? I'm not even going to entertain that silly notion. I don't have time for fairy tales. Besides, it's a school night, and you're still grounded, remember?"

"But…"

"That's enough. I've already said no."

"But what makes you think you can tell me that I can't go to the lake?" Gene points to his badge and asks Billy "What do you think this star means?"

Billy thinks for a few moments, but Terry already knows what he's going to say, so he grabs a chair and sits down while Billy says something stupid. Billy looks at the badge, then replies "You're Tinkerbell?"

"My decision is final, Billy. Now you and Terry go home right now. I have too much work to do and I won't be home until late. Now get going."

As they walk out of Gene's office, Billy whispers to Terry "We're still going to the lake, aren't we?"

"Yes. Casey and Allison will meet us there. They'll bring their cameras. You bring snacks. We might be there for a while."

"No way for me to back out of this, is there?"

"Nope."

"That's what I'm afraid of."

# CHAPTER ELEVEN

Darkness silently falls over the town of Littleroot, and Terry quietly opens his bedroom window after his parents go to sleep. Dressed in all black, he climbs down his bedsheet rope and jumps safely to the ground below. Armed with a backpack filled with a camera, flashlight, and spare batteries, he runs across town until he finally gets to the entrance to the lake, where Billy, Casey, and Allison are waiting for him.

"What took you so long, Terry?" Casey asks him.

"Sorry, but I had to wait until my parents were asleep." Terry replies. "So, what exactly is the plan?"

"Well, we were just going to walk over to the lake, but there are a few police officers keeping watch near the entrance. So, we're just trying to think of another way in." Terry looks over at Billy and says, "Any ideas?"

Billy shakes his head. "Don't look at me," he said. "I didn't want to be here to begin with, remember? If my dad finds out about this, I'll be grounded forever!"

"Keep your voice down, Billy!" Terry whispers. "Look, we're here, so we might as well get this over with."

"How can we do that?" asked Allison. "Those officers will see us."

"We just stay in the bushes and stick to the shadows. If we can do that, we should be able to get around the officers without being seen. If Billy keeps his voice down."

"Are you saying I can't keep quiet?" Billy whispered loudly, prompting the others to put their hands over his mouth and shush him. Terry looks over at the officers to make sure they didn't hear Billy; luckily, they seem to not hear a thing. He takes his hands off Billy's mouth, as do Allison and Casey. He looks at Billy and whispers "That's EXACTLY what I'm saying. If you keep making noise, you'll leave us no choice but to cuff you to a tree and shove an old sock in your mouth. Then we'll put duct tape over said sock."

"You wouldn't actually do that. Would you?"

Just remember this piece of advice, Billy. Silence is golden, but duct tape is silver."

"Point taken. Shutting up now."

Terry and the others crouch down into the bushes, trying to walk as quietly, and slowly, as possible without the officers seeing them. If they step on a branch, or sneeze loudly, their investigation at the lake will be over before it's even begun. They move past the trees, step over any puddles they see, and make sure not to make noise of any kind to avoid being seen.

Then, one of the officers turns on their flashlight, stopping Terry in his tracks and motioning for the others to stop. They manage to duck behind a bush before the officer shines the flashlight in their general direction. Terry wipes some beads of sweat off his forehead, knowing how close they are to being caught. When the officer turns his off his flashlight, Terry tells the others the coast was clear and they keep going, until they finally reach the lake. They walk a little closer until they come to the crime scene tape.

"Okay, guys. Let's take a five-minute break before we begin." Terry tells them, and they immediately sit on the soft grass beneath them. Billy opens his backpack and pulls out a handheld gaming device. He turns it on and starts playing whatever game he has in it, with the volume completely turned up. Terry quickly walks over to him, grabs the handheld, and turns it off, then takes the game out and puts it in his jeans pocket.

"What the hell was that for, Terry?" Billy whispered.

"The officers may not be able to see us right now, but they can still HEAR us, dumbass!" Casey exclaimed. "What were you thinking, bringing that stupid toy with you?"

"First off, it's not a stupid toy, it's a portable gaming device, useful for long waits at the doctor's office or when you're in the bathroom waiting for nature to run its course. Second, I was talking to Terry, NOT YOU!"

"You seriously need to let that go already! I was only trying to help! How many times do I need to explain it?"

"You can explain it until you're blue in the face, but I will never forgive you!"

"Will you two be quiet?" Terry snapped. "I am in no mood to listen to you guys fight like children while we are trying to find some evidence of what happened to Trent and the others."

"Sorry, Terry. So, what do you suggest we do?" said Casey. Terry takes a flashlight out of his backpack. "Let's split up," he says. "Two of us will look around the north side of the lake, while the other two stay here to search for any kind of evidence." Billy stands up, walks over to Terry and exclaims "Sweet! Partners?"

"Not this time, Billy."

"What? Why?"

"Allison and I will investigate the north side of the lake, while you stay here with Casey. If either of us finds anything, turn on your flashlights and wave it around long enough for the others to see it. Just be careful that it doesn't attract the attention of the officers. Now, let's do this already."

"But, Terry, I don't understand. Why are you doing this?"

"Because," Terry whispers, "at least this way you will have no choice but to talk to Casey. You two need to work out this situation and patch things up."

"But…"

"We'll be back later. Come on, Allison."

"Right behind you." Allison remarked. As the two of them walk off into the distance, Billy kicks a rock in frustration and walks back over to Casey, grumbling to himself along the way. *He wants us to talk things over?* he thinks to himself. *There's a better chance of being bitten by a radioactive spider and gaining spider-powers!*

As he sits down next to Casey, who doesn't say a word to him, he reaches into his backpack and pulls out a bag of honey barbecue flavored potato chips. He then pulls out a bottle of cola. Casey watches him as he tries to open the bag of chips without much success, and she rolls her eyes at him. He starts mumbling to himself, still not having any luck opening the bag, and she can tell he's about ready to scream, so she sighs and says "Oh, for Pete's sake, give me those!" And, without much effort, she opens the bag then hands it back to him. "Uh, thanks." Billy says without even looking at her.

"Yeah, well, it was either that or listen to you scream because you couldn't get it open. And I have no intentions of getting caught just because you couldn't go two minutes without a snack."

"If I must stay here with you, then I'd prefer not to starve. It's the only way to drown out your annoying voice."

Casey sighs. "Billy, I think's time we had a talk. We need to move past this already."

Billy shakes his head. "No. We don't," he says. "You got me in trouble. Everything was fine until you opened your big mouth. I liked my room the way it was."

"But how can you live in such a mess, Billy? It's not healthy." Billy looks away. "It's nothing, Casey."

"Billy, what's the matter? Terry seems to think you haven't been yourself lately, but you won't talk to him about it."

"Because there's nothing to talk about, especially not to you."

"Billy, if you can't tell Terry, you can tell me. You know that, right?" Billy shakes his head. He then looks at Casey and replies "…Okay. The truth is, since that night at Dr. Kaminko's house, I just haven't felt able to go outside. The room is my haven from the outside world. The one place where I feel safe, where nothing can hurt me."

Casey doesn't say a word. She couldn't believe he had kept these feelings bottled up inside, and he just needed to let them out. But she was the last person he would ever tell with the way she treats him. Perhaps he was afraid someone would judge him and think he's weird.

Okay, yes, he is weird, but if he had only told somebody what he had been feeling. She had no idea the night at Dr. Kaminko's house would affect him to the point where he was afraid to go outside. Then, without any kind of warning, she throws her arms around him in a tight, warm embrace. Billy finds himself speechless, which itself is quite rare.

*"What is going on here?"* he thinks to himself. *"Either Casey is hugging me, or she is preparing for the right moment to snap my neck and kill me. I wouldn't put it past her if she actually did that."* He puts up one of his hands and taps Casey's shoulder. "Uh, Casey," he begins, "wh-what are you doing?"

Casey says nothing. Billy prepares to make a joke, but instead, he soon finds himself being comforted by his cousin in a way he never expected. The way she was hugging him, it wasn't like she was his cousin. Instead, it was more like a hug from a close friend. Then, he hears Casey say "I am so sorry, Billy. If only I had known. I never should have said I wished you weren't my cousin."

Then, unexpectedly, Billy finds himself returning Casey's hug with one of his own. He feels a great weight lift right off his shoulders. He finds his anger at Casey start to disappear, and realized she was only trying to help. Then, with a goofy smile across his face, he whispers "Remember all those pranks I pulled on you in the past?"

Casey whispers back "Yes. Why?"

"When this is all over, I'd like to do them all over again." Then, Casey releases her hug and smacks Billy in the arm, which only makes him laugh, and she soon finds herself laughing, as well, without a care in the world.

Meanwhile, Terry and Allison continue their trek through the north side of the lake, and they start to hear Billy and Casey laughing their heads off. Allison smiles and says, "I guess they worked things out."

"I guess they did." Terry replies. "I knew they would. It was only a matter of time. They just needed the right push."

"And you were just the right person to do it, weren't you?"

"I knew something was wrong with Billy, I just needed him to talk about it with somebody. I picked the right person to do so." As they continue walking, Allison whispers "I just wish they wouldn't laugh so loud. They're going to alert the police officers that we're here." Terry yawns and responds "Yeah. I'm sure they'll stop soon, though." Allison turns to face Terry asks him "Are you feeling okay, Terry?"

"Yes. Why do you ask?"

"You just seem a little tired. Not sleeping well?" Terry stops in his tracks. "Not really," he says. "I haven't had a good night's sleep in months. I'm pretty sure it's the pain medication the doctor prescribed, but there's no way to prove it."

"Why don't you just stop taking the medication, then?"

"Because if I don't, I will be up for half the night. My arm always feels like it's on fire. It hurts to even raise it. The medication is the only thing that keeps it from becoming excruciating."

"Terry, that medicine can't be good for you. If one of the side effects is lack of sleep, then you need to stop taking it."

"I guess. But for now, we need to find some clues if we hope to prove, or disprove, that the Lady of the Lake is real."

Billy and Casey keep laughing, and soon Allison becomes nervous. "Maybe one of us should go back before they get us in trouble," she said. "Not until we find something." Terry replies.

"Terry, it's been almost ten minutes. We haven't found anything, and if we get caught, we never will."

Terry nods. "Good point. Let's go back before those two mess things up for us." They start walking back, but after about four minutes, Terry stops. "What's wrong, Terry?" Allison asks. Terry shakes his head. "The way Billy and Casey have been laughing, the officers should have been alerted and found them already. Something isn't right." He soon turns towards the direction to the lake entrance. "Come on, Allison," he says. "We need to check something out."

When they arrive at the entrance, they see the officers laying on the ground. "Are they okay?" Allison asks. Terry slowly walks towards them, but when he gets a good look at their faces, he is so shocked he falls to the ground and moves away from them. "Terry, what is it? What's the matter?" Terry, wide-eyed with a frightened look on his face, turns to Allison and says "Th-th-they're dead…"

"What did you just say?"

"The officers…they're dead. They suddenly look much older than before. It's like something suddenly sucked the youth right out of them."

"What does this mean, Terry?" Terry stands back up, still horrified at what he had just seen, but doesn't say a word. The shock hasn't completely set in yet, but he appears as if he had just seen a ghost. His face becomes frozen in fear. He finds himself unable to move a muscle; going into Dr. Kaminko's house was one thing, but seeing a dead body? That's another thing entirely. He finally turns to face Allison and says, "We need to go back to Billy and Casey and get out of here right now!"

"What?"

"Let's go! Now!"

Billy and Casey finally run out of breath, and stop their little laugh fest. Billy turns to Casey and says "Wow. Never knew you could laugh so hard."

"Well, if you laughed any harder, every house in the neighborhood would have broken windows by morning." Casey chuckles. Then, they hear a noise in the bushes. "Oh, crap!" Casey exclaims. "The police heard us! We're in trouble now!" Just as they start to run, Terry and Allison appear from the bushes. "Guys!" Terry shouts. "We need to get out of here now!"

"Terry, what's wrong?" Billy asks. "And where are the officers?"

"Dead. Something sucked the youth out of them." Allison replies. "We don't know what did it, but we need to leave before…" Then, at that moment, an eerie wind begins to blow, causing the nightly temperature to drop to a less-than-normal level. "Is it just me," Casey starts, "or did it just get really cold suddenly?"

"I'd rather not think about it right now." Terry said. "Let's go before anything else happens." Then, Billy points to the bushes and says, "You mean like a pair of glowing yellow eyes staring at us?"

"Billy, don't be silly. What yellow eyes?" Terry asks, then Billy screams "THOSE YELLOW EYES!" Terry and the others look to where Billy is pointing. At first, they don't see anything, but they soon take a closer look and realize that Billy was right. A pair of glowing yellow eyes stares at them intensely, and they soon start to move a bit closer. The group finds themselves frozen with fear. They want to run away, but they can't for some reason. Then, from out of the bushes, a woman with long white hair in an old dress appears before them.

The dress is old, stained by dirt and time with a few tears in it. She appears to be in her thirties, but something about her isn't right. The moonlight appears to be shining through her, as if she isn't even there. Terry thinks to himself *"There's something about her that seems really familiar, but I can't put my finger on it. Why can't I focus?"*

"Is…is…that the…Lady in the Lake?" Casey asks through chattering teeth. Allison replies "I honestly don't know. What do you think, Billy?"

Billy looks at her, but he can only mutter a simple "Meap!" Casey looks at him and says, "Did you just say 'Meap'?" Billy replies with another "Meap!"

"Billy, this not the time to be a chicken!" Terry shouts.

"Chicken? Chicken? At this point I'm ready to start laying eggs!" Billy exclaims, then he starts laughing nervously, but it soon turns from laughter into clucking noises. He folds up his arms and acts as if he's flapping his wings. "Aaaaaand there he goes." Casey mutters. Terry reaches into his backpack and tells the others "Quick! Grab your cameras!" They do as they're told, and pull out their cameras, ready to start taking pictures (except for Billy, who starts to peck at the ground like the chicken he claims to be). However, before they can even get one picture taken, the woman disappears. "Huh? Where'd she go?" Casey asks.

"I don't know," said Terry, "but keep your eyes peeled. She's around here somewhere." He feels his hands starting to tremble, making it hard to hold his camera. Was it simply adrenaline, or could it be fear that's causing the trembling? He never felt anything like this before; he had the courage to venture to Dr. Kaminko's house, sure, but never did he imagine would he find evidence of the lake being haunted. Is it possible they had finally encountered the legendary Lady in the Lake?

As it turns out, the others were experiencing the same feeling. Fear had taken control of their bodies, preventing them from moving a single muscle. How is it they could walk into Dr. Kaminko's house with no problem, yet are unable to face the ghostly image of a woman who may or not haunt a lake and may or may not have killed the officers who were supposed to guard said lake? Terry turns around, and soon finds himself staring into the eyes of the ghastly woman, who immediately lets out a blood-curdling scream right in his face. The scream pierces his ear drums, and he falls to the ground holding his ears in pain. Casey and Allison run over to him, trying to get his attention. They try talking to him, but all he can hear is a ringing noise in his head.

Casey turns to say something to Billy, hoping to snap him out of his chicken act. She runs over to him and slaps him in the back of the head, finally bringing back to his version of reality. She points to Terry, and they both go over to him. Billy tries talking to him, but just like Casey and Allison, all he can hear is a loud ring. He instead points to the woman, who turns her attention towards them with intent of harming them. She lets out another scream, which makes them cover their ears. The scream is painful, but it was worse for Terry because he took a direct hit when the woman was right in his face.

Then, the woman opens her mouth again, but instead of screaming, she says to them in an eerie voice "This is MY lake! This town shall pay for what it did to me, and I won't let anything get in my way, not even nosey children!" She raises a hand, getting ready to attack, but before she can get a chance, a pair of red and blue lights approach the area, followed by a loud siren. She turns her attention back to the group, and tells them "You are very lucky. But know this, if you ever come back to the lake, I will not spare you a second time. Heed my warning well, children."

Then, with a gust of wind, the woman vanishes, like she was never there. A few moments later, Sheriff Martin arrives and notices the group on the ground while Terry still clutches his ears. "What the hell are you kids doing here?" he asks Billy and Casey. "And what's wrong with Terry?" Billy looks at Terry, still clutching his ears, looks back at his dad and replied "Uh, he heard the first thirty seconds of the new Bieber song?" Gene just stares at them, unamused by his son's attempt to change the subject. "When the officers who were guarding the lake didn't check in, I had a suspicious feeling something wasn't right. But when I arrived, I heard a loud scream, and to my surprise, I find you kids here. Now, I'll ask again. Why are you here? You know this is a crime scene."

"Uncle Gene, I can explain." Casey says. "I convinced Terry and Billy to come here tonight. I wanted to find proof of the Lady in the Lake's existence."

Gene rolls his eyes. "Not that nonsense again," he says with an annoyed tone in his voice. "Billy, we've been over this. The Lady in the Lake doesn't exist."

"But we saw her, Dad." Billy exclaimed. "She appeared from out of nowhere and did something to Terry." Gene pushes the three of them out of the way, looks at Terry, and asks "Terry? Are you okay? Can you hear me?" Terry can see his lips moving, but can't hear any words coming out of them.

Gene turns on his radio, holds down the button, and says "This is Sheriff Martin. I need an ambulance at Littleroot Lake right away, and send another police vehicle. I have some children that need to be taken home." He gives the three of them a stern look, but they don't return his gaze. Instead, they look in different directions. Allison pretends to adjust her glasses, Casey wipes some grass off the back of her jeans, and Billy puts his hands in his jean pockets.

"Dad, I…" he starts, but Gene puts up a hand to stop him. "I don't want to hear it, Billy. I told you not to come to the lake, but you didn't listen to me. None of you did. We'll finish this discussion when I get home."

# CHAPTER TWELVE

Being caught by the police is never a good thing, but when the sheriff also happens to be your father, you can expect a pretty long lecture when you are brought home. That is exactly what Billy got when his mom saw him in a police car driven by Gene. They sat him down at the kitchen table and gave him a lecture about how stupid it was to sneak out of the house, especially since he was still grounded, going to a crime scene, and trying to find existence of something that couldn't possibly exist. They then grounded him for another two weeks and told him to go to his room. He let out a sigh of relief, glad the lecture was finally over; he thought it would never end and felt it took forever (even though it only lasted an hour).

Meanwhile, Terry was rushed to the hospital to make sure the damage to his ears wasn't permanent. Luckily for him, it wasn't, and his hearing would return in a day or two. The doctors chose to keep him overnight to make sure nothing else was wrong. His parents stayed in the waiting room in case their son needed anything. Julie tried to keep herself busy by reading a book while Marcus went to get her a cup of coffee. However, she couldn't focus on her book in any way; all she could think about was how her son got hurt again. She could barely contain her worries after Terry went to Dr. Kaminko's house and ended up breaking his arm. She stayed up the entire night, refusing to sleep until she knew he was going to be okay. It's bad enough his arm may never be at full strength again, but now he almost loses his hearing? Even though the doctors assured her Terry would be fine, she found herself making herself sick from worrying so much. She had hoped he would never do anything like this again. Perhaps this experience will convince him to stay home from now on.

Casey's parents, on the other hand, were quite angry. Not at her, but at Terry. They believed it was HIS idea to sneak out and go to the lake. Despite Casey's best efforts to convince them otherwise, they decided that Terry was a bad influence and forbade her from hanging out with him again. After being picked up at the station and brought back home, she immediately stormed up the stairs to her bedroom and slammed the door shut in her parents' faces. They refused to believe it wasn't Terry's idea to go to the lake. She wanted to go to the hospital and see how Terry was doing, but she knew her parents would try and stop her in any way possible. So, instead of attempting to leave, she decided she would just go see him after the school day ended.

Allison's mother Kimberly nearly had a conniption when she was told her daughter went to the lake, and decided to sit right outside her bedroom door to make sure nothing else happens to her. When David saw her, however, he told her to go to bed and leave Allison alone; she's a sixteen-year-old girl, not a prisoner trying to break out of their cell. They argued over an hour while Allison tried to sleep. Jake kept waking up because of the yelling, so Allison went into his room to keep him company until he finally went to sleep. Another hour passed until exhaustion finally kicked in, causing both Allison and Jake to fall asleep. If they stayed awake for another five minutes, they would have heard their father storming out of the house and deciding to stay at a motel for the night. When they woke up, they expected to see David making himself a cup of coffee before heading off to work. But when they saw only Kimberly in the kitchen, they instantly knew that something was wrong. Allison tried asking her where their dad was, but she refused to say a word. Instead, Kimberly just sat at the table, reading the newspaper. Allison motioned for Jake to sit at the table while she fixed him some breakfast.

The three friends met at the front entrance of the school, where the rumor mill quickly went from subtle to vicious in a matter of minutes. As they walked inside, they noticed their fellow students whispering to one another but didn't know why. Some even eyeballed them as they walked by, which finally prompted Billy to say "This is starting to feel a little familiar."

"Yeah, no kidding." Casey remarked. "Talk about some serious déjà vu."

"I guess it didn't take long for our classmates to hear about our little trip to the lake." Allison chimed in. "Who knows what they're saying us about right now."

"I'd rather not think about it." Billy said. "It might hurt my brain."

"EVERYTHING makes your brain hurt, Billy." Casey told him.

"Yeah, so? What's your point?"

"Never mind." Billy walks over to his locker, but before he starts to do the combination, he says "It's weird not having Terry here."

"Billy, I'm sure he's fine. We're going to be visiting him after school, anyway."

"You guys are, I'm not. My parents added two more weeks to my sentence. I'm really in the doghouse this time." He fumbles around with the padlock until he gets his locker open. He reaches for his French book, which makes Casey say "Billy, can I ask a dumb question?"

"Better than anyone I know."

"How come you don't bring your French book home?"

"Why would I?"

"If you're trying to impress Madame Granger, which, by the way, is totally gross, wouldn't it help if you actually brought your French book home and did your homework?"

"Hey. Gotta save SOMETHING for the marriage proposal, am I right?"

"Uh, no. That will never happen."

"The homework or the proposal?"

"Both."

"Meanie." He takes his French book out of his locker then shuts the door. However, before he can head to French class, he soon finds Jeremy Hodges standing in his way. "Hello there, Martin," he says. "Where's Welling?"

"Welling? Terry Welling? Black hair, blue eyes, works at Games 2 Go, went to Dr. Kaminko's house three months ago? That Terry Welling?"

"Yes."

"Never heard of him."

Jeremy shakes his head and replies "Really? You're going with the smartass routine today?"

"Sure, why not? I wanted to go the serious routine, but I was afraid I'd get lost."

"So, you're not going to deny you and your loser friends were at the lake last night?"

"Hey!" Casey and Allison exclaim.

"Littleroot Lake?"

"Is there any other lake in this town?"

"Is that what people are whispering about?"

"Duh." Billy moves Jeremy aside, with Casey and Allison trying to follow behind him. But Jeremy grabs him by the back of his shirt collar with one hand and blocks Casey and Allison's way with the other. "We're not finished here, Martin."

"I'm not really in the mood to listen to this right now, Jeremy."

"Too bad, Martin. Rumor has it you and your friends were at the lake doing something you weren't supposed to."

"Like what?"

"People are saying you're the ones who killed all those people and dumped their bodies at the lake, including Trent Alexander."

"WHAT?!"

Jeremy lets out a chuckle. "Oh, yeah. And apparently, your dad won't throw your asses in jail and is giving you a free pass to do whatever you want."

"That's not true. Now let go of me and let us get to our classes."

"Face it, Martin. Your dad's a loser. He won't even arrest his own wimpy son or his snobby niece because he's too nice."

"Don't you dare talk about my dad that way, Jeremy!"

"Why not?"

"Because none of it is true! And at least MY dad didn't walk out on his family drunk off his ass for some woman he met in a sleazy bar like YOURS did!"

At that moment, Jeremy releases his grip on Billy's shirt. It appears Billy has struck a nerve, which is not like him at all, because after a few seconds, Jeremy squares up and lands a fist right in Billy's face, causing him to fall to the floor. Casey and Allison run over to him to make sure he's okay, and they see drops of blood on the floor. They also notice that he's out cold. Every other student in the hall quickly rush over to see what's happening, and they see Jeremy Hodges standing above three other students with blood on his knuckles. Casey turns Billy over to look at him, and sees his nose is just covered in blood, as well as his mouth. Allison takes out a box of tissues from her backpack and hands it to Casey, who quickly takes one out to start wiping the blood off Billy's face. Jeremy begins to crack his knuckles and says "I'm going to enjoy this. A lot."

Casey hands the box of tissues back to Allison and stands back up to face Jeremy. He looks at her with delight and remarks "I've never hit a girl before."

"Funny," said Casey. "I was just about to say the same thing." Just then, Jeremy makes a fist and punches it into his other hand, ready to fight, while the other students gather around them to watch the massacre that was about to happen. Allison keeps cleaning blood off Billy's face, secretly hoping Casey would teach Jeremy a lesson he wouldn't forget anytime soon.

"Too bad Welling isn't here." Jeremy said to Casey. "I'm sure he'd love to watch me beat the snot out of his girlfriend."

"He is NOT my boyfriend!"

"Ah, whatever. I'm still going to enjoy this." Jeremy draws his fist back, ready to show Casey a thing or two, but before he gets the chance, he feels somebody from behind him and grab his hand, saying "That's enough, *Monsieur* Hodges." He turns to see Madame Granger smiling at him while holding his hand with a firm grip. "Now, what is the situation here?"

"No situation, Madame. Just having a little chat, that's all." Jeremy replied, while Casey mutters under her breath "Lousy, lying, little…" Madame Granger notices Billy on the floor and motions for everyone to move out of her way. She kneels beside Allison and looks Billy over. Her smile quickly turns to a stern look, then she says to Allison "Take *Monsieur* Martin to the nurse's office. I'll be there shortly. Everyone else, get to your classes immediately."

A few students grumbled, but they did as they were told and headed to their respective classes while Allison tried to wake up Billy. "Billy?" she said quietly. "Wake up, please." She gently taps the side of his face, hoping to get a response from him. He slowly begins to open his eyes, then he weakly asks "Nobody tried to kiss me, right?" Allison smiles and replies "No." Billy seemed a little disappointed, then he looks back at her and remarks "Could you?"

"Maybe later, you crazy fool."

As Allison helps Billy stand, Casey exclaims "What the hell were you thinking, Billy? You're lucky he didn't break your jaw. What made you decide to do something like that?"

"I lost my head in the heat of battle." Billy replied. Then, Madame Granger walks up to him and asks "Are you alright, *Monsieur* Martin?"

"Oh, yeah, I'm fine."

"Ms. Libby, please take him to the nurse's office right away."

"I'm fine, Madame Granger. Really."

"Let the nurse look at you, Billy. I'll be there soon." As Allison and Billy walk over to the nurse's office, with Casey not far behind, Billy whispers "Are you sure nobody kissed me?"

"I'm positive, Billy." Allison whispers back.

"Oh. I wish Madame Granger did." At that moment, Allison feels her heart drop down to her stomach, wishing Billy had kept his mouth shut for a few more minutes.

When the nurse started cleaning Billy's face, with Casey and Allison waiting outside, she told him how lucky he was that Jeremy didn't punch out any of his teeth, but he would have quite a headache for a little while. As he sat in her office, still a little dazed from the whole thing, he didn't notice Madame Granger walk in and talk to the nurse. She motions for the nurse to leave the room for a few minutes. She looks at Billy, then asks "Okay, *Monsieur* Martin, can you tell me what happened out there?" Billy holds his head, trying not to pass out, then replies "Uh, maybe his breakfast didn't agree with him?"

"Billy…"

"He just pissed me off, that's all. I guess I had enough of all of his B.S."

"There are other ways to deal with a bully. Why didn't you tell a teacher?"

"What would be the point? He'd still beat me to a pulp."

"Looks like he did a pretty good job this time."

"I guess."

"He's being suspended for a few days. You shouldn't have any trouble from him for a while."

"Thanks, Madame Granger."

Madame Granger waves her index finger. "What do we say, Billy?"

"Oh, uh, right. Uh, *merci*, Madame Granger. Hey, can I tell you a French joke?"

"Is it offensive?"

"No."

"Then go ahead."

"Uh, what do you call a crate of snails being delivered by ship?"

"I don't know, *Monsieur* Martin. What?"

"Es 'cargo'". Madame Granger doesn't say a word. Instead, she lets out a small chuckle, then she walks out of the office. Allison and Casey walk in to see Billy smiling. "What are you smiling about?" Casey asks him. "You just had the daylights punched out of you, remember?"

"Yeah," Billy remarked, "but I just made Madame Granger laugh with one of my legendary jokes."

"Was it the snail joke?"

"Yes."

"It was a pity laugh."

"Doesn't matter. It's increased my chances with her. I'm sure of it."

"You're delusional."

"She wants me. I can tell." At that moment, Allison walks out of the room, making sure Billy doesn't see the disappointment on her face. Casey immediately takes notice and says to Billy, "Be right back, cousin." She follows Allison as she makes her way to the hall.

"Hey, Alli!" she calls out. "What's the matter?" Allison turns to face her, doing her best to keep the tears from rolling down her cheeks. Casey puts a hand on her shoulder and says "Come on, you can tell me. What's wrong?"

"I just wish Billy would stop talking about that darn Madame Granger for one minute. It's all I hear from him; 'Madame Granger' this and 'Madame Granger' that. To be honest, I'm getting quite sick of it."

"Then perhaps you should tell him that instead of walking away every time he talks about her."

"And what good will that do?"

"Simple. You like him, he likes you, and the second he realizes he doesn't have a chance with Madame Granger, that will be your time to move in. Ask him to go to the school carnival with you."

"Do you really think he'd want to go with me?"

"I do, Alli. I really do. He just doesn't know it yet. Trust me, he'll come around." Casey places a hand on Allison's shoulder, knowing it was exactly what her friend needed, to keep her on her toes. Otherwise, she might lose her balance and fall flat on her face. With that gesture of reassurance, Allison and Casey decide it might be a good idea if they head back to their class before they get in trouble. Billy takes notice and shouts "Hey! Wait for me, guys!" Of course, they already knew he was doing it so he could try and flirt with Madame Granger again, and that was enough to make Allison and Casey want to throw up a little.

Being stuck in a hospital room is never a picnic. Uncomfortable beds, poor excuses for food, long waits for a doctor or nurse to check on you, and practically nothing to watch on TV. For Terry Welling, it was an absolute cure for insomnia. He hated being stuck in the hospital, but he hated missing school a lot worse.

He wouldn't be surprised if all his classmates were spreading rumors about the trip to the lake the previous night. What could they possibly be saying about him and his friends? Maybe they were telling stories about he and Casey or something. Or, what if everybody thinks they're the ones responsible for the deaths of their friends? There was no way to know for sure, since he couldn't go home until later that night. Hopefully his friends would stop by to give him the news. He wanted to scream from the sheer boredom, but he wasn't sure if he'd be able to hear himself since there was still a ringing in his ears.

Last time the doctors checked on him, they said his hearing was getting better, which made his parents happy, but he had a bit of a hard time hearing exactly what they were talking about because they were standing in the hallway and it was driving him crazy. All he wanted was to leave and go to school, but sneaking out wasn't exactly an option. His mom was essentially standing guard in the waiting room, and she would know if he tried to pull a fast one. *I swear she's like a worry ninja.* Terry found himself thinking earlier that day. So, in a vague attempt to pass the time, he decided to count the ceiling tiles in his room. He lost count after about seventy-five tiles, so he'd have to start over again. After many frustrating do-overs, he ultimately gave up and fell asleep.

He was sleeping for about two or three hours when the smell of food woke him up from his dream of being the lead singer for Dime Front. He looked over at the stand next to his bed and saw a tray of food. He peeked at the clock above his door and realized it was lunch time, so he grabbed the tray and opened the Styrofoam container to see what he was given. A grilled cheese sandwich in the main compartment, which made his nose curl up in disgust, because he hates grilled cheese sandwiches. He used to like them when he was little, but over the years he got sick of them. In another compartment was an apple that was slightly bruised. The smallest compartment contained a small dollop of applesauce. *"That's the only thing in this entire lunch that looks appetizing,"* he thought. *"I can't believe I actually want to eat whatever is being served at school today. It's got to be better than this crap they gave me."* He proceeded to grab the sandwich, get out of bed, walk into the bathroom, and throw the sandwich into the trash bin.

Just then, Julie walks in and notices him out of bed. "Terry," she begins, "what are you doing?" Terry turns around, eyes the trash bin, then replies "I'm saving my stomach from making the mistake of digesting this stuff." Julie rolls her eyes, points at the bed, and sternly says "Get back into bed, Terry. You need your rest." Terry doesn't argue with her, because he knew it would be pointless to even try, and slowly walks back toward the bed he swears is made from rocks and sandpaper.

As he reluctantly crawls back into bed, Julie says to him "I brought you something to keep you from going crazy," and hands him a book at least three hundred pages long. "I bought it at the bookstore," she said. "I figured you would want to kill some time while you're here."

"Thanks, Mom. This will help make this place a little more bearable. At least until the guys come visit." Terry replied. "But they probably won't be able to come. I'm guessing they're all in the doghouse for last night." As Terry flips through the pages of his new book, not ready to read it yet, Julie remarks "I'll talk to their parents and see if they'll give their kids time off for good behavior tonight."

"You don't have to do that, Mom. I'll be fine."

"Nonsense, Terry. I want to. Now, I have to leave for a little bit. But I'll be back later. Try to get some rest." As Julie walks out the door, Terry decides to do a little reading. After about an hour and reading two whole chapters, Terry starts to feel his eyelids getting heavy. He tries to fight it, but soon gives in and falls asleep.

He wakes up about an hour later, but feels a little uneasy. He gets out of bed after noticing the lights in the room have gone out, leaving him barely able to see where he's going. He bangs his toes against the bottom of the bed and lets out a tiny scream. He rubs his toe for a few moments until the pain subsides. He then takes out his IV drip and takes a few steps toward the small crack of light outside the door, feeling his way around the room to make sure he doesn't step or trip on anything.

He opens the door, checking for any doctors or hospital staff that might try to make him go back to bed. He looks to the left of the hallway, then to the right, where he sees his parents and friends sitting in the waiting room. When he's convinced there are no doctors around, he proceeds to walk. He figures it should only take a few steps until they see him, so he starts the short trek to the waiting room. As he starts walking, he thinks to himself, *"Just a few steps and they'll see me walking towards them. That way, they will see that I am okay."* He keeps walking, but he doesn't seem to be getting any closer to the waiting room.

*"Why is it taking so long to get to them?"* he thinks. *"I should have been there by now. What's going on?"* He looks down at the floor and sees his feet moving, but he's not going anywhere, as if he's trying to walk up on an escalator that's going down. He starts running, hoping to gain some movement, but to no avail. He cups his hands over his mouth and shouts "Mom! Dad! Billy! Casey! Allison! Look over here! I'm okay!", but they can't seem to hear him by any means, as if they aren't really there and they're just a figment of his imagination. But he keeps trying to get their attention by waving his arms and jumping up and down like a kangaroo; they still don't notice him, making him wonder what was going on.

Suddenly, the entire hallway starts shaking violently, as if there was an earthquake occurring, but earthquakes are extremely rare in the entire state of Maine, almost nonexistent. The shaking quickly becomes more intense, causing Terry to lose his balance. He stumbles, trying to stay on his feet, but he soon falls to his knees.

As he attempts to stand up, the floor around him begins to crack, and before he has time to react, he notices the cracks surround him, and he soon falls into a dark hole. He screams at the top of his lungs, but the pitch-black darkness seems to drown him out, as if somebody pressed the mute button in his voice box. He keeps falling down this dark pit like it's bottomless and it has no end, almost like he is destined to keep falling for the rest of his life without any sort of explanation.

He tumbles and twirls at high velocity, worried he will be smashed into pieces if the endless abyss does have an end he hasn't reached yet. Then, almost as quickly as he started his descent, he finds it's about to come to a complete stop as he sees the ground he is about to hit in just a few seconds. He closes his eyes, crosses his arms and puts them in front of his face to brace for impact. He immediately smashes into the ground with a loud bang that would startle a herd of elephants, but he is unharmed; not even a scratch or bruise. He is completely fine.

He stands up and starts to brush himself off, but he notices he is no longer wearing his hospital gown. He finds himself wearing some very familiar clothes; black t-shirt, dark blue jeans, brown boots, and leather jacket, as well as a backpack slung over his left shoulder. Within a few seconds, he realizes that he is wearing the clothes he wore the night he and his friends went into Dr. Kaminko's house. *"What is going on here?"* he thinks. *"I am so confused right now!"* He tries to get a good idea of his surroundings, since he doesn't know where he is, when he hears a mysterious voice say, *"What's the matter, Terrence? You look a little frightened."*

Terry tries to figure out where the voice came from, but nobody else is around. All he sees is darkness around him for miles, until a bright light shines from behind. He turns around to see, to his shock, an old house that was supposed to have been destroyed three months ago. *"That's not possible."* Terry thought. *"The house was destroyed! What is happening right now?"* He feels a strong urge of curiosity overcome him, convincing him to walk inside and look. He walks up the stairs, slowly opens the front door, and cautiously goes inside the house. He looks around to make sure he's not being lured into a trap, when he hears the same voice from earlier say *"Don't be shy, Terrence. Please, come in and make yourself at home."* He feels his heart racing, like it could jump out of his chest at any minute and he may need to catch it just in case. The door shuts behind him, which makes him almost let his bladder go.

Trying to keep his nerves from going crazy, he takes a few deep breaths to calm down, then he walks into the kitchen to look for answers. He doesn't get very far when he says quietly to himself "Why am I here? Billy and Casey checked in here three months ago and they didn't find anything helpful, so why would I hope to?" He pulls out a chair from the kitchen table and sits down, determined to keep himself from getting scared. He puts his hands over his eyes, hoping he was just in a very bad dream and would wake up soon.

*"I know what you're thinking. And, no, Terrence, this is very real indeed. You'll find out soon enough."* Terry immediately jumps up from the table, causing his chair to fall backward and onto the floor, turning into numerous little splinters upon impact.

"Who's there? Show yourself!" he shouts.

*"You know who I am. You also know where I am. It's only a matter of time until you figure it out."*

"What the hell are you talking about?!"

*"Poor, pitiful Terrence. You were so brave when you figured out my plan, but now you sound like you might be scared. What happened to the courageous little pack leader who broke into my home and exposed my schemes?"*

"Will you shut up and leave me alone?!"

*"Why? You didn't."* Just then, Terry hears another voice say, *"We never should have gone into that house!"* He recognizes it as Billy's.

"Billy?" he shouts. "Is that you? Say something else!" He waits a few seconds, then Billy shouts *"Terry! Where are you?"*

"I'm in the kitchen! Tell me where you are so I can find you!"

*"No! It's too dangerous! Stay away! Do not come into the basement!"* At that moment, the other voice remarks *"Yes, Terrence, stay away. Prove to your friends what a coward you are."*

"Shut up!" Terry replies defiantly. "I'm not listening to you, whoever you are! I am not scared!" He runs out of the kitchen and sees the door beneath the stairs. "Just where it was last time." He slowly opens the door, and it makes a loud creaking noise as he does. When the door is completely ajar, he looks down the stairs to make sure they're not rotting or falling apart. He carefully walks down into the basement one step at a time, his heart racing with every second. He finally gets to the bottom stair, prepared to help his friends if they are indeed in trouble.

But he soon gets a strange feeling in the pit of his stomach, and notices something is not right. The basement is empty; his friends are not here, nor are any of Dr. Kaminko's inventions, not even his portal to the ghost dimension. He seems to be walking in a dark abyss.

*"What? What's going on?"* he thinks. *"Where is everything? Where are my friends?"* He starts looking around for clues, but there isn't any kind of light to help him see where he's going. He doesn't get too far when he feels someone tap his shoulder. The second he turns around to see who it is, he feels a terrible, yet familiar, burning sensation in his chest. He looks down to see a hand inside his chest, as if he has just been stabbed. He can feel his insides being ripped apart, but he can't fight it. He looks up to see a familiar face staring right at him with evil intent. The face of the man whose corruption he and his friends exposed three months ago.

"Good to see you again, Terrence." Dr. Kaminko says with a devilish grin. Terry shakes his head, unable to believe what he is seeing.

"N-No!" he screams. "It's not possible! Y-you're dead!"

"Am I?" Kaminko replies. "Did you actually see me perish when you destroyed my house?! When you ruined my plans?!" Terry begins to feel himself losing consciousness and fights to stay awake. "Nobody could have survived that explosion," he exclaims. "It just isn't possible."

"It is VERY possible, Terrence. I am the great Dr. Ivan Kaminko. My resolve is so great, not even the realm of death can hold me back."

"This isn't real. It's just all in my head."

"That's it, Terrence. Keep lying to yourself, because you refuse to admit to yourself the truth."

"And what truth would that be?"

"That your fear is holding you back. I am the embodiment of that fear." Then, Dr. Kaminko moves his hand a little deeper into Terry's chest, making him cringe with pain. "What's the matter?" he asks. "Does that hurt? Good. Fear can be quite painful. It keeps you from reaching your true potential. You never really left the house. You may have destroyed it, but you're still in there. The little witch showed you."

"What are you talking about?"

"Instead of trying to avoid her scream, you just stood there frozen like a wooly mammoth. You proved how much of a coward you truly are, and I have no use for cowards." He then grabs a piece of Terry's spine. Terry lets out a bloodcurdling scream.

"STOP!" he cries out. "WHAT ARE YOU DOING?!" Dr. Kaminko pulls him in close to his face and stares at him with bloodshot eyes, then replies with a slightly demonic tone, "What I should have done three months ago. Goodbye, Terrence." He tightens his grip on Terry's spine, listening as it starts to crack, taking delight as Terry begs him to let go, until he hears a loud SNAP! He releases his grip, removes his hand, and watches as Terry's lifeless body falls into the endless abyss below.

"AAAAAAAAAAAAHHHHHH!!!!!!!" Terry wakes up screaming, drenched in sweat, causing his parents to run in and see what was wrong. "Terry!" Marcus shouts. "What's the matter?"

"Honey, it's okay!" Julie says. "It was just a bad dream!" A nurse comes in to check Terry's vitals. Other than an elevated heartbeat, he appears to be fine, but his parents know better. Terry starts sobbing uncontrollably, while his parents sit at his bedside and try their best to comfort him.

"What happened, Terry?" Marcus asks, but Terry doesn't hear him. He can't seem to calm down, until he finally manages to say through his tears "He won't stop torturing me. He'll never stop. He was right…"

"What are you talking about?" Julie asked, confused. "Who won't stop torturing you?" But Terry doesn't say another word; instead, he keeps letting the tears run down his face while his parents wrap him in a consoling embrace, refusing to let go for dear life.

# CHAPTER THIRTEEN

Terry found it difficult to get back to sleep after the experience he just had, so he makes the decision to stay awake for the rest of the day. His parents became increasingly concerned for him; they wanted to ask about his nightmare, but they were afraid he would give them the cold shoulder if they pushed too hard, so they decided to wait until he felt ready to talk about it. Or, if they were lucky, he would tell his friends and they would tell them afterward.

Julie called their parents, asking if they would allow their kids to visit Terry for a little bit. Billy's parents agreed to ease up on their son so he could visit. Allison's father said he'd bring her personally.

Casey's parents, however, refused to even think about it. They told Julie and Marcus their son was a terrible influence on their daughter, and would not allow him to get anywhere near her. Julie thought of a few choice words for Casey's mother, but held her tongue, knowing it wouldn't change anything. She and Marcus sat in the waiting room, trying to keep themselves busy.

A few hours passed, but they didn't even notice until they heard a voice say, "Hey there, Mr. and Mrs. W." They look up to see Billy and Allison signing the guest list. Marcus is the first to greet them.

"Hello, Billy. Hello, Allison." He shakes their hands. "Terry will be happy to see you. His day has been…less than ideal."

"What do you mean, Mr. Welling?" asked Allison. "Is he okay?"

"He's fine. Physically, anyway. His hearing is back to normal, but he seems to be a little shaken up by a dream he had earlier today."

"Did he tell you what it was?"

"No", Julie chimed in, "but we were hoping he would tell you since you're his friends. I just wish Casey could be here right now." At that exact moment, as if by magic, Casey walked through the door. "Did someone mention me?" she said coyly.

Billy opened his mouth to say something, but Allison stopped him before he could get a chance. "Don't start, Billy." Julie looks at Casey and asks, "I thought your parents said you couldn't come."

"They did say that," Casey begins, "but that is not going to stop me. Terry is my friend, and I want to make sure he's okay."

"You could always kiss him and make him feel better." Billy remarked, but by doing so he earned some stares from Terry's parents, as well as from Casey and Allison.

"I was only kidding! Lighten up!" he exclaimed sheepishly. Marcus lets out a small chuckle. "Come on, guys," he says. "I'm sure Terry will be happy to see you."

He leads them up the hallway until he stops at the door to Terry's room. "He's in here." Casey opens the door, and she sees Terry sitting up in his bed, flipping through channels desperately to find something worth watching.

She walks in, followed by Billy and Allison, but he doesn't notice until Casey sits on the side of the bed and says with a smirk "Boredom doesn't suit you at all, tough guy." He puts down the remote, turns to face his friends and replies, "If I have to stay here for another day, I will scream. I can't take another minute of being cooped up in this place."

Billy walks over, grabs the remote, since he seems to know what good shows are on TV at the right time, sits down in a chair by the room window, and starts flipping through channels. "I know what you mean," he tells Terry. "This is why I do my best to avoid hospitals at all costs. My immune system is unstoppable."

"Then why did you miss a whole week of school when the flu was going around earlier this year?" Allison asked.

"That was just a coincidence. I didn't have the flu. I had chicken pox."

Casey rolls her eyes, then remarks, "You had chicken pox when you were 8. You can't catch it again."

"Then I had the shingles virus."

"You're too young to get the shingles virus. Plus, last time I checked, it doesn't make you throw up or keep you on the toilet."

"You weren't there. You wouldn't know." Terry's face starts to turn green and he quickly clutches his stomach. "Can we change the subject, please?" he asks. "I don't want to hear any more about this."

"Sorry, Terry." Billy said as he continued flipping through channels, until he finally stopped on a show. "Sweet. Those *Impractical* guys. What a bunch of jokers!" He watches intensely, waiting for something to happen, until he lets out a loud laugh. "That's hilarious!" he howls. "That guy's skydiving! He looks like a screaming ferret!"

Casey rolls her eyes. "Billy, how can you watch that show?" she asked. "Those guys are so mean to each other!"

"That's why it's so funny!" Billy replied. It's what makes the show so popular! It just finished its sixth season. I'm already excited for the next one!"

"So," Allison interrupted, "how are you doing, Terry? Are your ears still ringing?"

"A little," said Terry as he tried to ignore Billy's laughter. "But I'll be going home later tonight, so I guess I'm A-OK. So, anything exciting happen at school today?" Billy quickly stopped laughing, as if somebody was reading his mind. "No," he quickly said. "Why, what have you heard?" Terry points to an area on Billy's face that appears to be slightly bruised and replies "What did you do to piss off Jeremy now?"

"Why do you always assume it was me?"

"You're right, Billy. I apologize."

"Thank you, Terry."

Terry looks at Casey and asks, "What did Billy do to piss off Jeremy now?"

"Hey!" Billy squealed.

"What do you think he did?" asked Casey.

"I'm standing right here!" Billy squeaked.

"He ran his mouth and got punched in the face?" Terry asked.

"Am I invisible or something?" whined Billy.

"Right on the nose with that one, Terr." Casey exclaimed. "Did you say something, Billy?" Billy covers his mouth, trying not to scream in frustration. Casey watches him as he starts stomping his feet like a wild animal. Terry and Allison start watching, as well, and they soon find themselves covering their mouths to keep from laughing so they don't disturb any other patients in their rooms.

Tears begin to roll down Terry's face while Billy continues his strange little dance, and soon a snort comes out of Allison's mouth. Terry and Casey stare at her as she covers her mouth and turns bright red, looking away so they don't see her face.

Billy finally stops his weird dance, speaks up and remarks "Did anybody else just hear a pig, or is it just me?" Terry and Casey roll their eyes. "It's just you," they both say at the same exact time. Allison attempts to compose herself, adjusts her glasses, then says "Sorry. I sometimes do that when something really funny happens, which isn't very often."

"So, all we need to do to make her laugh is have Billy do something stupid and immature?" Casey asked. Billy nods in agreement, then thinks about what Casey just said and snaps back "HEY! Not funny!"

Before Casey can get a chance to retort, there is a knock on the door. Everyone looks and sees Madame Granger standing in the entry way carrying a book and some papers. "Excusez-moi," she politely says, "Est-ce que je suis interrompue?"

"No, not at all, Madame Granger." Allison replied. "You're not interrupting." At that moment, Billy immediately shuts up, reaches into his backpack, then pulls out his beret and bubble pipe. Casey rolls her eyes. "Oh, no," she mutters under her breath. "Here we go again."

Billy proceeds to place the beret on his head and the bubble pipe in his mouth, then he quickly walked over to Madame Granger and immediately said in his Jacques Cousteau voice "Bonjour, Madame Granger, vous avez l'air incroyable cromme le gaz des marais au clair de lune."

At first, nobody says a word. Terry and the others feel their jaws drop; if they were cartoon characters those jaws would have probably dropped to the floor. They couldn't believe what they had just heard. Billy Martin, the one student dead set on never speaking another language for his entire life, actually spoke French! It felt like they were trapped in an episode of *The Twilight Zone*. Only in some bizarre reality could such a thing exist, since the only "French" Billy ever really paid attention was in those old cartoons with the skunk, and that didn't even count as the actual language at times.

Terry grabs a hold of his head, as if his brain just had some form of a short circuit. *"There is no way in Hell he just said that. It just isn't possible."* And he isn't the only one who was thinking it. Casey thought maybe somebody slipped something into her lunch when she wasn't looking. It could be the only explanation. How else could her cousin, who believed there were only forty-nine states in America, possibly speak the one language in the one class he absolutely refused to acknowledge even existed?

Allison, on the other hand, was a little hurt. She had a feeling Billy would do something like that the minute Madame Granger walked through the door, and he did. She wished that, for just one minute, he would use French on her instead. Then that changed when she, along with Terry, Casey, and obviously Madame Granger, figured out exactly what Billy just said. Terry shakes his head, as do Casey and Allison. Madame Granger, on the other hand, lets out a small chuckle; she too knows what Billy just said and decides to humor him. "Merci, Monsieur Martin."

Confused, Allison starts to say "Uh, Madame Granger, are you aware that he just said......", but Casey quickly places a hand over her mouth and whispers "Shush, Alli. I want to see where this is going." Billy blows into his pipe, causing tiny bubbles to come out, then he continues by saying "Permettez-nous de fuir ensemble et de cochonner des téléphones poreux."

Terry rolls his eyes, wishing Billy would stop and actually realize what it is he was saying. *"This has got to be the most embarrassing thing Billy has ever done."* Terry thinks. *"If Madame Granger slaps him, I don't think anybody would blame her."*

Instead, Madame Granger replies, "Non merci je suis intolérant à la télévision." Billy chuckles, blows into his pipe again, adjusts his beret, then tells Madame Granger "Vous faites mon coeur courir comme le dos de mon âne." Casey clenches her fists as she says to herself "Will someone please make him stop?" She keeps hoping Madame Granger will finally put an end to her cousin's sad (and disgusting) attempts at flirting. Instead, she continues to humor him by replying "Je suis heureux pour votre âne." Billy lets out a loud laugh, loud enough to make Terry and the other hold their hands over their ears.

"Billy, quiet!" Terry exclaimed. "You're going to disturb the other patients!" Billy doesn't hear him, and keeps howling, which soon makes Madame Granger wish she had earmuffs or something to drown out the noise. Finally, Casey approaches Billy, walks up behind him, raises one of her hands, and gives him a good hard SMACK in the back of his head. "OW!" he cries out. "What the hell was that for?!"

"Sorry, Billy, but…YOU WERE GETTING ON OUR NERVES!!" Casey screeches. "You were giving us all a damn headache! Somebody had to shut you up." Billy rubs the back of his sore cranium intensely. "Couldn't you have found another way of getting my attention?" he asked. Casey shakes her head and replies "Where's the fun in that? Hitting you in the head is one of our favorite past times."

Madame Granger proceeded to place the book and papers on the stand next to Terry's bed. "Anyway," she began, "I also wanted to drop off your book and assignment so you wouldn't fall behind. I asked Monsieur Martin to bring it to you, but I don't think he was paying much attention." Casey watches Madame Granger place the book and papers on the stand, then she makes a strange face that nobody seems to notice. *"Strange."* Casey thought. *"That doesn't look right."* She was about to say something, then decided to keep quiet for the moment.

"Well, merci, Madame Granger." Terry says. "I will work on it when I get home." Madame Granger smiles, waves to the others, then walks out the door. Billy sits back down, thinking he has finally won her over. "Well?" he asks. "What did you guys think of my French? Pretty impressive, right?" The group just looks at each other, silent, not sure what to say to Billy without hurting his feelings. Then, clearing his throat, Terry speaks up. "Uh, Billy," he begins, "do you know what you said exactly?"

"Does it matter?" Billy remarks. "I spoke French!"

"Except you said it all wrong!" Casey said. "How Madame Granger didn't slap you for what you said is a freaking miracle!"

"Why? What did I say?"

"Well," started Allison, when you greeted her, you said 'Hello, Madame Granger, you look amazing. Like swamp gas in the moonlight."

"What?! I didn't say that!"

"Actually, you did."

"You don't know what you're talking about."

"Well", interrupted Terry, "we do, since we actually pay attention in class and understand the language. You're the only one of us who has no idea what you said."

"If you're so smart, what else did I say?" Casey rolls her eyes. "You sure you want to know?" she asked. Billy nods, then she says "You also asked her to run away with you and pig out on fluffy televisions, to which she said 'No thank you, I am television intolerant.'"

Billy drops his head in shame. "Oh, crap," he quietly mutters. "What is wrong with me?"

"It doesn't end there, Billy." Terry chimed in. "Finally, you told her that she makes your heart race like the back of your donkey, and she said she's happy for your donkey."

Billy picks his head back up and starts waving his arms around like a maniac. "Why didn't you guys stop me?!" he shrieked.

"We tried, but we were kind of hoping you would've stopped talking long enough for us to say something."

"I feel like an idiot now."

"Now?" Casey remarked. "You should always feel like an idiot with the stupid stuff you do every day. Must I remind you of your infamous Squishies or your self-proclaimed 'Great Veggie Revolt'?"

"Those don't make me feel like an idiot. The day I walk out the doors of Littleroot High for the last time, my name will be remembered. My pranks will be legendary and future generations will try to top what I will have accomplished."

"Does that include the infamous chicken incident you pulled off last year?"

"The very same. And there is so much more I have yet to do."

"Like what?"

"A good prankster never reveals his secrets."

"That's magicians, Billy."

"Same diff." Just then, Julie walks in. She clears her throat and says "Sorry, guys, didn't mean to interrupt, but I was wondering if anybody would like to go down to the cafeteria and get something to eat. My treat."

Billy runs out the door, shouting "Nothing is better than free food!" Julie shakes her head. "He could have at least waited until I told him where the cafeteria is. Could someone track him down before he gets lost?"

Allison raises her hand and replies "I'll go."

While Allison begins her search, Julie remarks "Come on, Casey. Let's let Terry rest."

Casey nods and replies "Okay, Mrs. Welling." She then turns to Terry and says "Get some sleep, Terry. There is something we need to talk about later." She leaves with Julie, confusing Terry like never before.

*"What does she want to talk about?"* he thinks. *"I hope it's not serious. We haven't really had much of a conversation since…the ceremony. Is that what she wants to talk about? I thought maybe she would have forgotten about it by now. I know I can't. It's all I can think about lately."*

Instead of pondering about what Casey wants to discuss, he decides to get a head start on his French homework. He opens his book to see a page that Madame Granger marked so he would know what he needed to do. He spent the better part of about twenty minutes working tirelessly on the assignment, writing down answers with a pencil Madame Granger provided with the book, until he decided to take a break and try to watch some TV.

He notices it was still on the same show Billy was watching earlier. He watches as one of the people in the show is being chased out of a house by someone wearing a full body cat costume. He lets out a small chuckle and mutters "That's pretty funny."

Meanwhile, Julie, Marcus, and Casey sit in the cafeteria, but they haven't eaten yet; they're still waiting for Billy and Allison to arrive. Instead, they look out a window at separate tables, Casey at one, Julie and Marcus at another. They don't say a word. Casey finds herself twiddling her thumbs because she doesn't feel very comfortable for some reason.

She has never had trouble speaking to Terry's parents before, but that was because Terry was usually in the room with them. He helped break the ice quite a bit, but since he's resting right now, she finds herself unable to say anything and she doesn't understand why.

Luckily, Julie and Marcus feel the exact same way. When Terry was there, they could have a nice conversation, but without him, what could they possibly say to the girl they know has strong feelings for their son but acts like she doesn't? The room was so quiet you could hear a pin drop. Finally, Julie speaks up and says "You can sit with us, Casey. If you'd like."

"Uh, thanks, Mrs. Welling." Casey replies. "Are you sure it's okay?"

Julie chuckles and replies "Of course it's okay, Casey. Please sit with us." Casey gets up from her table and moves over to the one Marcus and Julie were sitting at. The second she sits down, she feels a little uneasy; they may have invited her to sit with them, but it doesn't make it any less awkward for her. What would she say to them? Or, rather, should she say anything at all?

"So, uh, how's the car dealership business going, Mr. Welling?" she asks nervously, wondering where on Earth Billy and Allison could be. She hopes Marcus didn't hear her question, but then he clears his throat and replies "It's going fine, Casey. Thanks for asking."

"Really? How so? Get any new models come in today?"

"Uh, yes, we did. We're actually thinking of expanding because we don't have enough space for them all."

"Have you spoken to the town council about it yet?"

"Not yet, but I will. After we bring Terry home."

"That reminds me. I've been meaning to ask, but I didn't want to be rude."

"What is it, Casey?"

Casey twiddles her thumbs again, takes a breath, and says "Well, I know you guys are quite financially stable, but I can't understand why Terry doesn't have a car of his own. I mean, you can certainly afford it, so why haven't you given him one yet?"

Marcus struggles to answer, but then Julie speaks up. "That is a very good question, Casey."

"It is?"

"Yes. You see, the reason is Terry wants to buy one for himself. We offered to do it, but he declined. That's why he got the job at Games 2 Go. He has his eyes set on a classic car, a 1973 model, red with black stripes. He feels that if he saves up his money and buys it himself, then he will know what it's like to truly earn something he worked really hard for."

"Why does he want an old car? I thought he would want one of the newer models from the dealership. Those look like some pretty amazing rides."

"We asked him that very same question, and his only answer was he prefers the classics. He said we could give Billy a car if we wanted, but then he took back what he said. Something about not wanting to cause the car any kind of suffering."

"He must've seen Billy play a racing game. I have, and he totally sucks at driving. Terry has saved countless people and animals from the horror of Mr. Crash & Burn."

They all let out a huge laugh, imagining Billy driving a car using a game controller as the steering wheel, to the point where tears start running down Julie's face. A minute later, once they have all had a chance to calm down, she wipes a tear off her cheek, takes a moment to compose herself, then looks around for Billy and Allison.

"Where are they?" she asks. "Shouldn't they have gotten here by now?"

Casey rolls her eyes. "Knowing Billy, he got lost in the elevator." She pulls out her cell phone and begins to dial Allison's number, but before she could hit the call button, Billy and Allison arrive. As they approach the table, Casey says "Where the hell have you guys been?"

"I was trying to find Billy." Allison replies.

"And where did you find him?" Casey asked.

Allison looks at Billy and says "Maybe you should tell her."

Billy sheepishly looks at the floor, not saying a word.

"Well?" Marcus said.

Finally, he says, "I thought it would be funny to hide in the morgue."

"What?!" Casey screeched.

"I was going to hide in the morgue. I planned to go into one of the slabs covered by a sheet, have Allison close it up, then when someone opened it, I would pop up and say 'Hey, shut the damn door!'" Casey smacks her hand on her forehead.

"Billy," Julie starts, "what were you thinking? Don't you know how dangerous that is? What if nobody found you? Those things can only be opened from the outside. Plus, considering what's been going on lately, I don't think it's a good time to be playing any practical jokes right now."

"I was only trying to lighten up the mood a little bit. Everyone's been so glum ever since they found the bodies of Trent and the other victims."

"I can understand trying to ease the tension, Billy." Marcus says. "But there has to be a better way of doing it."

"I guess."

Then, before they can continue their conversation, Jeremiah and

Angela Martin come storming into the cafeteria, and they definitely don't look very happy. They march right up to the table, then Jeremiah points his finger in Casey's face and shouts "Casey Martin! What the hell are you doing here? I thought we were clear when we specifically said we don't want you anywhere near that Welling boy!"

"Dad, I can explain…" Casey starts, but Jeremiah puts up a hand, refusing to hear a word of it.

"Casey, we tried to be as calm as possible," said Angela, "but you went behind our backs. That boy is nothing but trouble."

"I already told you time and time again that it was my idea to go to the lake, not Terry's! I convinced him to go, even though he was reluctant to. He is not a bad influence on me."

"You can stop covering for him, young lady. Only he would do something so foolish and stupid."

Just then Marcus chimes in and says "Now, hold on, you two. There is no reason to attack my son. If Casey said it was her idea, then don't you think you should listen to her reasons why she did it?"

Jeremiah sticks his finger in Marcus' face and shouts "You keep out of this, Welling! You're already on my you-know-what list, so don't make it any worse!"

"Uh, Uncle Jeremiah, Aunt Angela," Billy says, "is all of this really necessary? I mean, all Casey did was come to the hospital with us to visit our friend."

"Billy, this doesn't concern you. Please mind your own business."

"But…"

"Billy, if you were my son, maybe you'd learn to keep your mouth shut. Your dad's too soft on you."

"That seems a little harsh, don't you think, Uncle J?"

"I said be quiet, Billy." Jeremiah takes a closer look at Billy for a second, then says "And take that ridiculous beret off your head. You're coming home with us, too."

"What? Why?"

"Because we don't want you being influenced by the Wellings' punk son. He's a bad influence on Casey, and he's a bad influence on you too."

"Now wait just one apple-picking minute!" Marcus exclaims. "Whatever your problems with our son may be, that doesn't give you the right to boss your daughter and nephew around like they're soldiers. Billy's parents said he could be here."

"As I said, they're too soft on him. If they would actually discipline him, maybe he wouldn't be pulling childish pranks and causing teachers to quit. And don't even get me started on your son."

"And what is that supposed to mean?" Julie asked Jeremiah.

"Your son acts like he's innocent, but no 'innocent' person breaks into the mayor's house and then gets another one blown up the next night!"

"As Terry has already explained, he was not responsible for Dr. Kaminko's house being destroyed."

"That's another thing." Angela chimed in. "The whole 'Mayor Hamilton really being Dr. Kaminko' thing is a bunch of nonsense. We think he fabricated the whole story to cover his tracks."

"You can't be serious!" Marcus shouted. "You make it sound like Terry's some kind of criminal! He's not! He's a kind hearted and honest boy who loves to read and play video games and who dreams of becoming a History teacher someday! You have no right to insult my son!"

"THAT'S ENOUGH!" Casey screamed, shocking everyone in the cafeteria. "Dad, I wanted to check out the lake, not Terry. I convinced him to go, not the other way around. Allison and I wanted to investigate the legend of the Lady in the Lake. It's not a legend, Dad. The Lady is real. We saw her." Jeremiah rolls his eyes and scoffs.

"I'm serious! The Lady is responsible for the deaths of Trent and the other victims. We don't have any proof, but I know it's her. I just have to figure out how she's doing it."

"That's enough, young lady," Jeremiah replied as he grabbed Casey by the arm. "I don't want to hear any more about this Lake Lady nonsense. We're leaving right now." As Jeremiah, Angela, and Casey begin to walk out of the cafeteria, Jeremiah stops, gives Billy a look and says "Come on. I already said you're coming with us. Let's go."

"Uncle Jeremiah," said Billy, "I think I'll stay here with Terry's parents and Allison."

Jeremiah shook his head. "Perhaps you didn't hear me," he grumbled, "but you are coming home with us right now. Let's go."

"But my parents said I could be here. Terry's my best friend and I want to stay."

"Too bad, Billy. We're leaving."

"Actually," interrupted Casey, "we're not." Jeremiah and Angela notice Casey holding a cell phone in her hand. "You see, while you guys were arguing with Terry's parents, Allison gave me her phone and I called Uncle Gene. He was listening to your whole conversation the entire time, and he is on his way here right now."

"You can't be serious."

"I am very serious, Dad. I'd say he'll be here in about, oh, thirty seconds."

Then, like clockwork, Gene walks into the cafeteria, with a very sour look on his face. He marches right up to Jeremiah and angrily says "How dare you. I don't appreciate the way you've been talking about my son. And don't even get me started about how you insulted Terry. He's a good kid."

"If he is such a good kid," Jeremiah said, "then why did he drag my daughter and your son to the damn lake?"

"He didn't. She convinced them to go. If I know one thing about Casey, it's that she never lies. She's not very good at it." Gene then looks at Casey and says "No offense."

"None taken, Uncle Gene." Casey replies with a smirk on her face.

"Then how do you explain the stupid story about the Lady in the Lake?" Jeremiah remarked.

Gene replies "I can't. But the case is ongoing. We hope to have a clear answer soon so we can reopen the lake again."

"So, you're basically saying that you are completely incompetent at your job?"

But before Gene can deliver a retort, his phone rings and he answers it. "Hello?" A few moments later, he hangs up and puts his phone back in his pocket, but he doesn't say a word. He just stands there in silence, completely exasperated while everyone else just watches.

"What's wrong, Dad?" Billy asks.

Gene takes a deep breath and says "That was Deputy Judd. They just found another body at the lake. Another Littleroot High student." Small gasps are let out by everyone, then Casey asks "Who was it, Uncle Gene?"

Gene says nothing for another two minutes, then he finally answers Casey's question. "Jeremy Hodges."

# CHAPTER FOURTEEN

The news of Jeremy Hodges' death spread quickly, like a wildfire. He was found at the lake just like the other victims: suddenly aged rapidly and no defensive wounds, but the cause of death was still unknown. Gene was doing everything he could to ensure the town that there was nothing to worry about and he hopes to have a break in the case very soon.

Of course, the town's confidence in him was beginning to wane. Everyone was starting to believe that he was no longer competent enough to be their sheriff, but a few people were still believed in him.

The first person was Mayor Barbara Daniels, who in a recent interview stated that although the cause of the deaths had not yet been identified, she was confident that the sheriff would find one and finally close the case.

Another was Deputy Franklin Judd. Despite the town's misgivings about Gene's job as sheriff, Judd refused to give up on his partner and friend. Littleroot's overall crime rate dropped quite a bit ever since Gene and his family arrived from Bangor ten years ago.

Judd was essentially taken under his wing after he became sheriff and learned everything he knows from him. Gene considers him part of the family and Billy jokingly calls him "Uncle Frank", but he takes it to heart. He is sure Gene will finally crack the case, even if nobody else thinks so.

Billy, of course, is sure of his father's skills. He may not have had much to go on, but that hasn't stopped him from trying his absolute best.

He is determined to find the cause of these mysterious deaths and nothing will get in his way, not even a town that doubts him. Billy said he wishes he could help, but Gene told him not to interfere with official police business. He's still in trouble for going to the lake, after all.

Billy wasn't sure how to react to the news of Jeremy's death. On one hand, he doesn't have to deal with being bullied anymore, but on the other, he would never want that kind of thing to happen to anyone, even if they were a jerk who enjoyed tormenting the hell out of him. He decided it was best if he kept his feelings to himself so he doesn't offend anyone.

Terry returned to school the next day, his hearing fully restored, but he had the same mixed feelings as Billy. He didn't care for Jeremy much either, since he was always bullying the hell out of Billy, but he would never wish that kind of thing on his worst enemy. *"Nobody deserves that"*, he quietly thinks to himself as he approaches his locker, *"no matter how much of a heartless person they were."*

As he began the combination to open his locker, Casey walks up to him, but he doesn't notice until she taps him on his shoulder. "Hey, Terry," she says, "how are you feeling today?" He shrugs and replies "A little better, I guess. Didn't get much sleep last night."

"Because of Jeremy?"

"Not just him. It was…something else, something terrifying."

"What was it, Terry?"

Terry takes a deep breath, closes his eyes for a few seconds, then replies "I had a dream, more like a nightmare, that Dr. Kaminko was still alive. I was in his house, and he taunted me. Then, he…"

"What? What did he do?"

"I can't even say it. It's too awful to talk about." Then, he stops talking and looks away. He doesn't want to say any more, afraid to relive the whole experience all over again. It doesn't take long for Casey to find out what he's saying, or not saying in this case. She could never understand what he went through, but it wasn't hard to imagine, either.

Out of all four of them, Terry was definitely affected the most. Sure, Allison broke her wrist, Billy broke some ribs, and Cassey twisted her ankle, but Terry endured having Dr. Kaminko put his hand in his chest. Then he broke his arm in the most severe way possibly imagined. Of course, he would have such a terrible nightmare about Kaminko killing him. Who wouldn't?

Just then, Madame Granger can be seen approaching the two of them in a rather brisk pace. *"Oh, great."* Casey thinks. *"What the hell does SHE want?"* Madame Granger stands next to Terry and says "Bonjour, Monsieur Welling. How are you feeling today?"

"Fine, Madame Granger," Terry replies. "Just a little tired, that's all." Madame Granger chuckles. "Well, just make sure you don't fall asleep during class. I don't think you want one of Monsieur Martin's infamous spitballs waking you up. Do you?" Terry shakes his head at the thought of one of Billy's spitballs landing in his hair. "Definitely not. Mr. Elliot got one of those a few months ago, and he wasn't happy about it. At all."

"Well, I'd better get back to the classroom, so I'll see you and Monsieur Martin in a few minutes." Madame Granger then takes a quick but somewhat apprehensive look at Casey and flatly says "Ms. Martin."

As Madame Granger turns back towards her classroom, Casey screams "What the hell?! What is that woman's problem?!" Terry then starts rubbing his forehead and asks "Could you please stop yelling, Casey? No offense, but that's giving me a headache."

"Oh, sorry, Terry. But there was no reason for her to talk to me that way. She was so rude, yet she joked around with you? What's up with that?" Terry just shrugs his shoulders and opens his locker. "I don't know, Casey," he replies, "but it's probably best not to let it get to you. Plus, I saw the way you were looking at her in the hospital yesterday."

Casey lets out a small gasp. "And what do you mean by that?" Terry says nothing for a second, then takes out his books and remarks "You gave her this nasty look for no reason. All she was doing was being friendly to us. There is nothing wrong with teachers checking in on their students, you know."

Casey shakes her head in response. "You don't understand. There's something about her that I don't trust. Don't you think it was just a little strange that not long after she showed up, Jeremy's body was discovered at the lake?"

Terry rolls his eyes and scoffs. "Are you saying that Madame Granger had something to do with Jeremy's death?" Casey sighs. "No, I'm not saying anything of the sort. But I just think that it's convenient she shows up at the hospital and then Jeremy's body is found not long after."

"That was just a coincidence, Casey. Nothing more." Terry says nonchalantly. Just as he grabs his last book, he is about to close his locker when Casey places a hand on his shoulder.

"Terry," she starts, "I think we should go back to the lake and do another investigation." Terry takes a few steps back, shocked. "Are you kidding me right now?" he asked. "After what has happened, you seriously want to return to the place where all of those people died, AND the one place that is a crime scene at this very moment?"

"Yes. We need to find some answers."

Terry scoffs. "No. WE don't need to do ANYTHING. Your uncle told us not to go anywhere near the lake, and I intend to do what he says. I don't know if you've even noticed, but I'm kind of fond of my hearing, and I plan on keeping it for the rest of my life."

Casey rolls her eyes and places her hands on her hips in frustration. "I can't believe you, Terry Welling. Talk about a double standard!"

"What? What are you talking about?"

"When you wanted to investigate Dr. Kaminko's house, we went with you without question. And, thanks to our help, you found out the truth. But, apparently, the second I want to learn the truth behind the Lady in the Lake and the deaths, you immediately decide that it's not worth your time! Why is that?"

Terry doesn't say a word, because he knows she won't like his answer, but he finally clears his throat. "Look, Casey, investigating a corrupt politician is one thing, but we're talking about a ghostly witch who is haunting a lake and killing people. There's a huge difference between a mayor abusing his power and a witch's ghost."

"So, you won't help me?" Terry nods his head a couple of times. "Exactly. I hate to say it, but you're on your own. Count me and Billy out."

"What makes you sure Billy won't help me?"

"Have you met Billy? He's the one who called police when we were eight years old because he heard the Grinch stole Christmas, remember?"

"Good point. But this isn't fair, Terry. Brenna Kinsley thinks…" Terry holds up a hand to stop Casey from speaking.

"Let me stop you right there," he interrupts. "You talked to that stupid reporter? THAT'S your argument?"

"I didn't. Allison did, but that's not the point. What she told me was…"

"I don't want to hear about Allison's conversation with that nosey and annoying sad excuse for a journalist. She made my life miserable, and she got fired for it, so she is not exactly a reliable source of information right now."

Terry starts to put his hand down, but then Casey starts to speak, prompting him to put his hand back up. "Read my lips, Casey," he said. "I…am…NOT…getting involved in this ridiculous Lake investigation. End of story."

Casey can feel her eyes begin to fill up with tears, but she tries to fight them back as hard as she can when she screams "Go to hell, Terry Welling!"

She turns around and starts storming up the hallway, where Billy can see her. "Hey, Casey," he says, but she glares at him and shouts "Take a long walk off a short pier!" in response. She then proceeds to push him to the side, causing him to lose his balance and hit his shoulder on a locker.

"Ow!" he shouts, rubbing his shoulder as he continues to walk down the hallway and approach Terry, who's trying to calm himself down and released his clenched fists. He can feel his blood beginning to boil, and he can't understand why. He and Casey have disagreed before, but this is probably the first time they have ever argued.

"Hey, Terry," Billy says as he approaches his locker. "What's going on between you and my always-cheerful cousin?" Terry shakes his head as he grabs a few books out of his locker. "I don't know, but apparently me not wanting to investigate the Lady is considered selfish as far as she's concerned."

"It's selfish to want to stay alive?" Billy asks in response. "If that's the case, then I'm a real selfish guy!" Terry sighs and closes his locker while Billy starts to work on the combination to his. "I'm not in the mood for jokes right now, Billy, so can we just go to class?"

Billy opens his locker and grabs his Jacques Cousteau clothes, which Terry quickly notices and lets out a groan. "Billy…" he starts. "Yes, Terry?" Billy replies.

"I thought we agreed on no jokes today. We just finished talking about it."

"Yeah. And?"

"Can you please not become Jacques Cousteau today?" Billy looks at the clothes of his Frenchman alter-ego and lets out a small chuckle. "Don't worry, Terr. I'm not going to turn into Jacques anymore."

"Really?" Terry asks in shock.

"Yeah. To be honest, I'm actually getting a little tired of Jacques."

"Why?"

"He's served his purpose. Madame Granger seemed impressed, so it's time to become someone else."

Terry rolls his eyes. "Why not try being yourself for a change and maybe actually try impressing someone closer to your own age?"

"Where's the fun in THAT?" Billy laughs. "I'm so close to winning Madame Granger's heart, I can practically taste it."

"That would be the blood from after she punches you square in the mouth because you finally took your creepy approach to the utmost creepiest level."

"Nope. It's the taste of victory, Terry." He reaches into his backpack and pulls out his beret. "It's time for Madame Granger to meet…Pierre."

Terry seems completely dumbfounded by Billy's latest little scheme and gets a blank look on his face for a few seconds before saying "Pierre?"

Billy smiles and remarks "Yep."

"Why Pierre?"

"Because my bladder's empty." At that moment, Terry finds himself letting out a small but loud groan. "Billy, that is just terrible. One of the worst jokes you have ever said!"

"Well, it was better than Francis."

"Francis?"

"Francis Fulloffrenchpeople."

Terry says nothing. Instead, he grabs Billy by his shirt collar and begins dragging him to French class, hoping to avoid any more of his friend's horrible puns. "No more of your bad play on words, Billy. Let's hurry before we're late to class. Again."

Billy shrugs his shoulders. "Sure, whatever. You'll see that I will soon succeed in my mission to win Madame Granger's love. Pierre is prepared."

French class seems to be going slower than usual, at least it is for Terry. He can't bring himself to focus on anything Madame Granger says while Billy is being very attentive, which is very unlike them. *"I must be in the Twilight Zone or something,"* he thinks, *"because that can be the only explanation to why Billy's paying attention in class and I'm not."* He opens his notebook and starts doodling random images on one of the pages.

*"Maybe Casey's right. Maybe I do have some kind of double standard when it comes to Kaminko and the Lady. I don't know. Maybe she's overreacting. Maybe I'm underreacting. Maybe I should stop using the word 'maybe' all the time. Okay, mental note. Replace 'maybe' with 'perhaps'. That could work. Maybe. Ugh! I thought I was going to stop using that word. Maybe I should… there I go again! Stop it!"*

"Excuse me, Monsieur Welling."

Terry, still lost in thought, continues drawing in his notebook and doesn't seem to notice Madame Granger and the entire class staring at him. As he keeps drawing, he faintly hears the sound of the other students laughing. When he looks up, he sees Madame Granger standing right next to his desk which makes him throw his notebook in the air in surprise and it lands on Billy's head. "Ouch!" he cries out.

"Sorry, Billy. Uh, hi, Madame Granger. Is something wrong?" Terry said. Madame Granger picks the notebook up from the floor. "Just wondering as to why you seem to be having an out of body experience while I'm trying to teach a class, Mr. Welling."

She stares at Terry's doodle. "Is this supposed to be a porcupine or a monkey wearing a wig?" She hands the notebook back to Terry, who replies "I honestly don't know. I was just doodling. Wasn't trying to draw anything in particular."

Madame Granger shakes her head. "I expected better from you, Terry. This is not like you at all. Please pay attention or I'll have no choice but to give you detention. Do I make myself clear?"

"Yes, Madame Granger." As Madame Granger walks back to her desk, Billy puts a hand on Terry's shoulder and whispers "Dude, what's the matter with you? Normally I'm the one getting in trouble. Are you okay?"

"Yeah, I'm fine. I was just thinking, that's all."

"About what?"

"We need to figure out how Jeremy and the others died." Terry whispers back. "We need to get to the bottom of this."

"And how do you plan we do that?"

"I'll let you know as soon as I think of something."

The rest of the school day goes on as well as can be expected after a student has died. Many went home after seeing the guidance counselor, and some were even taken out of school by their parents; they felt nobody would be safe until the causes of the deaths was found and the person responsible would be arrested. The fear wasn't unjust; the school had no reason to dispute the parents' concerns for the safety of their children, so it was suggested the building be closed until further notice.

However, Mrs. Doyle refused to shut down the school just because of something nobody could find a solution to. She said to let the police do their job and hopefully they can close the case as fast as possible. At some point during the day she received a phone call from superintendent Michael Dunlap. When asked why she didn't close the school, she stated she didn't believe it would make much sense when there was only a month left in the school year.

If she closed it down and a month went by without any kind of answers then the students would have to make it up over their summer vacation, and she could think of quite a few students who had no intention of spending their summer in a classroom; particularly, one whose father was also the town sheriff. Plus, she didn't really want to put up with his antics during that period either.

The final bell rings, and nearly less than half of the student body walked outside since many were already home thanks to their parents. Casey and Allison are among the first outside, much to their relief. As they walk to the corner, waiting to cross the street, Allison's phone rings. She takes it out of her pocket and sees the Caller ID is her mother. She puts it on vibrate and puts it back in her pocket.

"Who was that?" Casey asks as she sees it's safe to cross. As they cross Allison replies "Just my mom."

"It's not like you to ignore her calls. What's up?"

"This morning I told her I was going to be stopping by the shelter today and check in on Maverick. She had a problem with that." They finish crossing and begin walking up the sidewalk. "Isn't Maverick the dog Trent was spending time with?" Casey asks.

Allison nods solemnly. "Trent wanted to adopt him, but I'm afraid if he doesn't find a home soon, the shelter will have no choice but to…" She begins to feel her eyes fill with tears but tries to hold them back. Casey gives her a hug, trying to comfort her the best she possibly can while the tears finally roll down Allison's face. "It's going to be okay, Alli. He'll find a home, I'm sure of it." Then, an idea comes to her mind. "Why don't you adopt Maverick?"

Allison shakes her head. "I can't. My mom hates dogs, which is one reason she doesn't want me spending time at the shelter."

"Well, I'd adopt him if I could, Alli, but my mom is allergic to dogs so it's not an option."

"I know." Just then, Allison notices something unusual. "Uh, Casey?" she asks. "Where are we going? Home is the other way."

"I know," Casey replies. "But we aren't going home." Allison gets a look of confusion on her face. "Then where are we going?"

"We're going to the medical examiner's office and find some answers."

Upon walking into the hospital, Allison began to feel a little uneasy. Nobody in their right mind would think of sneaking into the morgue to look at a dead body for any reason, but Casey didn't seem to notice. She was just curious and wanted to know what could have killed Trent and the others. She knew the Lady had something to do with it, but she wasn't sure how she was doing it.

"Casey," Allison whispers as they continue their trek to the morgue, "this is wrong. We shouldn't be going down there." Casey rolls her eyes. "Allison, relax. Everything is going to be fine. We are not going to get caught."

"What makes you so sure? Have you been in the morgue before?"

"Well, no, but I've seen it done on TV many times. How hard can it be?"

Before Allison can reply, Casey stops in her tracks in front of a door. "Okay, this is it. The morgue is right here." She tries to open the door, but finds that it's locked. "Shoot!" she cries out. "How do we get inside?"

"I don't think we should even try, Casey. Obviously, we don't have any kind of clearance to get in there." Allison remarked. "Let's just go home."

Before Casey can say another word, she hears footsteps coming down the stairs and starts to panic. Two pairs of footsteps, to be exact. "Uh, oh. I think we're in trouble. We have to hide." As she and Allison search for an unlocked door to hide in, the footsteps start getting louder. And louder. Casey and Allison manage to open a closet door and hide inside. By the time they close the door, the footsteps stop.

Casey cracks the door open slightly to take a peek, then hears a familiar voice say "Ready or not, here we come!" She then pushes the door wide open to see Terry and Billy standing there. "What the hell are you guys doing here?" she asks angrily.

"I thought we were playing hide and seek." Billy replied. "Did we win?" Casey shakes her head while Allison slowly walks out of the closet. "How did you know we were here?" she asked.

"We saw you headed this way after school, and I assumed you were thinking the same thing we were." Terry said. "You're looking for answers too, right?"

"Well, actually, Terry was thinking it. I was thinking of tacos, but he made me come." Billy shudders. "This is just so wrong. So many dead people. And no tacos."

"Billy," Casey said, "if I even think you're going to say that you see dead people, I will not hesitate to slap you upside the head." She approaches the morgue door and remarks "Besides, I thought Terry made it perfectly clear that he didn't want to investigate the Lady."

"I gave it some thought, and you were right." Terry replied. "I didn't want to admit it at first, but I couldn't get what you said out of my mind. I did have a double standard when it came to Kaminko and the Lady, but I'm over it. The Lady is taking innocent lives, and we must figure out how and why."

Casey lets herself smile at Terry's response. "Now that sounds like the Terry I lo...uh, think is pretty cool." She turns her attention back to the door, hiding the redness in her face. "So," she says, clearing her throat, "how do we get inside?"

Allison points to a scanner on the side of the door and says "Looks like we need a security pass to get in. Where are we going to get one of those?"

Just then, Billy shouts "Ta-da! One security pass, at your service!" Stunned, Casey asks "Where the hell did you get one of those, Billy?"

"Terry and I managed to take it right out of Dr. Taylor's coat pocket. She really needs to wear it around her neck or something. You never know when a couple of guys will steal it so they can look at some dead bodies."

Casey takes the pass out of Billy's hand and runs it through the scanner. A few seconds later, the door unlocks and the four teens go inside the morgue. There is an uneasy feeling upon entering the room, almost as if you're being watched with suspicion even though there is nobody else in the room.

"Uh, this is so creepy." Billy said with a slight tremor in his voice. "Perhaps I should wait outside. This place is a……"

"Don't say it's a dead end, Billy." Terry whispered. "This is neither the time nor the place for that joke. Besides, we won't be staying here for very long. We just need to find a clue as to how the Lady is killing her victims."

"Maybe she feeds them food from the cafeteria and makes them suffer a slow, painful death. That stuff is nasty."

"Or maybe she makes them listen to one of your horrible puns and cheesy jokes." Casey chimed in. "I swear I die a little inside every time I have to hear them." Billy, not at all amused, rolls his eyes and replies "Oh, that is SO funny! I almost forgot to laugh!"

Allison whispers "We need to be quiet, Billy. We don't have much time before Dr. Taylor realizes her pass is missing, so we must hurry."

Terry nods. "Agreed. Look over there." They approach an autopsy table that clearly has a body on it, but is completely covered by a sheet. Terry stands at one end where the head is supposed to be while Casey stands at the other end, leaving Billy and Allison to stand at one side of the table."

"Okay, guys." Terry grabs the sheet. "I'm going to lift this so we can take a quick look and hopefully find a cause of death. Be ready." He takes a deep breath, and folds the sheet down just enough to see the victim's face. The group just stands there, completely flabbergasted.

"Who the hell is this old geezer?" Billy remarks. "I thought we were looking for Trent and the others."

"I was just thinking the same thing." Casey said. "This doesn't make much sense." She takes a closer look at the body. "I guess Dr. Taylor hasn't started her examination of the body yet." She pulls the sheet down a little further, exposing the man's upper torso. "Just as I thought. See? No incisions were made. If this body was already examined, there would be a large Y-shaped scar from when she sewed the incisions back up."

"So, what now?" Allison asked.

"Let's go home." Billy chimed in. "This place is obviously a…"

"Billy…" Terry gives him a stern look. "What did I say about making that joke?"

"Party pooper."

Casey looks back at the body. "Do you think…this is Jeremy?" Billy shakes his head. "That's impossible!" he exclaims. "This guy has got to be over a hundred years old! I'm pretty sure Jeremy was nowhere near that age!"

"Who else could it be, Billy? There's nobody else in the room."

"No", said Allison, "but there could be more in the refrigeration units."

"The what?" asked Billy.

"The refrigeration units." Terry began to explain. "They're essentially lockers to preserve the bodies of the deceased until they are transferred."

"Why would they be kept in lockers, anyway? Wouldn't they start to stink after a while?"

Casey rolls her eyes. "No, dummy. They're not like your gym locker. As Terry already said, they are used to preserve bodies until they can be transferred, pending an autopsy and or identification. Besides, didn't you want to hide in one not too long ago?"

"Yeah, but I didn't actually know what they were used for."

"They're used to store dead bodies, you goober."

"But how do they work? I don't get it."

Allison clears her throat. "The lockers work in either one of two different ways, positive temperature or negative temperature."

"What's the difference?" Terry asked.

"Well, in positive temperature, bodies are kept between 2 and 4 degrees Celsius. While this is usually used for keeping bodies for up to several weeks, it does not prevent decomposition, which continues at a slower rate than at room temperature."

"And what about negative temperature?"

"In negative temperature, the bodies are kept at between -10 and -50 degrees Celsius. Usually used at forensic institutes, particularly when a body has not been identified. AT those temperatures the body is completely frozen and decomposition is very much reduced."

"So, do you think any of the other bodies found at the lake are in the lockers?" Casey asked Terry.

"It's possible," he replies, "but we won't know until we take a look. Everybody pick a random locker and open it up; maybe we'll be lucky enough and find a clue."

"Wait a minute." Billy says, holding his hands up. "You want us to just open a cold chamber thingy, and look at more dead bodies?"

"That's what I said."

"I'd really rather not do that, Terry. That's how a lot of zombie movies end badly. I'll just watch you guys from the sidelines."

"Billy, there is no such thing as zombies."

"You also said there was no such thing as ghosts when we were checking out Dr. Kaminko's house, remember?"

"Just open a locker and check out a corpse already!" Casey shouts.

"Fine. But if a body sits up and tells me to shut the damn door, I'm out of here."

"Deal." The group go to different corners of the room, each one standing in front of a locker door. As they grip the handle on their respective door, they each feel a little funny. They know they have to find some kind of answer, but to just look at dead bodies in their search is somewhat unsettling; some would call it disturbing, but they all agree that it needs to be done.

"On the count of three," Terry begins, "we open our doors at the same time. Everybody ready?"

Casey and Allison nod in agreement. "We're ready."

Billy puts a hand up. "Can I get a second opinion?"

"One......two......three!" At that moment, they all pull their doors open with slight force and speed. What they find is truly bizarre.

"Uh, anyone else open a door that had an old person in it?" Billy asked the others.

"Sure did." Terry replied.

"Same here." Casey added.

"I didn't." Allison remarked.

"Who the hell are these guys? Was there an old geezer convention in town we didn't know about?" Terry takes a closer look at the body he discovered while Billy continues his rant that everyone chooses to ignore. He can't put his finger on it, but there is something about the body that seems familiar, so he pulls the slab out a little further until he sees something on the body's foot.

"What is it, Terry?" Casey asked.

"It's a toe tag. Maybe the victim's name is on it." He grabs a hold of the toe tag and looks it over. A few moments later, his eyes widen with sheer terror and shock. His lip quivers as the others notice him just standing there, not saying a word to them.

"What's wrong, Terry?" asked Allison.

"Who is that man?" Casey chimed in.

Finally, Terry manages to gather the courage to speak, though he doesn't want to say anything because it's impossible to believe. "I-it…it's Trent Alexander."

"Are…are you sure, Terry?"

Terry reluctantly nods his head. "The toe tag has his name on it. I don't think Dr. Taylor would make a mistake like this. Which means…" He looks back at the body on the autopsy table. "That must be Jeremy."

"But who are the other victims?" Allison asked as Terry looked over two more two tags. "Hmmm… Wallace Paisley and Henry Reeves, the victims before Jeremy. But I can't think of what could have caused this."

"That makes two of us, Mr. Welling," said a voice from the outside of the door. The group sees Dr. Taylor standing there, with a clipboard and a stern look on her face. "I had a feeling you guys would want to find some kind of answers. That's why I let Billy take my security pass. I knew your curiosity would get the better of you."

"How did you know it was me who took your pass?" Billy asked her. She lets out a small chuckle. "I detected the faint smell of cherry soda and fear."

"I suppose you're going to tell my dad now, right?" Dr. Taylor shakes her head. "No, Billy, I'm not. Granted, I could get into serious trouble just for letting the four of you in here, but I suppose it wouldn't hurt to have an extra hand with this bizarre mystery." She walks over to Terry and hands him the clipboard. "You were right, Terry. The victim on the table is indeed Jeremy Hodges."

Perplexed, Terry asks "Any idea what caused this?" Dr. Taylor replies "Not yet," as she walks over to a filing cabinet and pulls out three files, "but Jeremy and Trent, as well as the other bodies found at the lake, all had the same thing happen to them." She hands the files to Billy and the others. "At first I thought that maybe they had a very advanced case of progeria."

"Progeria? What's that?" Casey asked, to which Billy cheerfully replied "That's the little blue pill some men like to use." Terry rolls his eyes. "No, Billy, that's something else entirely. Progeria is a disease."

"To be precise," Dr. Taylor adds, "progeria is an extremely rare autosomal dominant genetic disorder in which symptoms resembling aspects of aging are manifested at a very early age. Those born with it typically live to their mid-teens to early twenties."

"So, what are the chances that every victim found at the lake would all have the same advanced aging disease?"

"Very slim. It's rarely inherited since those with the disease never long enough to reproduce and pass it on. But just to be safe I tested them for progeria."

"And? What did the tests reveal?"

"They all tested negative for progeria. But that's not the only strange thing I found during my examinations. It's in my reports." Terry and the others open the files Dr. Taylor gave them, start to read them very carefully, and notice something she highlighted. "Are you sure this is accurate, Dr. Taylor?" Terry asked.

"Yes. The pituitary glands of all of the victims were empty."

"So, it sounds like whatever, or whoever, is responsible sucked the youth right of them." Casey remarked. "That's quite morbid, to say the least."

"What do you mean 'whoever is responsible', Casey?" Dr. Taylor asked her.

"We have reason to believe the Lady in the Lake is responsible for these mysterious deaths. We encountered her recently, but nobody will believe us." She stares into Dr. Taylor's eyes, lets out a sigh, and continues, "And I'm guessing by the look on your face that you don't believe it, either."

"You have to admit that it does sound a little far-fetched," replied the doctor. "But I'm willing to keep an open mind, considering what has been happening lately. This is way beyond my expertise. I can't find any other way to explain it."

"I know what you mean, Doc." Terry remarked. "Exposing a corrupt politician is one thing, but a witch who steals someone's youth and vitality? That's a little hard to explain."

"But why?" Allison asked. "Why is the Lady stealing someone's youth? For what purpose could it possibly serve?"

"That," said Terry, "is the mystery we need to solve. And I think I know who can help us." He takes out his phone and dials a number. Everyone stays quiet while the phone rings, then Terry says "Hi, it's me. I was wondering if you could do us a quick favor."

"Who's Terry talking to?" Billy whispered.

"Shhh!" Casey said. "I'm trying to hear what he's saying."

"Right." Terry continued. "Could you please look up anything you can find on the Lady in the Lake? I know it sounds bizarre, but it might be helpful to what we need to know. It would be a great help."

He stops talking for a few moments, then says "Really? That'd be great! Yeah, we'll meet you as soon as you let us know what you found. Thanks a lot. Bye."

He hangs up, puts his phone away, and notices the others staring at him. "What?" he asks.

"Who were you just talking to, Terry?" Casey asked back.

"That was Mr. Elliot." Terry replies. "He said to call him if I ever needed anything, and I decided that now would be the best time to do so."

"But why?" asked Allison.

"Being a history teacher, he probably knows more about the town and its urban legends then we do. Come to think of it, perhaps I should have asked him for help on Dr. Kaminko. I never really paid much attention to the legend until my dad told me and Billy about it."

"I told you about it first!" Billy exclaims.

"Yeah, I know. But you tend to blow things out of proportion. Remember the Grinch incident?"

"I was eight! When are you going to let that go?!"

"Probably when you call the police because you think your grandma got run over by a reindeer. But you're not that gullible. I hope."

"What makes you think Mr. Elliot can help us?" asked Casey.

"We're not getting anywhere looking for answers on our own, Casey. We keep hitting dead ends." Terry quickly looks over at Billy, who stares at him with his mouth hanging in disbelief, and says "Yes, I know what I said, Billy. No need to rub it in."

"Why does he get to say it and I don't?? That's not fair!" Billy screams.

"Because he didn't use it out of context, which is something you would obviously do." Casey told him. "Now will you please stop screaming?"

"If your teacher can help us," Dr. Taylor says, "then it would definitely be a big step in this case. Otherwise…"

"Otherwise," Terry finishes, "this is going to get a lot worse before it gets better."

# CHAPTER FIFTEEN

Being a high school history teacher in a small Maine town isn't the most exciting job in the world, but that's not why Mr. Elliot took the position. He loves teaching, and he enjoys inspiring students to learn about the state and its past. Prior to his job at Littleroot High, he had been offered a position at a university, but he turned it down for personal reasons. He preferred to teach in a smaller classroom because he felt more comfortable not having to teach so many students.

Over his twenty five years of teaching at Littleroot High, he has had the pleasure of meeting some amazing students who he hoped would be inspired to pursue their dreams, no matter how small or difficult they may be. He would take time to help them with their issues or tutor them if they were falling a little behind. But recently, there has been one student in particular who has been an absolute joy and experience. The student's name is Terrence Harper Welling.

Prior to Terry's freshman year at the school, Mr. Elliot felt trapped. He was beginning to think the students didn't care to learn anything he was trying to tell them. He wanted to retire and move to a different town at the end of the next school year, but then on the first day, he met Terry and his friends. He was surprised at how polite and knowledgeable Terry was. The minute Terry walked into the classroom, he immediately walked up to Mr. Elliot's desk and offered up a handshake.

Surprised by the gesture, Mr. Elliot wasn't sure what to do at first, but decided to return the handshake, seeing that the young man was being very genuine with it. He immediately had a feeling that Terry could be one of his most attentive students. As soon as the students had sat at their desks, Mr. Elliot immediately introduced himself by writing his name on the board.

"Welcome to History class," he began, "my name is Mr. Elliot, and I shall be your teacher for the next four years. I must warn you in advance, I will not go easy on you. The assignments and projects I give you will be no walk in the park. I expect you to give 110% on everything you do in here."

He then proceeded to write a question on the board. "Before we begin, I like to kick off each school year with a simple question." The second he was done writing his question, he then read it out loud to the class. "What year did the Korean War begin and what year did it end?"

Just then, a boy with blonde hair, sitting in the very back row, raised his hand in excitement. "Oooh! Oooh! I know this one!" he said with enthusiasm. "Okay, then." Mr. Elliot replied. "What is the answer?"

"The Korean War started in 1972 and ended in 1983," the boy said. "That was easy."

Mr. Elliot shakes his head, lets out a sigh, and says "That's wrong."

"What? How can it be wrong? My dad and I watch that show all the time!" Mr. Elliot raises an eyebrow, looks over to see Terry sitting next to the blonde haired kid, and says "Mr. Welling?"

"Y-yes, Mr. Elliot?" Terry replies nervously.

"Perhaps you can answer the question without involving sarcastic meatball surgeons. Would you like to give it a shot?"

"Uh, sure." Terry clears his throat, and says "The Korean War began in 1950 and ended in 1953."

"That is correct." Mr. Elliot looks back at the blonde haired kid and asks him "What is your name?"

"Uh, Billy Martin. My dad's the sheriff." Mr. Elliot points to an empty desk at the front of the class. "Perhaps you should sit here, Mr. Martin, so I can keep an eye on you and you can learn something."

"But that's not fair. Why do I have to sit up front? Because I got one little question wrong?"

"One question can make the difference between passing and failing this class, Mr. Martin. Now hurry up. We don't have all day." Billy gets up from his desk, grumbling something under his breath, and starts to slowly drag his feet across the classroom.

Eventually he gets to the front of the room, and sits at the desk. But right after he sits down, he puts on a pair of sunglasses, to which Mr. Elliot doesn't seem to notice, but Terry certainly does; he knows what Billy is going to do, but thinks it would be best not to say anything. If Billy wants to pull something like that, then he'll have to deal with the consequences himself.

"Okay, class, today you'll be given your textbooks, and your first assignment will be to…" Mr. Elliot then notices Billy wearing the sunglasses with a huge grin on his face. "Uh, what do you think you're doing, Mr. Martin?" Mr. Elliot asks.

"I'm just ready to learn, that's all." Billy replies.

"Why are you wearing those sunglasses?"

"It's bright in here. My eyes are very sensitive."

"It's not that bright."

"Well, the light's reflecting off the top of your head and I don't want to be blinded." The whole class begins to start snickering; some trying to keep themselves from laughing by covering their mouths with both hands, some snorting, the rest burst out laughing, except for Terry, who just put his head in his hands thinking to himself *"I can't believe he just said that. It was nice knowing him."*

At that point, Mr. Elliot began to feel he was losing control of his students thanks to Billy's little remark. He closed his eyes, took a deep breath, counted to ten, then let out a long sigh. He looked at Billy and asked "Do you think you're some kind of comedian, Mr. Martin?"

Billy takes off his sunglasses and replies "That all depends. Are we talking stand-up comedian or prop comedian? If we're talking prop comedian, I'm going to need a watermelon and a large mallet." Mr. Elliot gives him a slight smile, almost devilish, and says "Alright, class. Thanks to young Mr. Martin and his sharp wit, your first assignment will be to read the first FIVE chapters in your History book and do the reviews at the end of every one." At that moment, the class let out a loud collective groan, as well as a few colorful choice words for Billy.

To say having Terry and Billy in his class for the past couple of years would be an understatement for Mr. Elliot. While Billy would complain about every assignment and project they were given, Terry wouldn't say a word and just do the best he could to finish each one. Despite a slow start, Terry grew to be one student Mr. Elliot had high hopes for and envisioned a bright future for him. He even found himself going out of his way to help Terry with any assignments he might have been struggling with.

The night Dr. Kaminko's house was destroyed, he was sitting at home grading papers when he got a call from another teacher telling him to turn on the news. To his shock, one of the town's most iconic landmarks was up in flames, but grew concerned when he learned four of his students were at the house before it was destroyed. He immediately got in his car and drove to the site of the explosion.

He quickly started looking around the destruction for any survivors, then noticed someone being loaded onto an ambulance. He quickly ran over and his concerns grew when he saw it was Terry, then realized the other students must have been Billy, Casey, and Allison.

Since that night, he found himself keeping an eye on the group, making sure they were adjusting and trying to move on from their traumatic experience. He even gave Terry his personal cell phone number if he ever needed anything, which is something he never did for any of his other students. But Terry told him he would not call unless it was absolutely necessary.

Three months later, and Terry hadn't called him once. He would stay after school every so often and talk to him face to face, but only for a few minutes, mostly if he needed some help with an assignment. Terry tended to keep to himself ever since the night at Dr. Kaminko's house, and Mr. Elliot respected his space. When he wanted to talk about it, Mr. Elliot would be ready to listen.

He knew Terry had it rough over the past few months ago, but he didn't want to push the subject. Instead, he simply kept a quiet eye on his student, and only stepped in when Jeremy Hodges was harassing him and Billy. Aside from that, he didn't really have to do anything, which made him assume Terry was trying to handle the situation in his own way, even if it wasn't really working. But he chose to let Terry figure it out on his own.

Then, a few hours ago, as he was getting ready to go home for the evening, his phone rings. He takes it out of his pocket and checks the caller ID. To his great surprise, it was Terry. He answers. "Hello?" he says.

"Hi, it's me." Terry says on the other end of the line. "I was wondering if you could do us a quick favor."

"Of course, Terry." Mr. Elliot replies. "But it might help if I knew what exactly kind of favor you need. Does it anything to do with the mysterious deaths at the lake?"

"Right. Could you please look up anything you can find on the Lady in the Lake? I know it sounds bizarre, but it might be helpful to what we need to know. It would be a great help."

"The Lady in the Lake? The old urban legend? Well, Terry, I don't know much about it, aside from a few tidbits, but I'm sure I can dig up some more information. If it can provide some insight into what's going on at the lake, I'd be happy to help."

"Really? That'd be great! Yeah, we'll meet you as soon as you let us know what you found. Thanks a lot. Bye."

"You're welcome, Terry. Bye." He hangs up, walks out of the classroom, locks the door, and leaves the school to go home to look for clues on what might be one of the biggest mysteries in the history of Littleroot, Maine.

# CHAPTER SIXTEEN

Terry found himself unable to sleep after learning what he and the others had discovered in the morgue. He just couldn't wrap his mind around it; how is the Lady stealing the youth of her victims? Why was she even doing it in the first place? Revenge maybe? Does she harbor a decades long grudge against the town? If so, what could it possibly be? What could have happened that would cause a woman to take the lives of innocent people at the Lake? And that leads to another question. Why is she only killing at the lake? There had to be some reason for it.

When he woke up to get ready for school, he saw his parents sitting at the kitchen table. They didn't seem to notice him. "Uh, good morning, Mom and Dad." Terry said. Marcus looked up from his newspaper. "Oh, good morning, Terry," he replied. "Did you sleep well?"

"Not really. Had a few things on my mind. I was up for most of the night."

"I had a feeling that was the reason." Julie said. "I could see your light was on in your room. Something must be bothering you."

"Yeah. I guess you could say that."

"Would it have something to do with the Lady in the Lake?" Marcus asked.

"Is it that obvious?" Terry replied as he went to the fridge. Marcus slightly nods and says "We can sort of read your face like a book, son. We know when something is bothering you." As Terry proceeds to grab a carton of milk from the fridge, he lets out a small sigh. He takes the carton over to the counter and grabs a glass from the cupboard. He pours the milk into the glass.

He puts the carton on the counter, grabs the glass, and takes a sip of milk. He then lowers the glass and says "It just doesn't make any sense, Dad. I've only heard bits and pieces about the legend of the Lady. I'm familiar with most of the town's urban legends from stories Grandpa told me. Dr. Kaminko, the Phantom of Littleroot High, the Monster of the Marshlands, the Witch Doctor. I think I even heard something about Littleroot Mountain, but I know nothing about the Lady in the Lake."

Marcus folds the newspaper and half and pushes his chair out. "Well, son," he begins as he gets up from the table, "there have been many conflicting stories about the Lady, and none of them really add up. It's been told in so many different ways that there is no definitive version, just like the legend of Dr. Kaminko. At least until you and your friends discovered the truth."

Julie then chimes in and says "I'm sure you will find the truth about the Lady, honey. You just need to keep digging for more clues. Something will come up eventually."

Just then, there's a knock on the door. "That must be Billy." Terry remarks. "Come on in, Billy." The door opens and Billy peeks his head inside. "Is it safe?" he asked.

Terry rolls his eyes and replies "Yes, Billy. It's safe. Get in here." Billy steps into the house, closes the door behind him and exclaims "Howdy, Mr. and Mrs. W! How's it hanging?" Marcus pours himself a cup of coffee. "Morning, Billy," he replied. "Been a while since you've come to the house."

"Really? How could you tell?" Billy asked him.

"We still have food on the table." Marcus said with a chuckle.

"Are you hungry, Billy?" Julie asks. "We have plenty of sausage left." Billy, holding his stomach, eyes the sausage on the table, remarks "Thought you'd never ask! I'm starving!" He sits down at the table, grabs a few sausage links, and starts eating. "Guess I don't get have to any breakfast this morning." Terry remarked as he watched Billy devour the links. "I'll just grab a donut."

Terry opens a box of chocolate donuts and takes one out. He takes a bite while Marcus and Julie watch Billy enjoy his breakfast. Finally, Billy puts the links down and says to Terry "So, what were you guys discussing before I arrived and graced you with my presence?"

"Nothing important. Just, you know, the Lady." Terry replied as he sipped his milk.

"Oh. Can we change the subject? Let's talk about my dad and when he trained to be a silent mime."

"Billy," Julie says, "we asked your dad about that and he said it never happened."

"Of course, he would say that. He signed a non-disclosure agreement. He's not allowed to talk about it." Billy then tries to keep himself from smiling at his latest witty remark while Terry rolls his eyes and says "Billy, that was just horrible." Billy takes a hand and pats himself on the back. "That just means I'm doing a great job with my amazing sarcasm."

Julie grabs Billy's plate. "Your dad told us you made up that story when you were nine years old," she says. "Apparently he said something about people training to be mimes and how he sometimes wished you would do the same thing, but you heard something completely different."

"Kind of like the time he told the class why there was a crack in the middle of his bottom." Marcus chimed in. "That was a funny story."

"My mom said she wouldn't tell anybody that!" Billy exclaimed. "She lied to me!"

"Billy, relax. It wasn't that embarrassing. Terry had done some funny things when he was a kid, like when he swallowed sixteen cents thinking it was candy."

"I forgot he did that." Julie said with a laugh.

"I did?" Terry asked. "Why don't I remember this?"

"You were only three years old at the time, son." Marcus replied. "Your mother panicked and we took you to the hospital. Luckily there was nothing to worry about."

Billy lets out a loud laugh. "So, let me get this straight," he said between howls. "He swallowed loose change, and I guess you had to wait until he passed it. Does that mean on the funniest things he's done, swallowing loose change would be number two?" Terry rolls his eyes again, and replies "That was a crappy joke, Billy." with a smirk, then he too starts laughing.

Marcus and Julie shake their heads, watching as their son and his best friend laugh at the terrible joke. Tears start rolling down their cheeks, unable to contain their laughter. For a few moments, the thoughts of Dr. Kaminko and the Lady disappear from their minds, as if they never happened, and things go back to the way they used to be, when they could just hang out and goof off, not worry about corrupt mayors, haunted houses, or evil spirits at a lake. They could just be regular teenagers playing video games, reading comic books, and hang out with their friends.

Terry stops to catch his breath. He wipes the tears from his eyes and takes a look at his watch. "Oh, shoot!" he exclaimed. "Billy, we're going to be late for school!" Billy stops laughing, lets out a sigh, and replies "Aaaand the fun is over. Do we have to go to school?"

"Yes, Billy. We do. We don't want to be late."

"What is this 'we' stuff? I wouldn't mind being late. Heck, I wouldn't mind skipping school altogether!"

"Then your parents will make you sign up for summer school. Again. Do you really want to repeat that?"

"Good point. Let's get going." As Terry and Billy head for the door, Julie says "Have a good day, sweetie. Love you." Before Terry can respond, Billy remarks "Aww, I didn't know you cared so much, Mrs. W!" Terry rolls his eyes, pushes Billy outside, and shuts the door behind them.

As the two friends begin their short trek to school, Terry takes his phone out of his pocket to check if he had any messages, only to find that he has none. "Nothing?" he mutters to himself. "I was hoping he would have at least texted me or something…"

"You say something, Terry?" Billy asked him. Terry shakes his head and replies "Just talking to myself, Billy. It's nothing." They continue their walk to school, mostly talking about the latest video games and movies; pretty uneventful, until they are approached by a familiar face, one that Terry wishes they didn't run into.

"Mr. Welling, Mr. Martin." Brenna Kinsley says as she walks closer to them, much to Terry's annoyance. "I need to speak to the two of you. It's important."

"Why?" asked Terry. "Did you run out of people to harass about Dr. Kaminko's house? And did you forget that you're not supposed to talk to us?"

"Maybe I can call my dad and tell him about this." Billy chimed in. "I'm sure he'll be more than happy to arrest you again."

"Wait, please. I just need a minute of your time." Brenna pleaded. She took a deep breath and said "I want to help you solve the murders at the lake. You know as well as I do that the police have no idea what they're dealing with."

"I'm not sure how to respond to that." Billy flatly said, clearly offended by Brenna's comment. Terry crosses his arms, also showing that he doesn't appreciate what he interpreted as an insult toward his best friend's father, whom he has a great deal of respect for. "You're obviously trying to make a point, Ms. Kinsley," he said. "I suggest you hurry up and get to it before Billy calls his father."

"As I just said," Brenna replied, "we need to work together to solve the murders. If this keeps up, then the mayor will have no choice but to close down the lake, and we all know what could happen if that happens."

"Yeah. The lake is a big tourist attraction, and the town would suffer if it were shut down. Without the money from tourists, a lot of small businesses would probably have no choice but to close their doors for good. We can't let that happen."

"So, can we work together? I might have a few sources who can help us if we need them. What do you say?"

Terry, with his arms still crossed, begins to ponder about the idea of working with the former reporter who had hounded him and his friends about Dr. Kaminko's house. He was reluctant to accept her help, but perhaps her sources could provide them with some answers about the Lady and why she's only killing at the lake.

"Okay, we'll work together...on ONE condition. You don't publish anything about the murders until we have definitive proof. Deal?" Terry sticks out his hand. Brenna looks at it for a second, then returns the handshake. "Deal," she replied. She then reaches into her pocket and pulls out a card. "Here's my number. Call me if you have anything, or if you need help."

Terry takes the card, takes out his wallet, and puts it inside. Brenna smiles, says "Thanks! You won't regret this!", turns and walks away. Billy looks at Terry, waits until Brenna is out of earshot, and says "Are you sure we can trust her, Terr? She might go back on her word."

"Maybe, maybe not." Terry replied. "But we're not getting anywhere on our own. If she can help us, despite what her motive might be, I say we don't have much choice at the moment. With her help, and Mr. Elliot's, we might be able to shed more light on the story of the Lady."

"Or…we can ignore it and let them do all the work so we can pretend it never happened. Yeah, that sounds good. Let's do that!"

"Billy…"

"What? I don't like talking or even thinking about it. The whole thing is creepy as hell. The thought of a ghostly woman killing people at a lake. Makes me not want to go back there!"

"If we have to, we will."

"You guys can. I'm not getting anywhere near that place again! Count me out!"

"I'm sure with the right motivation you will. Come on, let's get going." The duo then resume their walk to school, unaware that somewhere in the shadows, they were being watched with dark intent.

Outside the main doors of Littleroot High, Casey and Allison wait patiently for Terry and Billy to arrive. Well, Allison waited patiently; Casey was pacing back and forth, checking her watch every thirty seconds. Allison passed the time by double checking her homework to make sure there weren't any errors.

Finally, Casey spoke up and shouted "Where the hell are they?? They should have been here by now! Billy must have done something stupid to slow Terry down! That's the only reason!"

Allison looks up from her homework and says "They'll be here, Casey. I'm sure they lost track of time. You know how those two are. They probably grabbed a snack at the store on their way to school."

"I guess you're right, Alli. I just want Terry to get here before the bell rings so I can ask him something."

"You mean you want to ask him to go to the school carnival with you. I know, Case. You've mentioned it a few times."

"Well I can't take the chance of him getting asked by some other girl!"

Allison finally puts her homework away, takes a deep breath, and calmly replies "Casey, as your best friend, I'm going to be honest with you. Out of every single girl in this entire school, Terry has eyes for only one. You."

"Really?"

"Yes. We've all seen the way he looks at you. Billy doesn't care too much for it, his best friend flirting with his cousin, but everyone else knows you two like each other. I'm pretty sure he wants to ask you to the carnival, too."

"Then why hasn't he?"

"Well, actually, he tried. Remember? You practically turned him down. He hasn't really talked about it since."

At that moment, Casey's heart sank. "Oh, no…I'm such an idiot. I can't believe I did that to him. He must have been upset. I have to make it up to him somehow."

"You will, but after we solve the mystery of the Lady. Hopefully Mr. Elliot will be able to provide some answers."

Just then, Casey sees Terry and Billy approaching the school, which makes her heart skip a beat. As soon as the pair reach the bottom step, Allison asks "What took you guys so long?"

"Ah, you know how it is," Billy replied. "One minute you're at a bar throwing back a few shots of whiskey and the next thing you know you're late for school because you got into a fight with some roughnecks." Terry just rolls his eyes and smacks his forehead.

"Very funny," Casey said. "Where were you guys?"

"We got a little sidetracked," Terry responds. "Brenna Kinsley approached us about working together to solve the mystery of the Lady. She said she had resources that might be helpful if we need them."

"And what did you say to that?"

"I said I'd accept her help as long as she doesn't publish anything we find before asking for permission first. She might be trying to gain fame and fortune for the story, but we can deal with that when the time comes."

"I'm sure she just wants to find the truth." Allison says. "She approached me about the Lady first, and even though I was reluctant at first, I decided to hear what she had to say. She's convinced there is some kind of connection between the Lady and Dr. Kaminko's house."

"If there is," Terry began, "then we haven't found it yet. It's kind of doubtful, considering the legend of the Lady supposedly occurred a couple of decades before the events at Dr. Kaminko's house. We just have to wait until we can get some more evidence."

"But can we really trust Kinsley?" Casey asked. "All she's done is harass us about Dr. Kaminko. She can't just be doing this out of the kindness of her heart. Besides, wasn't she fired from the station?"

"She was," Allison replied, "but she's not doing this to get her job back. She wants to find the truth, that's all."

Billy shakes his head and chimes in, "That can't be it. I agree with Casey. She must have another reason."

"And what would that reason be?"

"Maybe she wants to defeat the giant mole men and save the Ninth Dimension." The rest of the group roll their eyes and ignore Billy's theory. For a few moments, they just stand there silently, each thinking of why Brenna Kinsley wants to help them. Then, Billy looks out of the corner of his eye and sees Madame Granger walking up to the building.

He wets his hand, slicks his hair back, walks over to Madame Granger, and says in a deep voice "Bonjour, Madame. How are you doing this fine morning?" Madame Granger just stares at him, not saying a word. Instead, her gaze seems to be cold and distant, is if she's a completely different person.

Billy feels a chill run down his spine, and immediately walks back over to the others. He stands next to Terry, who has the same uneasy feeling as he does. Madame Granger walks past them and up the stairs, when something catches Casey's eye. She notices one of Granger's hands seems to be different than the other; pale, slightly wrinkled, and just looked disturbing. Terry clears his throat and says "Good morning, Madame Granger." She looks at him, giving him the same icy stare she gave Billy, then says "You two are going to be late for class if you don't get moving."

"Is something wrong with your hand, Madame?" Casey asked her. She quickly put it in her pants pocket and replies "It's fine. Just a little cold, that's all. Mind your own business, Ms. Martin." As she opens the door and goes inside, Terry squirms and says "Is my shirt too big or is that my flesh crawling?"

"That was bizarre," Allison remarked. "She didn't seem like herself at all. Is she okay?"

"Maybe she finally got tired of Billy's creepy flirting, like the rest of us." Casey said.

"Hey!" Billy exclaimed.

"That's not it," Terry replied. "Allison's right. Madame Granger seemed like a completely different person. Plus, her hand looked really strange." He thought quietly for a few seconds. "So, I was right…"

"What was that, Terry?"

"A little while ago, during class, I noticed that her hair had a few grey strands. I thought I was being paranoid, because I hadn't been getting much sleep, but I'm convinced that something is going on with her."

"I think you're right." Casey added. "When she came to visit you in the hospital, I noticed that her hand was a little discolored. Not as bad as what we just saw, but it was still quite noticeable. I didn't say anything because it didn't seem like a big deal at the time."

"You guys aren't making any sense!" Billy shouted. "Perhaps she's just having a bad day. Just because she wasn't herself doesn't mean anything! She's a wonderful person!"

"Actually," Allison said, "we don't even know what kind of person Madame Granger is. We never see her outside of school, and we know absolutely nothing about her background. She's an enigma."

Billy rolls his eyes. "What does her religion have to do with it?"

"We mean her entire life is a mystery, Billy," Terry responded. "We've never heard her mention a life outside of work or where she lives. Very strange."

"It is. But we can figure it out after we deal with the Lady." Casey says. "Perhaps we can try to sneak a peek at her records when we're done."

"Sounds like a good idea to me." Terry said.

Billy becomes furious and immediately says "Are you guys serious?? You really think she has something to hide??"

"It's something we can do in the meantime until we actually have something on the Lady, Billy. In case you haven't noticed, finding information on her isn't easy. It's a needle in a haystack."

"But there's no reason to waste our time with Madame Granger! She hasn't done anything wrong!"

Casey gets between them and says "Billy, think about it. She just happens to appear out of the blue, and nobody knows where she came from. That doesn't seem suspicious to you?"

"No. It doesn't. So what if she doesn't talk about her life? That doesn't mean we need to dig into her past! Let's just leave her alone!"

"Billy…" Terry begins, but Billy puts his hand up, refusing to listen. "You want to stick your noses into Madame Granger's business," he says, "go ahead. But I won't have any part of it! Count me out!" Billy brushes past Casey and Terry, then Allison, as he walks up the stairs, then he angrily opens the door and quickly slams it shut, almost breaking the glass in the process.

Casey tries to catch up with him, but Terry grabs her shoulder and shakes his head. "Let him go," he says. "He just needs time to cool down a little bit. He'll be okay in about an hour or so." Casey nods and begins to walk inside the building before the bell rings. As she does, Allison and Terry decide to follow suit, and hope the day will be as normal as possible. However, in the back of their minds, they know that it will be anything but normal.

# CHAPTER SEVENTEEN

The second Billy walked inside the building, he immediately walked down the hallway and went straight to his locker, still fuming over his friends' insinuation that Madame Granger had something to hide. He couldn't believe they actually thought she had some sort of dark secret. So what if her hand was a little pale? Perhaps she was just cold, or she forgot to apply moisturizer on it or something.

And what does it matter that she had a few grey hairs? That's not a really big deal. She still looked perfect to him, no matter what imperfections she may have. Webbed feet? No problem. Gap in her teeth? Not a deal breaker. Big ears? Funny looking, probably, but it wouldn't bother him at all. Then again, the way she was looking at him was a little disturbing. Why did she stare at him like that? Had he done something wrong? Did he say something inappropriate without realizing it?

Before he could ponder it any further, he heard Terry and the others walk inside and down the hall to their lockers. He doesn't look at them, refusing to even acknowledge that they may be right about her hiding a secret. Instead, he fumbles with the padlock on his locker, trying to remember the combination so he doesn't have to ask Terry for help.

While Billy attempts to get his locker open, Terry starts working the combination to his own. He struggles for a bit, but eventually he manages to get his locker open. He grabs his books, and notices Billy is getting frustrated with getting his locker open. "Damn it!" he hears Billy exclaim, which was quite surprising for him. Casey and Allison notice, as well, but they feel it would be best not to say anything for now; they were unsure if Billy would lash out at them for simply trying to help.

Billy again tries to open his locker, but to no avail. Getting to the point of becoming irritated, he grabs the latch on the door and starts pulling on it, letting out a loud scream of anger in the process and garnering the attention of every student walking down the hall at that very moment.

He soon earns the attention of a few faculty members immediately afterwards, and they are none too happy about a student potentially damaging school property. It doesn't take long for Mrs. Doyle to hear the commotion all the way from her office. She quickly leaves her office and heads down the hall to see what was happening. When she sees the commotion, she finds herself a little surprised that Billy Martin is responsible for the outburst.

Nonetheless, she couldn't let Billy continue with this spectacle. Just as she was about to walk over to him and take him into her office, Terry notices and grabs Billy by the shoulder. "Billy", he whispers. "You need to stop and calm down. You're making a scene. Mrs. Doyle is going to give you hell if you keep this up."

"I don't care!" Billy snaps. "This stupid locker keeps pissing me off! I'm so sick of never being able to get it open! Just once I'd like to open it without any kind of problem!"

"Billy!" Terry shouts. "Calm down before Doyle gives you detention for damaging school property!" At that moment, Billy begins to loosen his grip on the door latch. He takes a deep breath, and releases his grip entirely. Mrs. Doyle approaches the two of them and says "What the hell is going on here??"

Billy looks around, sees all of the students and teachers staring at him, and tries to come up with a response. He sees Mrs. Doyle quickly losing her patience, and begins to think of every possible excuse he knows. Terry whispers "Better think of something fast, or you're a dead man."

Billy quickly starts knocking on his locker door, much to Mrs. Doyle's annoyance, and screams "WILMA!!" Mrs. Doyle rolls her eyes, sighs, and announces "Okay, everyone, there's nothing to see here. Move along."

The rest of the students and faculty members proceed to go into their respective classrooms and begin the day, some a little disappointed they didn't get to see Billy have a total meltdown and turn into a basket case;

the rest just assumed he was trying to be funny and failed miserably. Either way, they decided it was best not to ask questions, unless they want Billy to give them a smart answer.

Billy took a few moments to compose himself, takes a couple of deep breaths, then notices Terry and the others just staring at him, confused at they had witnessed. He doesn't say anything; instead, he simply looks away, not wanting them to stare at him.

But Terry doesn't say anything. Instead, he walks over to Billy's locker, works his magic on the padlock, opens the door, and hands Billy his French book. Billy takes it from him, then says "Perhaps we should get to class now."

Terry nods in agreement, then looks at Casey and Allison and motions for them to get to their class. They don't say a word, and leave for their class. Allison feels she should stay behind and talk to Billy, but knows she should just do what Terry said and give him space, even though she doesn't want to.

Once Casey and Allison have left, Terry turns his attention back to Billy. "You okay?" he asks, but Billy doesn't answer. He seems to be lost in his own little world at the moment, as if he's not himself. "I'm fine, Terry," he finally says. "Let's just hurry up and get to class before Madame Granger gives us detention or something."

"Are you sure you're okay, Billy?"

"I said I am fine, Terry. Can we get to class, please?"

They head to the classroom as quickly as they can, with Billy in the lead. He opens the door, and sees Madame Granger sitting at her desk, and eyeing the two of them with a strange look. Terry notices, and a chill runs down his spine; something about Madame Granger just didn't sit right with him. She was like a completely different person, not at all the cheerful teacher who usually greets the class every morning.

"Hurry up and take your seats. Now." Madame Granger said in a cold, emotionless tone. "I won't tell you again." Before Terry can ask her a question, Billy glances at him and says "Do what she says, Terry. Sit down." Terry says nothing and walks over to his desk while Billy does the same. The second they sit down Madame Granger says to the entire class "It would seem some of you have not been doing what you were asked. I give you simple assignments, and you don't turn them in. You don't even attempt to do them!"

Terry immediately raises his hand, and Madame Granger coldly says "What do you want, Mr. Welling?" Surprised by her question, he replies "Well, Madame, it seems kind of harsh to assume nobody is doing the assignments you give us. Some of them have been quite difficult, if I'm being honest."

A few other students nod their heads in agreement with Terry, muttering that some of the assignments Madame Granger had been handing out were a little hard to do, let alone finish. The chatter in the room begins to grow louder, with Madame Granger growing impatient every second, until she has finally had enough. She stands up, slams her hands on her desk, and shouts "SILENCE!"

The entire class immediately goes quiet, surprised at their teacher's outburst. That is, except for Billy. He doesn't move a muscle; he just sits there, not saying a word or even batting an eyelash. Terry turns around and notices Billy, frozen like a statue. Billy catches Terry staring at him, shoots him a nasty look and whispers "What?"

Before Terry can respond, Madame Granger snaps "Mr. Welling! Do we have a problem here?"

"No, not at all, Madame Granger," Terry replies. Granger gives him the same exact look as Billy did, then says "This is your last warning, Mr. Welling. Do NOT disrupt my class again." She clears her throat, regains her composure, and announces to the class "Since every one of you little ingrates think the homework is too difficult, I think I will make it even more challenging for you. You must all write a book report, three-thousand words, entirely in FRENCH. And it will count as a quarter of your final grade."

The entire classroom lets out a collective groan, except for Billy. Again, he doesn't say a word. Terry whispers "Billy, didn't you what she said? Book report? Three thousand words? Completely in French?"

"Yes, I did hear what she said, Terry," Billy replied in a flat tone. "It sounds both challenging and delightful. I cannot wait to get started."

"Even if you fail? Because it's a quarter of our final grade, you know!"

"And your point would be what, exactly?"

"Well, I just assumed you would complain or make some sort of smartass remark about the whole thing, that's all."

"There is nothing to joke about, Terry. Madame Granger is a wonderful woman, and she just wants what is best for the class, despite what you and others may think of her."

"Billy, what's going on? You're not acting like yourself. You're not making jokes, you're actually paying attention in class, and you're actually excited about homework? Are we in some kind of backwards reality or something?"

"No, Terry. I'm just trying to stay focused on Madame Granger's lesson. Now please be quiet so I can learn something."

"Are you still mad at us for what we said about her? I'm sorry we hurt your feelings, but something isn't right with her. You have to at least know that."

"There is nothing wrong with her, Terry. She is perfectly fine."

"But, Billy…"

"WILL YOU SHUT UP ALREADY?!"

Billy's outburst catches the attention of everyone in the room, including Madame Granger, who is already not happy with Terry anyway. "What the hell is going on, Mr. Martin?" she asked.

"Terry is bugging me and he won't shut up!" Billy snapped. "I just want him to leave me alone, for crying out loud!"

"Mr. Welling, I warned you," Madame Granger growled. "But you wouldn't listen, and you have tried my last nerve. Detention after school!"

"What?!" Terry exclaimed. "I didn't do anything wrong, Madame! I was just…"

"Be quiet, Mr. Welling! I've had enough of you disrupting my class! No more!"

"But the book report is utterly and completely stupid! You're being completely unfair!"

"And you are being extremely disrespectful! I will not tolerate such behavior in my classroom, especially not from you!"

Terry gets up from his desk, grabs his books, and heads for the door. "Don't worry," he said. "I won't be in this toxic classroom anymore. I'm leaving."

"If you walk out that door, you'll be serving more detention, Mr. Welling! I'm warning you!"

Terry opens the door, not caring about Granger's warnings, and replies "I'll consider myself warned, then." He then walks into the hallway and slams the door behind him.

He takes a moment to calm his nerves, and proceeds to walk down the hall to clear his head. As he's walking, he doesn't notice he's walking by another student, A.J. Cookson, photographer for the school's newspaper the Littleroot Weekly. Quiet, a little competitive, but generally a nice guy. He notices Terry walking by him, confused, and says "Hey, Terry, where are you going?"

Terry stops walking, looks at A.J. and replies "Oh, hey, Cookson. I was just walking to clear my mind. Getting a little toxic in the classroom, so I decided to leave. What about you? Why aren't you in class?"

"Oh, I have first period free. I usually spend the time looking over the pictures I took for the next issue of the paper and decide which ones would be the best ones to use. But I figured I should stretch my legs for a little bit today." He looks around for a second, then asks Terry "Which classroom were you leaving, anyway?"

"French. I don't know what Madame Granger's problem is, but I just couldn't be in there for another second. She threatened me with detention, but I didn't care. Something's going on with her. I just don't know what."

A.J. doesn't say anything for a few moments. He looks to his left, he looks to his right, then he looks back at Terry motions for him to come closer. Terry takes a few steps forward, though he's not so sure why, but his instincts tell him to trust whatever A.J. has to say.

"Listen," A.J. whispers, "I think you're right about Madame Granger. She's been acting weird for a while now, and not just what you described."

"What do you mean?" Terry whispered back, but A.J. goes silent again. "Come on, what do you know about Madame Granger?"

"I can't tell you. Not out here, anyway. Follow me. The evidence is on my computer in the newspaper office." He points to a room further down the hall, and starts walking, with Terry not far behind.

A.J. reaches into his pants pocket and pulls out a key. As they get closer to the office, Terry asks "What's with all the cloak and dagger stuff, A.J.? Is this really necessary?"

"Yes," A.J. replied. "Because what I have to show you is important. Nobody has seen it. You will be the first. Well, actually second, besides me."

"If it's so important, why haven't you shown it to anyone else, like Doyle?"

"Because I don't exactly have concrete proof yet. I was afraid Doyle would simply dismiss my theory and shut down the paper in retaliation."

"Makes sense to me. You can't accuse teachers of anything without any way of backing it up."

The two reach the door, and A.J. proceeds to put the key in the doorknob and undo the lock. He turns the knob and pushes the door open. "Welcome to the office of the Littleroot Weekly," he announces proudly. "It isn't much, but we don't let that stop us from giving the school a quality paper."

Terry looks around the room, and can't believe what he sees; a few desks, chairs, some slightly outdated computers, and a printer that looks like it should have been thrown into the scrap heap ten years ago. How anyone can work in such conditions didn't make sense to him, but he knew it wasn't his place to say anything. He was only interested in seeing A.J.'s evidence against Madame Granger.

A.J. walks over to his desk, where the computer he used was still on, and opens a file marked "Photos". At that instant, Terry saw a list of at least a hundred or more photos. He finds himself a little overwhelmed. "That's, uh, that's a lot of pictures," he managed to say.

A.J. lets out a chuckle. "Yeah, I know. I have to take a lot and then go over the best ones with the team to determine which should be used. But I'll make it easier for you and show you a few you might find interesting." He proceeds to scroll through the photos until he stops and clicks on one from a couple of weeks ago. Terry examines the picture closely. It shows the lake, late in the afternoon, and what appears to be a woman with brown hair standing near the edge.

"Is that…Madame Granger?" he asked suspiciously, and A.J. nods. "What is Granger doing at the lake when it's been closed off?"

"That's just it," A.J. replied. "She was at the lake a couple of weeks before it was closed off, before the mysterious deaths occurred."

Terry puts his hand up. "Hold the phone. Why were you following

Madame Granger to the lake in the first place? And how did she not know you were following her?"

"Because of this." He clicks on another picture, and what Terry sees makes his heart sink a little. He actually does a double take, hoping what he was seeing was only a figment of his imagination. "Is…this…accurate, A.J.?" he asked nervously.

"It is." A.J. replies sadly. "This is a picture of Madame Granger talking to Trent Alexander…the last day anyone saw him alive."

"This doesn't make sense. Trent wasn't even in her class. What could they have possibly talked about? He was in a different part of the building, nowhere near her classroom! This is just beyond bizarre!"

"I wish I had the answers for you, Terry."

Terry's shock quickly turns to anger towards A.J. "Why didn't you tell Sheriff Martin about this? Why didn't you say anything about it? This could have saved Trent's life!"

"Don't get mad at me! I didn't have any reason to believe she had something to do with Trent's death. I just assumed they were having a simple conversation." He goes back to the other picture. "In case you haven't noticed, she's alone in this picture. Either Trent hadn't arrived yet, or…"

"Or what?"

"Or maybe…his body had already been hidden by the time I arrived."

Terry calms himself down, writes down his e-mail address on a piece of paper, and hands it to A.J. "Send me those photos to my e-mail, along with any others you think are important."

"Why?"

"Because they may uncover another piece to the puzzle."

"You think so?"

"Yeah." He then heads to the door, before turning back to A.J. and saying "Thanks for the help, Cookson. You have a real knack for photography."

"Thanks. Anytime, Terry."

As soon as Terry shuts the door, he immediately takes out his phone, and sends a group text to both Casey and Allison:

***"Meet me in the library ASAP."***

He then puts his phone in his pocket, and quickly heads up the stairs to the school library.

$$\diamond \, \diamond \, \blacklozenge \, \blacklozenge \, \blacklozenge \, \diamond \, \diamond$$

Fifteen minutes went by as Terry sat in the school library, waiting patiently for Casey and Allison to meet him. He checked his e-mail every few minutes for the pictures from A.J., but he hadn't received them yet. Another twenty minutes passed, but Terry managed to pass the time by reading a book on George Washington. Somehow reading up on history seemed to relax him a little, and by the time he was nearing the end of the book, Casey and Allison arrived with confused looks on their faces. He waves them over to the computer he was using, and they are even more perplexed as to why he wasn't in class.

"Okay, Terry, what's going on?" Casey asked quietly. "And where's Billy? Is he hiding somewhere in here?"

Terry shakes his head. "Billy's not here. He's probably on his way to Mr. Elliot's classroom by now."

"And you're not going with him?" asked Allison.

"Something more urgent has come up." He checks his e-mail and sees a message from A.J. "Finally!" he exclaims. He opens the message and clicks on the pictures attached to it. He looks at the girls and says "Look at these and tell me what you see."

They examine the pictures, very closely, and have the same reaction Terry did when he saw them. They feel their legs getting weak, and Allison tries her best to fight back the tears in her eyes. "This is a joke, right?" Casey asks, but Terry shakes his head.

"I wish it were, Case," Terry said. "But it's the truth. Madame Granger was the last person to see Trent alive the day he disappeared."

"That makes no sense. Trent didn't take her class. What could she have possibly talked about?"

"I have no idea. But look at this picture." Terry brings up the photo of Madame Granger at the lake. "A.J. followed Granger to the lake. He thinks it was after Trent vanished, but I highly doubt that."

"Why is that, Terry?" Allison asked. Terry points to a section of the photo and replies "Look at the angle of the sunlight. Judging by that, I'd say it was sometime in the afternoon. A little after school, but not too much. It takes at least twenty minutes to get to the lake from here. Granger must have left school early and waited for Trent to arrive."

"But there's no way Granger could have killed Trent! She doesn't possess the ability to drain the youth out of people!" Casey exclaimed, causing the librarian to shush her.

"Maybe she's not doing it willingly. Maybe the Lady put her under some kind of hypnotic spell to make her do her bidding. It's the only explanation."

"Or maybe she is working for the Lady on her own accord. As we said, we don't know that much about her. Think about it. She shows up sometime after Dr. Kaminko's house gets destroyed, and Doyle just hires her on the spot? Doesn't make sense to me."

"That's a good point, Casey. Perhaps there's a way to find out." Terry takes out his phone, the card with Brenna's number on it, and begins dialing. He waits a few seconds, then hears "Hello? This is Brenna."

"Brenna, this is Terry Welling. We may have a lead on the Lady for you."

"Really? Lay it on me, Terry."

"It's a bit of a stretch, but is there a chance you might have a contact in the superintendent's office? We need some information on a teacher. Abigail Granger."

"How is that a lead on the Lady, exactly?"

"Just trust me on this. We think she might be working for the Lady, either willingly or unwillingly. We just need some more info on her."

"Well, luckily I know a few people who work for the school district. Give me a little time, and I'll call back with any information I can get."

"Thanks, Brenna. Bye." Terry hangs up and looks back at the girls. "All we can do now is wait and hope Brenna comes through for us."

"I still don't trust her." Casey tells him.

"We don't have much choice. We have no way of getting the information on Granger by ourselves. We can't just sneak into the office and peek at her records."

"So, what now? Do we just wait here and twiddle our thumbs until Brenna calls back?"

Terry reluctantly nods. "I'm afraid so. It's important we stick together right now. If Granger is working for the Lady, we can't risk getting separated and forced into a trap."

An hour passes, and the trio try to keep themselves busy; Allison and Casey look over their assignments for the day, while Terry stares out a window. He occasionally checks his watch, knowing he is missing Mr. Elliot's class, but decides it's for the best when the town might be in serious trouble.

They finally decide to go downstairs to the cafeteria and get some lunch; upon arriving at the door, they notice Billy is nowhere in the room, not even in line, which was bizarre. Normally he would be looking for something edible or at least complain about, like a burger the size of a hockey puck and tasted like rubber. Terry quickly becomes concerned, and he's not the only one.

"Where is Billy?" Casey asked. "This isn't like him at all. He should be here. Something's not right."

"I hope he's okay," Allison added. "I'm getting a weird feeling in the pit of my stomach."

"I know what you mean, Alli," Terry remarked. "Billy's been acting really strange since this morning, and he won't even talk to me about it. He says he's fine, but I don't buy it for a second. We have got to get to the bottom of this."

Then, like clockwork, Billy appears behind them and says "Get to the bottom of what?", scaring them.

Terry turns around and replies "Oh, hey, Billy. We were just discussing, uh, Mr. Vaughn's latest assignment. From what the girls told me, it's very difficult, so we were just trying to decide where we should meet up and work on it together." The girls nod in quick agreement, knowing very well Terry was trying his best not to anger Billy regarding Madame Granger's possible involvement with the Lady.

"Oh. That sounds interesting." Billy said. "But you have detention after school, remember? I'm afraid your little study group will have to do the assignment without you."

Terry then takes a look in Billy's eyes. They seem to be dark, as if he's in a trance; his pupils were essentially missing. All Terry could see was dark blue irises, and it raised his concerns by a large margin.

Before he could say anything, Madame Granger walks in and stands next to Billy, as if she was trying to protect him from his own friends.

"What do you think you're doing, Mr. Welling?" she asked angrily. "Haven't you gotten yourself into enough trouble today?"

"What time is it?" Terry replied with a hint of sarcasm in his voice, while the girls stare at Granger with suspicion and anger in their eyes.

"Terry, there is no need for hostility," Billy chimed in. "You don't want to get any more detention from Madame Granger, do you?"

Terry shakes his head. "I did nothing wrong, Billy. Madame Granger is just being completely unfair because she obviously holds a grudge against students who think her assignments are unjustly difficult."

"That's enough, Mr. Welling," Madame Granger snapped. "Stop acting like an entitled brat and grow up, for goodness sakes. Not everything is about you." She then looks at Billy and calmly says "Oh, Mr. Martin, there is something I need to discuss with you later. Please come by the classroom when you get some free time."

"Of course, Madame Granger." Billy replied. "Anything you want." Madame Granger smiles and turns to walk back to her room, ignoring Terry and the girls as if they were invisible.

Billy watches as Granger heads up the hallway to return to the classroom, then he looks back at the others and remarks "I'm feeling a little hungry. I should get some lunch and prepare my brain for the rest of the day. Excuse me." He walks past them and gets in line, giving Terry an angry look as he does.

As Billy steps in the lunch line, Allison whispers "Did anyone else get the chills, or is it just me?" She lets out a slight shiver, clearly creeped out at she and the others just witnessed. "I think whatever's wrong with Billy is getting worse. We have to figure out what is going on and fast, for Billy's sake."

"I agree. We must find a way to help him and hopefully snap him out of his little trance or whatever it is that's making him act like that."

At that moment, as if it were some sort of divine intervention, Terry's phone starts ringing. He checks the caller ID, sees that it's Brenna, motions for the girls to follow him, then they go into the hall. He answers the call and puts Brenna on speaker so the girls can hear her.

"We're here, Brenna," he says. "What do you have for us?"

"Well," Brenna began, "I asked my contact to give me all they had on Granger. They were reluctant at first, but they eventually agreed and begun digging up anything they had."

"And?" Casey asked. "What did they find?"

"That's the thing. There was no record on her."

"Wait. What?" Allison exclaimed. "What are you talking about?"

"They don't have a record of an Abigail Granger ever working in the district. So, I did a little digging of my own, hoping to find something about her."

"Did you find anything?" Terry asked, sharing the same feeling of confusion as the girls. "Anything that might help us?"

"Unfortunately, no. I couldn't find a single thing about her. No school history, no form of education, no hometown, nothing. Not even a driver's license or birth certificate."

Terry shakes his head and says "Are you sure, Brenna?"

"I'm sure." Brenna replies.

"But that doesn't make any sense!" Casey screamed. "There has to be something on her! People don't just appear out of thin air! Are you sure you didn't dig deep enough?"

"I dug as deep as I could, Casey, but I'm telling there is nothing about her. The simple truth is, your Abigail Granger doesn't exist. I'm sorry."

"Don't be sorry, Brenna," Terry says sadly. "You did the best you could. We appreciate the help. Thanks." He ends the call and just stands there in complete silence along with the girls. If Madame Granger doesn't exist, who has been teaching French for the past couple of months? Furthermore, how could she have possibly gotten the job if she didn't have any experience or even a teacher's license? It just didn't add up at all.

Feeling defeated, they decide to just grab some lunch and call it a day. They walk back into the cafeteria and notice Billy has already left, but before they can look for him to tell him about Granger, Mr. Elliot appears next to them.

"Mr. Welling. Ms. Martin. Ms. Libby," he says, a little out of breath. "I'm glad I found you three." He looks around for a second then asks "Where's Mr. Martin? Normally he'd be eating or complaining about what he's eating."

"He's a little indisposed right now, Mr. Elliot." Terry tells him. "What do you need?"

Mr. Elliot smiles and says "I found what you've been looking for. I found the story of the Lady in the Lake." Terry's eyes widen at the news, and the girls let out a collective gasp. "Are you serious, Mr. Elliot?" Terry exclaimed.

"I am very serious, Terry. It took me all night, but I finally discovered the true story behind the legend of the Lady. I was going to tell you after class, but you never came and I assumed something was wrong."

"Sorry about that. It's been a weird day. I just needed some time to myself. So, what do you have on the Lady?"

"I printed everything you need and left it in the classroom. Let's go there immediately." He turns and begins walking back to his room, with Terry and the girls not far behind.

The four of them reach the door to the classroom, and Mr. Elliot proceeds to unlock it. He walks inside and heads over to his desk while the others follow him in. He opens a drawer and takes out a small pile of papers stapled together. "I haven't had a chance to read it all, but this is the story of the Lady in the Lake." He hands the papers to Terry, who quickly begins reading them.

After reading a paragraph or two, Terry says "According to the legend, the Lady's real name was Genevieve Dubois. She and her sister Jacquelyn immigrated from France to Littleroot in 1921. Supposedly they were healers, using nature and special herbs to treat the sick when traditional medicine didn't work. They would treat the townspeople near the lake as they believed it had magical healing properties."

"So, they were witches?" Casey asked.

"Not exactly," Mr. Elliot interrupted. "They were most likely Wiccans."

"What's a Wiccan?" Allison asked.

Terry replied "A Wiccan, I believe, is a person who is tune with the forces of nature, using them for healing purposes. They believe in using herbs and other natural elements to draw on the power of the earth to heal the sick."

"That is correct, Mr. Welling," Mr. Elliot said. "And because of their non-traditional approaches and eccentric ways, they were often accused of practicing witchcraft. In fact, the word 'witch' comes from 'Wicca'.

"So they were burned at the stake like in Salem, Massachusetts?" asked Allison.

"No. The Salem Witch Trials ended in 1693, 228 years before the Dubois sisters moved to Littleroot. The town didn't do anything of the sort. At least, not until 1926."

"What happened in 1926?"

Terry keeps reading. "For the next four years, the town welcomed the Dubois sisters' gift of healing. They set up a small area at the lake where people could see them for any type of ailment. Headaches, fever, nothing was off-limits. Then, in 1926, Alden Littleroot, founder of the town, became gravely ill. Hoping to find a cure, he went to the doctor first, but when they couldn't help, he went to Genevieve."

"What happened next?" Casey inquired.

"The normal treatments weren't working, so Genevieve begun to try using black magic, practicing various spells in hopes of saving Alden's life. Jacquelyn became concerned, begging her to stop before she got them in trouble. Unfortunately, Genevieve became obsessed with saving Alden, and ignored her sister's warnings. She focused her time and energy practicing her spells, before becoming consumed by them. Unfortunately, someone witnessed her practicing, and immediately went to the sheriff to tell him."

"That doesn't sound good." Allison muttered.

"The sheriff didn't believe them, but shortly after, the entire town learned that Alden passed away in his sleep. The witness told everyone they saw Genevieve practicing witchcraft, which prompted the entire town to come to the conclusion that she must have killed Alden, so they immediately demanded she and her sister be arrested and tried for practicing witchcraft and the murder of the man who founded their town."

"Oh my..." Casey said in a low voice.

"There's more." Mr. Elliot tells them.

Terry clears his throat. "The townspeople went to the lake and surrounded Genevieve, but Jacquelyn was nowhere to be found. The trial started the next morning, where Genevieve was charged with murder. They brought her to the lake, and tied her up, with the intent to burn her at the stake. Despite her greatest efforts, her desperate pleas fell on deaf ears, and she was quickly sentenced to death. The sheriff took a torch and set the stake on fire. With her last words, Genevieve cast one last spell and vowed to one day return to get revenge on the town that betrayed her."

"So, she was accused of murdering a man she was only trying to help," Casey remarked. "That's just horrible. No wonder she hates the town so much. She feels she was dealt a terrible injustice for trying to do the right thing."

"But I don't get something," Allison chimed in. "If she wanted to get revenge on the entire town, why did she wait nine decades to do it? And whatever happened to her sister Jacquelyn? Did they ever find her?"

Terry scans another couple of pages, then shakes his head. "There's no other mention of Jacquelyn Dubois in these pages, except she was never seen or heard from again after Genevieve's death. As for why Genevieve waited so long, I don't know. But I might know why she chooses to kill her victims at the lake."

"And what would that reason be, Mr. Welling?" Mr. Elliot asked him.

"Well, since the sisters believed the lake possessed mystical properties, perhaps it's the only place she can really use her dark magic. Plus, her spirit is tied to the lake, so maybe that's the best place to do it."

"But why is she stealing the youth of her victims? What purpose could that possibly serve?" Allison asked.

Mr. Elliot chimes in. "Well, the logical reasoning behind it could be is her advanced age. She needs to stay young to be at full power, otherwise she would most likely wither away and turn to dust if she can't steal any youth."

"Well, we know the story of the Lady," Terry remarked. "But we don't know how to track her down. If only we had a picture to go by, then she would be easy to spot."

Mr. Elliot grabs another piece of paper and hands it to Terry. "This is a picture of a painting of the Dubois sisters an artist did as a thank you gift for saving his daughter's life," he said. "Perhaps that might help."

Terry looks over the picture. He doesn't see anything out of the ordinary at first, but then he takes a closer look at one of the sisters, and he is immediately overcome with a feeling of dread. "Oh, no…" is all can say, until a few moments later when he screams "No, no, no, no, NO!!!"

"Terry, what's wrong?" Casey asked him, but he doesn't respond. He feels his legs become weak, and quickly drops to his knees, still holding the picture in his hand until the girls grab him and hold him up.

"What's the matter, Terry?" Allison asks.

"Terry? What is it? Are you okay?" Mr. Elliot asked.

"It…it all makes sense now…" Terry replied weakly.

"What does?" asked Casey. "What are you talking about?"

"The absences, the murders, the strange behavior, the grey hairs, the discolored hand, Billy acting like he was under a spell…" Quickly regaining his composure, Terry immediately runs out of the room and down the hall, hoping to find Billy still in the cafeteria. The girls and Mr. Elliot follow behind him, confused about what was happening.

Terry runs as fast as he can, but when he gets to the cafeteria, he finds Billy has already left. "Damn it!" he shouts. "Where the hell is he?!" The girls, along with Mr. Elliot, finally catch up to see Terry frantically scanning the cafeteria.

"Mr. Welling, what are you doing?" Mr. Elliot inquired. "What's the emergency?"

"We have to find Billy right now! He could be in serious trouble!"

"Billy? Are you sure?" asked Allison as she adjusted her glasses.

"Yes!" Terry quickly turns back and starts running back up the hall, with the girls and Mr. Elliot right behind him, becoming concerned for Billy's safety and well-being while also worried about Terry. What had come over him?

*"Come on, Billy, where are you?"* Terry thinks as he continues running through the hall. *"You have got to be around here somewhere!"* He keeps running until he reaches the main lobby of the school, stopping to catch his breath as sweat drips down his face. He scans the faces of every other student in the lobby as they walk to their classes, but doesn't see Billy anywhere.

The others stop and do the same thing, trying to find Billy in the small puddle of Littleroot High students, but they don't see him. Casey hands Terry a handkerchief to wipe the sweat off his forehead. He takes it and dries his face, getting increasingly worried about his best friend. "Where is he?" he asked between breaths, feeling his eyes begin to fill with tears. Casey notices and puts her arms around him, doing her best to fight back tears of her own, prompting Allison to do the same.

Then, Terry asks a passing student "Hey, have you seen Billy Martin around here anywhere?"

"Yeah," the student replied. "I saw him at lunch, and then I saw him talking to Madame Granger afterward. Something about the lake, I think."

Suddenly, Casey grabbed the picture from Terry's hand and showed it to Allison. They look at it, and added the clues together. It all made sense now; Terry figured it out. The truth of the Lady was right under their noses the whole entire time. And now Billy could be in serious danger.

"The lake? Are you absolutely sure?" Casey asked the student.

"I'm sure. I heard her mention the lake, loud and clear. No doubt about it."

At that moment, Terry immediately headed towards the main doors, with the girls right behind him, and Mr. Elliot shouts "Where are you three going?"

"No time to explain, Mr. Elliot!" Terry exclaimed. "We have to get to the lake immediately, before it's too late!" And with those words, the three friends run outside and head in the direction of Littleroot Lake.

# CHAPTER EIGHTEEN

Littleroot Lake, such a calm and tranquil place, where the citizens of the town can go to relax and unwind after a long hard day at work or school. The kind of place where you can have a nice picnic or read a book by the water. At least, it used to be that kind of place.

Ever since the deaths that had been occurring and the bodies of the victims kept appearing at the lake, as well as it being closed off by the police, nobody dares to even go near it, believing it to be cursed; as if something dark and sinister was brewing beneath the normally calm waters, which could very well be something only seen in the latest horror movie or television show. For Billy Martin, however, none of that mattered to him in the slightest.

He stood at the edge of the lake area, staring at his reflection in the water. Normally he wouldn't be caught dead wandering any place rumored to be haunted or cursed, but because of the way he's been acting he doesn't seem to care about any of that stuff. He just stares at his reflection, waiting for something. Or rather, someone.

He hears a noise coming from behind, turns around and sees movement in some bushes. A wild animal, perhaps? Or maybe even someone foolish to come to the lake despite the fact it's a crime scene? He focused his gaze on the bushes, prepared for whatever comes out.

Madame Granger steps out of the bushes, and he quickly drops his guard. "I'm sorry for being late, William." Granger says in a soothing, yet creepy, voice. "I had to make sure we weren't being followed."

Billy smiles. "It's okay, Madame," he said. "All that matters is you're here now. I am pretty sure nobody will be bothering us. I have been waiting with much excitement, m'lady."

"I am glad to hear you say that, William. I am also looking forward to this moment, but I had to wait until we could finally be alone. We could both be in a lot of trouble if we were to be caught by your father or your friends."

"We will deal with them if necessary. I'm not worried about it right now. All I can think about is this moment."

Madame Granger starts walking closer to Billy, albeit slower. "You know, William, I've had my eye on you for quite some time. Ever since we first met after I became the new French teacher. I pretended to ignore your attempts to impress me, but I thought they were very sweet. It's been a long time since I've been impressed by a gentleman trying to court me."

"Anything for you, Madame Granger. You are an amazing woman, and you deserve to be treated with the utmost respect and admiration."

Madame Granger keeps walking closer, biting her bottom lip as she does. Soon she is mere inches away from Billy, who can feel his heart beating faster than normal. This woman in front of him, whose affection he tried so hard to win, was actually right in front of him with nobody else around to witness what could be the greatest moment of his young life, and that was just the way they both wanted it.

"Madame," he began, "I have a small question I must ask you."

"Of course, William," Granger said. "What would you like to know?"

"I'm just curious. Why did you choose to meet at the lake after everything that's been happening?"

Granger softly places both hands on Billy's face, and he feels a wave of anticipation come over him. She then whispers, "This is where my magic is at its most powerful." But Billy doesn't hear her; all he can feel is being pulled in closer towards her, his lips mere inches away from touching hers…

Just then, a voice from out of nowhere screams "BILLY, DON'T!" And it causes Billy to look away from Madame Granger and investigate where the voice came from. He sees Terry, Casey, and Allison come out of some bushes on the left edge of the lake with worried looks on their faces. "What do you guys want?" is all Billy can ask.

"Billy", Terry pleaded, "listen to me. Granger is not who she claims to be. She's dangerous! You have to get away from her before she kills you!" But Billy rolls his eyes and scoffs.

"That's a good one, Terry," he says, "but it's not going to work. When are you going to drop this nonsense and leave us alone? Can't you see we're busy?"

"That's it!" Casey shouts. She runs as fast as she can, approaches Billy and Granger, grabs Billy by the arm, raises a hand, and smacks him across the face as hard as she can. The slap is so loud Terry and Allison can hear it from their side of the lake. Billy places his hand on his cheek, blinks a few times, then Terry and Allison join up with Casey.

"Billy?" Terry said. "Are you okay?" Then he notices something in Billy's eyes. The dullness in his irises begins to vanish, and his pupils slowly but surely return. He blinks a few more times, then shouts "Ow! What the hell, Casey?! Why did you slap me so hard? What did I do to deserve such hostility?!"

"Billy, you're back to normal!" Terry exclaims. "Thank goodness!"

"Well, about as normal as Billy can be," Casey said with a chuckle. Billy stares at them, confused, takes a look around, and notices something different. "Uh, what are we doing at the lake?" he asked. "Weren't we at school a few minutes ago?"

"It's a long story, Billy," Allison chimed in, "but we need to get away from Madame Granger as fast as we can."

"Wait, she's here too?" Billy sees Granger standing behind the others, letting out a low growl. "What's wrong with her?"

"She just tried to kill you." Terry told him. "She's not who she says she is." He then turns his attention to Granger, who is getting angrier by the second. "It's over!" Terry exclaims. "We know everything! We know who you are! You aren't killing any more people, Genevieve!"

"Her name is Abigail!" Billy shouted, but Terry shakes his head.

"Her real name is Genevieve Dubois, but she's better known as the Lady in the Lake!"

Billy could not believe what he was hearing. How could Madame Granger be the ghost of an ancient witch? It didn't make sense to him at all.

"But," he struggled to say, "if she's the Lady, then that means she…"

Terry sadly nods. "Yes, Billy. She's the one who killed Trent and the others. We discovered the truth a little while ago. That's why we came here. You were going to be her next victim."

"She was going to kill me?"

"I'm afraid so. She doesn't love you. She doesn't even like you. She was just using you. She put you under a spell and made you come here so she could steal your youth." Before Terry could say anything else, Billy looked back at Granger, clenching his fists so hard they begin to tremble, and screams "How could you?! You lied to me! You used me as a mind puppet! You killed Trent, and Jeremy, and the others! Are you crazy?! Do you know what you are? You're an *ananas!* Yeah, that's right! You're nothing but a heartless *ananas!*"

Terry rolls his eyes. "Billy!" he said.

"What?" asked Billy.

"You just called her a pineapple!"

"I did? Well, then, what's the word for…"

"SILENCE!" Granger screamed. "I've heard enough of your incessant babbling!"

"She obviously doesn't know Billy well enough." Casey muttered, causing Allison to let out a small chuckle, which in turn caused Granger to glare at them.

"Well, it's true." Casey tells her. "Billy never shuts up."

"Yeah, that's right!" Billy exclaimed, only to think about what Casey said for a minute and say "Wait, what?", which caused Terry to roll his eyes and smack his forehead.

Then, Granger began to undergo a strange transformation. Her eyes began to glow yellow, her brown hair started changing color, a mysterious purple aura surrounded her entire body, and the sky turned pitch black, is if it were a sign something dark and ominous was about to begin.

Terry and the others could only watch as their teacher began to change right in front of their eyes; her clear complexion turned into pale and disturbing features. Her cheeks sunk in, so her face almost resembled a skull. Her brown hair turned to white. Her hands now looked skeletal, her teeth grew longer and sharper, and her clothes shredded away to nothing, only to be replaced with a long, white torn up dress. She quickly let out a loud scream that caused the group to cover their ears as it echoed throughout the entire town.

Granger soon turns her attention back to the group and says in a chilling voice "You have witnessed my true form once before, you little maggots, but you will not survive the experience again!"

Terry looks at the others and screams "Everybody RUN!" Without questioning it, the group immediately runs into the woods, with the Lady letting out another loud scream and pursuing after them. She forms a magical ball of purple energy in her hand and immediately throws it, missing Allison's head by mere inches and destroying a tree branch along the way.

Terry struggles to find the way out of the woods; the combination of trees, bushes and the dark sky made it very difficult to see where he was going. As he continued to fumble his way through the woods, the others are having the same amount of luck as he is. He hears the faint sound of another energy ball coming towards them. He looks back at the others and shouts "Guys, get down!"

At his word, they immediately slide down to the ground covering their faces and don't even watch as the fireball zooms by above their heads, destroying everything in its path. Terry looks up for a second and sees they're almost out of the woods; a few more steps and they'll be back in town. But he knows that would be the worst thing to do right now.

"Look! We're almost back in town!" Billy exclaims as he looks up. "Let's hurry up and get out of here!" But Terry shakes his head.

"We can't do that, Billy," he says as he and the others stand back up. "If we lead the Lady into town, then she'll only make things worse. She could find some random person on the street and kill them. We have to keep her by the lake."

"How can we do that if she's chasing all of us at the same time?" Allison asked.

"Exactly. She can't chase us all at the same time if we split up. We just have to keep her busy until the right time comes along."

"Are you nuts, Terry?!" Billy screamed. "She's right behind us and we'll be her next victims if we stay here! We have to leave right now!"

"Trust me, Billy, I don't like it any more than you do. But it's the only way we can stop her and save the town." He looks at Allison and says "Alli, come with me. We'll go to the north side of the lake while Billy and Casey go to the south side."

Just then, the Lady appears, ready to attack again. She prepares yet another fireball, prompting Terry to scream "Now! Split up!" The Lady watches as Terry and Allison run in one direction while Billy and Casey run in another. "You think this little plan is going to stop me?!" she screams. "It matters not. One way or another, I will find and kill every single one of you interlopers!"

"You'll have to catch us first, you crazy old bat!" Casey remarks as she and Billy vanish from the Lady's line of sight. She throws her fireball in their direction, but misses them completely. Casey and Billy keep running, with Billy feeling like he could pass out at any moment. Casey points to some big trees they could hide behind and catch their breath for a minute. They get to the other side of the trees and Billy peeks around it to make sure the Lady didn't see them hide.

"How can someone who's so hot also be a murderous witch?" he said between breaths, which earns him a nasty look from Casey.

"You still have the hots for that woman?" she snapped.

"A little bit, yeah." Billy replied sheepishly.

"You do know she's over a hundred years old, right?"

"So she's a cougar? Cool."

"She's a sabretooth tiger, you moron!"

Just then, they hear a strange noise that sounded like whispering. A chill fills the air, causing Billy and Casey to begin shivering. "What's going on?" Casey asked through chattering teeth. "Why is it so cold all of a sudden?"

"Maybe the Lady forgot to pay her heating bill?" Billy joked. Before Casey could respond, she felt something grab her. She looked down and noticed the tree limbs were wrapping themselves around her waist, slowly crawling up her torso, getting a little tighter.

"Casey!" Billy exclaimed, but before he could try to help his cousin, the same thing began happening to him. He struggles to escape the tree's hold on him, but the limbs are too strong to break free. "I've heard of wanting to branch out," he shouted, "but this is just ridiculous!"

The Lady then appeared in front of them, her eyes glowing brighter than before, making it obvious she was using her magic to control the trees. "You can't hide from me," she told them. "I know these woods inside and out. I am familiar with every tree and bush around here. Did you really think you could escape from my power?"

"Well, we did," Billy told her, "but then we decided to go out on a limb." Casey rolls her eyes at both Billy's joke and their possible demise. "We are so screwed," she said. The Lady moves toward Billy, placing her hand on his chin, prompting Casey to scream, "Get away from my cousin, you witch!"

"You are in no positions to make threats, you stuck up little girl," the Lady sneered. "I have all the power, and there isn't a thing you can do to stop me."

"You're crazy! You won't get away with this!"

The Lady begins to press her lips against Billy's, when a sudden blast of bright light came from out of nowhere and sent the Lady deeper into the woods. The limbs then returned to normal, allowing Casey and Billy to escape. Casey runs over to Billy and asks "Are you okay, you bonehead?"

"Yeah, I'll be okay." Billy replied. "What was that?"

"I have no idea. Now let's get out of here before Genevieve decides to trap us again." And with that, the two cousins change directions and decide to head back to the lake, hoping Terry and Allison are okay.

Meanwhile, at the other end of the woods, Terry and Allison stop to catch their breath. They find a decent sized bush and decide to hide behind it. Allison drops to her knees, saying "I don't think I can take another step. Can we stop here, Terry?"

"Good idea," Terry said. "These woods are pretty big. The Lady won't be able to find us. At least for now." Terry sits down and looks up at the blackened sky and notices the sun is nowhere to be seen. He wipes a few beads of sweat off his forehead, and says "I hope Billy and Casey are okay."

"I'm sure they are," Allison said. "Casey will keep Billy safe from harm. She might find him to be a little immature and annoying, but she won't let anyone hurt him."

"Yeah. That's one of her best qualities."

"What is?"

"How much she cares for people, even if she doesn't show it, especially to Billy."

Then, they notice a bright light. Allison says "Did the sky clear up already?" Terry shakes his head and points up toward the sky, which was clearly still dark. "No. The sun is still covered by darkness."

"Then where did that light come from?"

"I have no idea." He thinks for a moment, then says "Isn't that where Billy and Casey were running to?" Allison feels her heart drop, then replies "It is! They could be in serious trouble!" She stands back up, as does Terry, and they head in the direction of the light, worried for the safety of their friends.

They run as fast as they can, hoping nothing has happened to Billy and Casey. Allison struggles to keep her glasses on with each sprint, while Terry tries to keep himself from tripping over his own two feet. Then, they hear a voice from behind scream "You will not escape my wrath!" They stop and turn to see the Lady, hovering in the air and glowing a deep, intense purple color. Terry motions Allison to get behind him, and she obliges. Terry stares at the Lady with a steely-eyed expression, refusing to back down.

"What do you think you're trying to do, Welling?" the Lady asked him with a chuckle. "Do you think you can stop me? You're nothing but a child! A weak-willed one, at that!"

"We know the truth, Genevieve. We know you were only trying to help Alden Littleroot find a cure for his ailment."

"That may be true, but it matters not."

"What are you talking about? Of course, it matters! A great injustice was done to you! What happened shouldn't have!"

"But it did! All I wanted was to save Alden's life! None of the normal treatments worked, and I was desperate to save him! I loved him!"

"Wait, what? What do you mean?"

"Alden and I were in love, destined to be together. I would have done anything for him, so when he told me he was dying, I was determined to save him so we could finally begin a life together. But when none of the normal treatments failed, I decided to go even further."

"By using black magic?" Allison asked, still hiding behind Terry.

"I had no other option. My sister tried to dissuade me from using such powerful magic, but I didn't listen. Nothing was going to stop me from saving the life of the man I loved!"

"Until someone saw you using black magic." Terry said sadly.

"That fool believed I was the one who killed Alden! The entire town believed his lies! They persecuted me, completely convinced I was responsible for Alden's death and put me on trial for witchcraft and murder! They felt the lake was a proper setting for my death sentence! They refused to listen to my side, and my sister was nowhere to be found to defend me! She ran away and hid like a coward! Our lives were taken without probable cause!"

Just then, Terry became confused, as did Allison. "Did she say 'our lives'?" she asked him. Terry nodded, then he asked "What do you mean? I thought you said your sister wasn't there."

"Not my sister," the Lady said, then tears started to fill her eyes. As the tears ran down her face, she screamed "MY BABY! THEY KILLED MY BABY!" Terry and Allison gasped at the sudden revelation. "Baby?" Allison asked. "That wasn't mentioned in the story."

"The townspeople obviously didn't know anything about it." They watch as the Lady continued sobbing, obvious the pain she felt was more than sentenced for a crime she didn't commit. He had a feeling the tears in her eyes were very much real. They weren't for Alden's death or even for the crime she was unfairly accused of; they were for something far more painful, the kind of pain that never leaves you.

Before Terry and Allison could say anything, the Lady quickly made a waving motion with her right hand, letting out a gust of wind that caused Terry and Allison to be blown away, quite literally, and through the woods, feeling themselves scraping against the trees and bushes, their clothes getting slightly torn along the way.

They soon hit the ground and slide a little bit, kicking up dirt, tumbling and rolling, until they finally stop. Terry lets out a scream of pain as he lands on his arm. *"I don't need this right now,"* he thinks as he struggles to stand up. He looks around and notices the lake off in the distance, then realizes something isn't right. "Allison?" he says, looking for her. "Allison?!" He begins to panic, frantically looking around for her.

He hears a faint sound in the distance, like someone groaning. He gets to his feet, but quickly falls to his knee. He has trouble standing up, and realizes he must have twisted his ankle during his little flight through the woods. He clenches his teeth, and slowly stands up, trying his best to ignore the pain, and begins limping toward the sound. *"Allison must have been somehow blown towards the north side of the lake. She could be in trouble. I've got to get to her as fast as I can."*

He continues limping through the dark woods, being careful not to make any noise to attract any attention that could potentially help the Lady find him. The pain in his arm and ankle are almost unbearable, but he doesn't let it stop him. He knows he must keep going, for the sake of his friends; if he can talk some sense into Genevieve, maybe he can convince her to let go of her pain and leave the town alone. It's a long shot, but it's a risk he has to take. If it doesn't work, then maybe his backup plan will.

He makes it out of the woods, and reaches his destination, the north side of the lake. He sees Allison near the edge of the water, not moving a muscle. He limps over to her as fast as he can, fearing the worst. He manages to reach her before the pain in his ankle is too much for to bear any longer. He places his left index and middle fingers against her neck, and finds a pulse. Just then, he hears Billy's voice say "Terry!"

He sees Billy and Casey approaching him from the woods. The run over and sees he's been injured. "Terry, what happened?" Casey asked him. "Are you guys alright?"

"We're fine." Terry replied.

"What happened to Allison?"

"She's okay, she's just unconscious. What about you guys? I thought you were going to the south end of the lake like we planned."

"We were, but the Lady stopped us from doing that. Guess splitting up isn't going to work."

"Then let's get out of here!" Billy screamed. "Look what she's already done to you and Allison! She's going to do much worse if we don't leave!"

Terry shakes his head. "I can't. I don't have the strength to walk out of here. I twisted my ankle and we need to protect Allison the best we can."

"How?"

"I don't know. But we have to try."

The Lady soon appears in front of them, as if out of thin air. She holds two fireballs in her hands, intent on using them with every fiber of her being.

"Genevieve," Terry pleaded, "please don't do this. I'm sorry for what the town did to you. You didn't deserve to be punished for something you didn't do, and neither did your baby. If there were a way to undo what happened all those years ago, we would do it. But you can't take your pain and anger out on the entire town." Casey and Billy listen, confused by the mention of the baby.

But the Lady is unmoved by Terry's words. "This town took everything from me. My love, my life, the life of my baby. It doesn't matter when it happened, it still happened!"

"But wait a second!" Casey exclaimed. "Something doesn't make sense."

"What's that?" Billy asked.

"If she wanted to get revenge for what the town did to her, why did she wait ninety years to do it?"

"I would have done it a lot sooner," the Lady explained, but there was something keeping me from leaving the lake and using my power. Then, a few months ago, I was finally freed from whatever shackles held me back, and I began my plan immediately."

"So, you put Doyle under a spell so you could get a job at the school and plot your revenge?" Terry asked her.

"It was working out so brilliantly, until you four decided to stick your noses in my business." Allison wakes up, dazed, and says "What's going on?" She starts fumbling around, looking for something. "I can't find my glasses. Where are they?"

"I-I think we have other things to worry about right now, Alli." Billy tells her, clearly terrified.

The Lady lets out a laugh. "Just look at the four of you!" she said. "You clearly can't comprehend the magnitude of the situation, and two of you are in no condition to try to escape me! You thought you could save this pathetic little town, but you can't even save yourselves!"

Then, Billy places a hand in the lake, then flings a few drops of water at the Lady's face, and she is very clearly not amused in the slightest.

"What...was that?" she asked as the water dripped down her face.

"Wait, you're not melting?" Billy asked. "It worked in *The Wizard of Oz!*"

"That was your plan??" Casey snapped at him. "Can't you be stupid somewhere else?"

"Not until four."

Allison keeps fumbling around, until she finally finds her glasses and puts them on. They're a little cracked, making it hard to see, but at least she had a better idea of what was happening. She noticed the Lady holding the fireballs in her hands, preparing to throw them.

"What are we gonna do?" she whispered to Casey.

"I don't know, Alli," Casey replied. "Just stay calm. We'll think of something. I hope."

Terry glares at the Lady, with a look of sympathy and anger. "You know this isn't right, Genevieve," he says. "The town has changed a lot since that day. You have to stop this. You have to let go of your pain and move on."

The Lady screams "I will never forget! This town will pay for what it did, and nobody shall stand in my way any longer!" She throws one of the fireballs, and it hits the ground. The shockwave causes Allison to fall into the water.

"Allison!" Casey cried out. Before she could jump in to help her, however, Billy beats her to it, diving into the water. With every second, the situation grows even more tense, until the two of them emerge to the surface, with Allison's arm wrapped around Billy's neck. He swims to the edge and puts Allison on the shore. But when he looks up, he says "Uh, guys? Something's not right here."

The others look and notice Genevieve has vanished. A sense of dread overcomes them rather quickly, and it becomes very clear that it won't be going away anytime soon. Allison opens her eyes, looks around for a few moments, then notices her arm around Billy's neck. She looks up and stares at him as he tries to keep his composure, not knowing why he looks so worried. She places her other hand on his cheek, to which he takes notice of. He looks down at her, feeling a little relief outweigh the feeling of dread. She gives him a smile, tears running her face, and quietly says "You saved me."

Billy feels his face turn red while Casey and Terry notice the interaction between them, and then he nervously replied "Well, I…I couldn't let anything happen to you, so I just, you know…" Before he could finish his sentence, Allison pressed her lips against his, and for a brief moment time stops; nothing else that was happening mattered to them for those brief but prolonged ten seconds they were caught up in their embrace.

Casey rolls her eyes in disgust, then notices Terry staring at her with a smile across his face, which makes her blush and quickly turn away.

Before Terry could say anything, he felt the ground beneath his feet begin to tremble. The others soon feel it, too, making Billy and Allison snap out of their kiss and back into reality. "Get ready, guys!" Terry shouts. "I think we're going to be getting some company pretty soon!"

And, like clockwork, he was right. Genevieve reappeared in a flash of light, briefly blinding the group. She immediately grabs the dazed Terry by his neck and brings him close to her face, intent on finishing what she started. Billy and the others attempt to help him, but Genevieve merely shrugs them off with a blast of wind, knocking them to their feet. "TERRY!" Casey shouts. "Let him go, you crazy old bat!"

"Oh?" Genevieve replied defiantly. "And what if I refuse to comply with your petty demand, you little jezebel?" She turns her gaze back to Terry, who struggled to break her grip around his neck but was quickly losing strength. He could not get free, and felt the world around him getting dark as he began to lose consciousness. But he then feels himself being released from Genevieve's grasp as he falls to the ground. He lifts his head up off the ground and tries to stand, but is too weak to move. He looks up and sees Billy putting Genevieve in a headlock. She begins to flail around, trying to throw Billy off of her. "Get off me, you annoying little whelp!" she screamed as Billy continued to have a hold of her, desperately trying to hang on.

"Billy, get out of here!" Terry tried to yell, but his voice was too raspy for Billy to hear him thanks to Genevieve's strong grip. Casey runs over to his side, places a hand on his shoulder, and says "Terry, are you okay?" He lets out a few coughs, clears his throat and replied in a hoarse voice "I'll be okay, but Billy needs to let go of Genevieve. She's far too strong for him to handle."

"We need to get you out of here first!" She picks him up with what little strength she had left, wraps his arm around her shoulder, and proceeds to help him walk away from Billy and Genevieve. Terry struggles to keep pace with Casey as his legs feel like they aren't there at all. He looks back and sees Billy finally lose his grip on Genevieve as she manages to force him off with a quick blast of magic. He falls to the ground, but before he can stand up, Genevieve places a hand around his neck and lifts him off the ground. "You can't get away from me!" she screamed.

"Wow," Billy snapped back. "I waited all puberty for a girl to say that to me and now it's a complete bummer." Genevieve spins around and faces the lake with her hand still around Billy's throat. She places her other hand near his torso as it begins to glow. She pulls him in closer and snarls "You die first." She releases a fireball and sends Billy flying straight into the lake as he makes a huge splash upon hitting the water.

"BILLY!" Terry and Casey screamed.

"NO!" Allison shouted. "BILLY!"

The three teens turn their attention back to Genevieve, who returns their gaze with her own. She creates two more fireballs as her eyes begin to glow. She moves slowly toward the group, unable to gather the strength to try and escape. They all close their eyes, prepared to accept their inevitable fate. Genevieve raises one hand and prepares to throw the first fireball.

The teens keep their eyes closed, waiting for Genevieve to finish them off, but nothing happens. Confused, Terry opens his eyes and notices something odd, as do the others. They watch as Genevieve lowers her hands, the fireballs fade away, and her eyes stop glowing. She drops to her knees, but she can't seem to get back up. "What's happening?" she asked weakly, but Terry and the others are just as confused as she is.

She looks at her hand and watches in horror as it starts changing in front of her eyes. It begins to become bonier and more wrinkled as it begins to get covered in liver spots, then she notices the same is happening to her other hand. She crawls over to the edge of the lake and stares at her reflection, realizing what was happening to her.

Her hair begins to become thinner and whiter, then it begins to fall out one strand at a time. Her face begins to change as well; her cheeks sink in, her eye sockets become bigger and her skin begins to change to a ghastly white color. She screams in agony as her body rapidly deteriorated. "Why is this happening?!" she shouted, but before the group can answer, they watch as Genevieve suddenly turns to dust, dress and all. The dark skies over the lake fade away, revealing the bright warm sun, and the wind begins to blow, carrying the remains of the infamous Lady in the Lake away.

Then, a bright light from the center of the lake catches the attention of Terry and the others. They turn around and to their delight, they see Billy being carried out of the water by a mysterious figure. The figure approaches them and places Billy on the ground next to their feet. It then waves its hand over his body, and a few seconds later, he begins to cough up water.

He opens his eyes and sees his friends standing over him, and in typical Billy fashion says "What the hell happened? Please tell me nobody tried to kiss me." Allison kneels down and wraps her arms around his neck, tears streaming down her face.

Terry and Casey follow suit and hug him, glad he's okay. "Billy!" Terry exclaimed. "Thank goodness you're okay!"

"What the hell were you thinking?" Casey asked him sternly. "Are you crazy?"

Before Billy could answer, Terry stared at the mysterious figure, who was just standing there. He says "Thank you for saving our friend, but I have a question. Who are you?" The figure points to the center of the lake, and the group notices the strange sculpture that normally resided there was missing. They look back at the figure, who proceeds to remove its hood, revealing the face of a young woman. She then says "My name is... Jacquelyn Dubois."

Terry and the others stare at her in complete shock at the revelation. They found it hard to believe, at first, except Billy, who had no idea who that was. Terry clears his throat and says "You're Jacquelyn? Genevieve's sister?" Jacquelyn nods solemnly, saddened by the tone in Terry's voice. "Indeed I am. I know you must have a lot of questions."

"I don't." Billy muttered, resulting in Casey smacking him in the arm.

"We sure as hell do!" Casey exclaimed. "Like, how can you be the statue in the middle of the lake? And where were you when your sister was being held on trial and she had no one to defend her?"

"Casey..." Terry started, but Jacquelyn stopped him and raised her hand. "I know how it must sound, but I was there the day my sister was on trial. Fearing they would arrest me as well, I hid from the villagers while they persecuted her for Alden's death. I listened as she vowed to get revenge on the town. I feared she would carry out her scheme, so after the villagers left the lake, I decided to protect the town the best way I knew how."

"And what was that?"

"Using black magic, I converted my body into stone and used my life force as a barrier to keep Genevieve's spirit trapped in the lake. And it was successful, until..."

"Until what?" asked Allison.

"A few months ago, I felt a powerful surge of energy spread throughout the town. As soon as it reached the lake, the barrier weakened, until it eventually shattered. I could no longer keep my sister's spirit contained within the confines of the lake."

Terry becomes puzzled, trying to figure out what could have caused Jacquelyn's spell to be broken. What could have been so powerful it would shatter a magical barrier? He thinks back to the past few months. What happened that destroyed the spell? Then, it hit him. "Dr. Kaminko's house!" he exclaimed. "That's what destroyed the barrier!"

"What are you talking about, Terry?" Billy asked.

"It all makes sense now," Terry elaborated. "We all assumed the house was simply destroyed after Kaminko's portal malfunctioned, but what if the energy that powered the device was spread throughout the town? Who knows what kind of power that thing contained? Brenna was right. The night at Kaminko's house and the deaths at the lake were connected."

"I feel absolutely terrible about this," Jacquelyn said. "If my barrier hadn't been broken, then none of this would have happened."

"No, it's our fault." Terry explained to her. "We were trying to investigate the mayor and find proof of his corruption. Instead, we got in over our heads and unleashed a terrible evil upon our town. So, if anyone is to blame, it's us." The group look at Jacquelyn, who says nothing for a few moments, then she shakes her head and says "You are not to blame, young ones. I knew my spell would one day fail and my sister would have eventually carried out her plan for revenge for the death of her unborn child."

"You knew she was pregnant?" Allison asked her.

Jacquelyn nodded. "Yes. I was the only one she told. I vowed to help her raise the child, but sadly that never happened. I was devastated when they put her on trial for a crime she did not commit. If only I had said something in her defense, then you four would have never been in any danger. But you also put an end to this terrible tale. You have my thanks."

"By the way," Billy asked, "what exactly happened to Genevieve? Why did she turn to dust?"

"She ran out of energy," Terry told him. "She needed to steal youth to stay strong, but I guess the more of her magic she used, the weaker she became, and she wasn't able to steal any of our youth. I had hoped to keep her busy until she became too weak to do anything, but I wasn't expecting her to turn to dust."

"Whatever the case," Jacquelyn chimed in, "the story of the Lady in the Lake is finally over. The town is safe now that my sister can no longer harm any innocent people, which means I can finally rest."

"What do you mean?" Casey asked Jacquelyn.

"I spent nine decades keeping the town from my sister's wrath, and vowed I would not stop until she was no longer a threat. And having spent most of my life force keeping her spirit contained, I am afraid I cannot remain in this world for much longer." And with those words, Jacquelyn's body began to glow. The light enveloped the area, causing the teens to cover their eyes from the intensity. The light spreads to and blankets the town, so much that it attracts the attention of Sheriff Martin and Deputy Judd at the police station.

"What's that light?" Judd asked.

"I don't know, but it's coming from Littleroot Lake." Sheriff Martin replied. "Let's go!" They grab their coats and run out the door as fast they can to the lake.

Back at the lake, the light begins to subside, and the teens faintly hear Jacquelyn say to them, "Thank you, young ones. The town is safe. My sister is gone, I can finally be at peace knowing the town has such brave heroes looking out for it. I shall never forget what you have done today. Farewell." With those final words, Jacquelyn fades away and the light finally disappears. The teens open their eyes and notice Jacquelyn is gone; even the rock formation she appeared from has vanished, as if it was never there to begin with.

The second the light subsided, Sheriff Martin and Deputy Judd arrived in their car. They get out, and Sheriff Martin yells "What the hell is going on here? And what are you kids doing here? This place is a crime scene!"

"It's okay, Dad," Billy tells him. "The Lady is gone. Thank goodness. I don't think I could date an older woman."

"What are you talking about? There is no Lady in the Lake! It's an urban legend! But that's not the point! You four are in huge trouble! Again!"

"Uh, Sheriff?" Deputy Judd said.

"Not now, Judd."

"But, Sheriff! Look!" Judd points to the center of the lake, and Martin notices the strange rock statue was missing. "What the hell happened here?" he asked, glaring back at the teens.

"Trust me, Dad," Billy said sheepishly, "you wouldn't believe me if I told you!"

# CHAPTER NINETEEN

It took a few hours of convincing, but eventually Sheriff Martin decided his son and his friends were telling the truth about the deaths at the lake, and how Brenna Kinsley was right the entire time about how the deaths were connected to Dr. Kaminko's house. But, for official purposes, he decided it was best to leave out the part about a witch trying to kill the townspeople by stealing their youth. He had enough publicity with Dr. Kaminko's house being destroyed; the last thing he needed was another media circus, but he held a press conference a few days later to declare the case officially closed.

"After much investigating," he began, "we have determined the identity of the Lake killer to be Abigail Granger. For reasons still unknown, she lured her victims to the lake and proceeded to kill them using methods still not known. Ms. Granger was a teacher at Littleroot High, which was a clear and obvious cover for her while she committed these heinous murders."

"Sheriff Martin," the newly rehired Brenna Kinsley shouted, "where is Ms. Granger now? Any leads on her whereabouts?"

"We currently have no information as to where Ms. Granger might be," Sheriff Martin replied, playing along with Brenna's questions. "For all we know, she is in the wind. But I can safely assume she will no longer be a threat to the town or anyone else, for that matter. We are declaring this case officially closed."

After the press conference had finished and the press had begun to leave, Brenna approached Sheriff Martin. "That was clever," she told him.

"'In the wind'? That was a good way to put it." Sheriff Martin lets out a chuckle. "I guess my son's habit of telling bad jokes is rubbing off on me. Besides, it's best the people don't know what      really happened at the lake. I don't want my family and their friends to be hounded by the press again. No offense."

"None taken. I learned my lesson. There's a difference between getting the truth and obsessing over it. Thanks for helping me get my job back, by the way."

"No problem. You helped my son and his friends solve the mystery of the lake. It was the least I could do. They wanted to thank you in person, but they had school and I'm sure they've missed enough of it."

"They're great people, solving two of the town's biggest mysteries. Your son could be a great detective one day if he applies himself."

"I know. But after what happened these past few months, I'm sure he wants to be a regular kid again for a little while."

"And that concerns me."

"How so, Ms. Kinsley?"

"What if the first thing he figures out is the truth as to why you left the Bangor police department? How do you think he'll react to the news?"

"What are you talking about?"

"After I was fired, I did some digging into your career. I know why you transferred to Littleroot, and I think it's time you told Billy the truth."

"Why were you looking into my past?"

"I was angry with you. I was trying to find some dirt on you to use as leverage, but I had a change of heart. I couldn't go through with it. I am so sorry, Sheriff." Sheriff Martin groans and places his head in his hand. He looks back at Brenna and says "How much do you know?"

"All of it. You have to tell your son the truth." Sheriff Martin crosses his arms, thinking about what Brenna said, then realizes he can't hide this secret from his son forever. "You're right. I'll tell him." He checks his watch. "But right now, I have somewhere else to be." With that, he walks over to his car, intent on getting to his next destination.

Life seems to slowly return to normal for the students at Littleroot High, except they now know their French teacher was nothing more than a heartless killer who took the lives of so many people, including one of their own. Mrs. Doyle was still dumbfounded as to how Granger convinced her to give her a job without even so much as a resume or reference. As far as everyone was concerned, there was no Lady in the Lake; she was nothing more than an urban legend like Dr. Kaminko, except Dr. Kaminko was a real person as opposed to the spirit of a witch that supposedly haunted a lake. The sheriff convinced the town Granger was the true killer, not some ancient 20th century spirit.

The town had no idea who helped crack the case, and that was just the way Terry and the others liked it. They wanted to stay out of the spotlight, though they were credited as "anonymous sources" by the police. Some of the students believed Terry and the others were the sources, but they couldn't get them to confess they were the ones who solved the case. Terry felt relieved by the anonymity. Now he could go back to work without some reporter looking to make themselves famous with another story on him and his friends.

Billy was still a little sore from being blasted by the Lady, but he decided he should get out of the house and not sit in his room all day. He cleaned up the rest of his room, and his mother returned his collection of Sherlock Holmes books. He started buying things from Games 2 Go in-store again, which made Terry happy; they could chat and goof off when he was on break like they used to, even if his boss was slightly annoyed by it.

Allison was convinced her mother was going to lock her in her room for the rest of her life, but much to her surprise, her mother realized she couldn't keep watching and protecting her forever, so she decided to let up on the reins she had on her daughter. Allison never felt so relaxed since the night at Dr. Kaminko's house. Now she could get back to doing what she loved best; going to the library and volunteering at the animal shelter.

Casey's parents, on the other hand, were not so forgiving. They still blamed Terry for taking her to the lake even though she told them over and over again that it was her idea in the first place. They did, however, agree that perhaps Terry wasn't as bad an influence as they initially thought and allowed Casey to keep hanging out with him. Of course, she planned on doing that, anyway.

The school day finally comes to an end. The bell rings, and the student body rushes out the door like a stampede of wild buffalo. All except four of them. They decide to calmly walk out the door and take the time to relax for a few minutes.

"What a day!" Billy exclaimed. "I can't believe Mr. Elliot wants us to read five chapters on the American Revoltion!"

Terry sighs and says "That's the American Revolution, Billy."

"What's the difference? Didn't they both make people sick and throw up?" Casey shakes her head, knowing that Billy is back to his old annoying self. "No, you dummy," she said. "Do you ever pay attention to anything Mr. Elliot says in class?"

"Not really. As soon as he starts talking history my mind wanders and I fall asleep. That's why I always feel so refreshed after each and every class."

"Sad thing about that statement," Terry said to Casey, "is that it's all true." Casey rolls her eyes, then notices Allison taking out her phone. "What are you doing, Alli?" she asked.

"I'm calling the animal shelter," Allison replied. "I'm going to spend time with Maverick and try to adopt him. He needs a good home, and I'm going to give him one." She dials some numbers, then waits for someone to answer. When someone does, Allison says "Hi, this is Allison Libby. I was calling to schedule some time with the dog Maverick and was wondering if…" She stops for a few moments, then says "Oh, okay. No that's fine. Thanks anyway. Bye." She hangs up, and tries to keep herself from tearing up.

"What's wrong, Alli?" Billy asked her.

"Someone came by the shelter earlier today and adopted Maverick. They just left."

"Who was it?" asked Terry. Allison shakes her head, letting the tears roll down her face. "I don't know. The shelter isn't allowed to give out that kind of information."

"But that's a good thing, right?" Casey said. "You were worried he wouldn't be adopted, and now he's going to a good home."

"Yeah, but I was hoping to be the one to adopt him, like Trent planned to. But as long as he's in a loving home, nothing else matters. I just wish I could have seen him one more time before his new owner picked him up."

Just then, Sheriff Martin pulls up in front of the doors in his squad car. He opens his door and steps out. "Hi, kids," he said cheerfully. "How is everything going?"

"Dad, what are you doing here?" Billy asked him. "We didn't do anything wrong. We are totally innocent. Well, most of us. I don't know about Casey."

"Hey!" Casey exclaimed, but Sheriff Martin lets out a chuckle and replied "Relax, Billy, nobody is in trouble. I just thought you would all like to see the surprise I have in the car."

"What surprise?" asked Terry."

"Just wait. I think you're going to like it." Sheriff Martin proceeds to walk around the car and stands at the rear passenger side door. He opens the door, and a dog jumps out. The dog runs over to Billy, knocking him off his feet, and proceeds to give him an endless supply of licks on his face. Allison is surprised at what she's seeing. "Sheriff Martin, you're the one who adopted Maverick?" she asked gleefully.

"I saw his picture on the shelter's social media, and I thought he would make for a good family dog, and someone to keep an eye on Billy so he doesn't get into too much trouble. Turns out my instincts were right." As Maverick continued to lick Billy's face, the others let out a loud laugh as they hear Billy say "Okay, that's enough! No more licks! Yes, you're a good dog! Now stop it!" Maverick finally ceases his barrage of doggy kisses on Billy, who manages to push him off and stand back up, wiping his face in the process. "So, he's going to be our dog?" Billy asked his father.

"That's right, and you are going to help take care of him. Feed him, play with him, bathe him, walk him, clean up after him…" Allison looks at Billy and says "You're going to do fine, Billy. I can tell Maverick already likes you." She then looks at Maverick, kneels down and says to him "You found a very nice home, buddy. The Martins are a great family, and you are going to love them." She wraps her arms around Maverick's neck and kisses the top of his head.

"Come on, Maverick," Sheriff Martin said. "Let's go to the store and get you a nice warm bed, a big bag of food, and lots of toys you can play with." He looks at Billy and asks "You want to come with us, son?"

"Sure," Billy replied. "Let's get him the biggest bone we can find!" Billy and Maverick run to the car, with Maverick jumping into the back seat and Billy shouting "Shotgun!" He looks at the others and says "See ya guys later!" as he shuts his door. Sheriff Martin gets back into the car, and the others watch as they drive off.

Allison wipes the tears from her eyes and says "Well, I guess I'd better head down to the shelter and see if there are any animals who want some play time." She looks at Casey, points to Terry, and says "And I think you two have something to discuss?" She walks down the path, so Terry and Casey can have some alone time.

Terry just stands there, not looking at Casey. Instead he just checks his watch while Casey looks up at the sky. The awkwardness between them begins to grow, with their faces turning red, until Terry finally speaks up and says "Uh, Casey?"

"Yes, Terry?" Casey replied enthusiastically, before clearing her throat and saying in a calmer tone "Yes, Terry?" Terry wipes some sweat from his forehead, looks at Casey and nervously says "So, the school carnival is coming up…"

"Yeah. In a few weeks, actually. Billy and Allison are going together, you know."

"Yeah. What about you? Are you going with anyone?"

"Well, there is this one guy I was hoping to go with. If he wants to go with me."

"What's he like?"

"Smart, caring, honest, determined, funny. Kind of cute."

Terry smirks and says "Kind of cute?"

"Okay, he's very cute." Terry takes Casey by the hand as softly as he can, looks deep in her eyes and says "Casey, would you like to go to the school carnival with me?" Casey returns his gaze, then presses her lips against his, and when she's done, she says "I thought you'd never ask, Terry Welling." He says nothing, and instead gives her a smile. Still holding her hand, he walks her down the stairs, and she says "Don't you have to go to work?"

Terry says "I don't have to go to work for another hour. I'd like to spend the time with you, if that's okay." Casey blushes, kisses Terry on the cheek and replies "That sounds good to me." She places her head on his shoulder, and they both stare off into the sky, taking in the calm surroundings of their quiet little town of Littleroot, wondering what new adventures await them.

# ABOUT THE AUTHOR

J.M. Sewall has had a love of reading and telling stories from a young age. In 2016, he wrote and published his first book "The Legend of Dr. Kaminko". He lives in a small town in Maine with his dog Ziva.

Printed in the United States
By Bookmasters